CW01669148

3.8

Kevin Cookson

en Press

ISBN 978-1-78003-144-6

First published in Great Britain by
Indepenpress Publishing Ltd
25 Eastern Place
Brighton
BN2 1GJ

Cover design Jacqueline Abromeit

Acknowledgements

This book would not have been possible without the full support of my family and friends.

The following people made a significant contribution to the making of this book: Lynne Starkey, James Donaldson, Linda Barley and Reginald Bailey.

Thanks, everyone!

For James Lovelock
(I believe, and for sure: Gaia lives)

Contents

Information about Kevin Cookson can be found on his website: www.kevincookson.com

barn, in front of the holographic recorders and play gigs, just like we did in the past, and guess what?"

She placed her hands on her hips and leant over.

"We don't have to travel or stay in hotel rooms, this saves money, and the next day we're with the kids on this beautiful island. We're not travelling or breathing in exhaust fumes from the traffic jam the whole world is in. At the same time we can project the holographic images into as many countries and venues, as we wish. This earns us ten times the amount of money we used to earn doing a single gig. Not only that! We get to go home to the kids every single night."

"Whoa!" said Razor. "These arguments are a little bit one-sided, if you ask me. Let's take the cash issue. There's nothing stopping us from taking the holographic recording gear on the road and recording a real gig these days. Judith tells me they've sorted out a new lightweight battery system for both the transmitter and the receivers – they'll run for a week on one charge. So we could transmit the real gig to 20 locations, just like we do from the sland!"

Razor paused to see Mary's reaction. There wasn't any. e continued.

"You know we might actually play a little better with me real adrenalin running through our veins. That's at a live audience does for you, yes? And remember ying overnight and meeting real people? Well, that gave naterial for writing the songs, so it was well worth the n expense, wasn't it?"

ary could sense he wouldn't drop the idea of gigging f she was being honest with herself, there was a lot nse, as usual, in what Michael was saying. "OK! I'll about it!"

anks, love!" He got off his seat and kissed her on eek. "Now we've calmed down a little, how about around the island with the kids. It's going to be a l sunset."

walked along the beach, lazily kicking the football f them, for the children to chase, Mary said, "You

Preface
(by the author)

I think that in her song *Slender Thread* (*Poet's Heart*), Kate Wolf summed up, in a very succinct and powerful way, the dependence of the human race on serendipity.

She didn't intend to.

The way I see it, the survival of our species hangs by such a slender thread. Just close enough to the sun not to freeze to death – just far away enough not to fry – a liquid core that produces a magnetic bubble that protects us from the sun's radiation – a large Jupiter to protect us from rogue comets – large asteroid impacts in the past favouring our species.

Who says there's no God?

And when does our luck run out? For one day it surely will!

– Chapter One –

Near Zero

Z-Day minus two weeks...

"It's not that I don't like touring but why would I war change this lifestyle for a life on the road again?" said forcibly.

"Come on, you've gone soft in your old age," calmly replied.

"No, I haven't. Look, I get up at 9:00am 'cause come and wake me. The sun's shining every d down to the beach and have a swim and we la with the children for an hour or two. Then w back from the beach, dinner has been prepa eat alfresco – with the kids, mind! Nanny tak afternoon, which allows us to get in the stud of the day if necessary. What the hell's wror sounds wonderful to me, Michael!"

"I admit this life does have its advan having that routine for nearly three year just getting a tad bored?"

Mary didn't want to answer that que doubt, it was definitely boring at time tack.

"OK! Think of our pockets. We u world. Then Judy found the holog we set up in our specially-const used to tell me that gigging stifled your creativity, because you were too busy doing the mundane tasks or checking harmonies or guitar lines you'd already invented. So what's changed?"

"Me! I was wrong. I've found out it's important to mix reality with comfort and creativity. We need to balance one with the other and at the moment there's no balance. We're living a life of make-believe out here. It was a brilliant idea that Judy had and she had it for the right reasons – but it isn't working. This state of play has to be temporary, or in the end, it's going to kill the group. We must get back out on the road."

Razor, Mary and the children carried on their walk along the sea shore and as Mary glanced at the setting sun and the children laughing at the water's edge, she had the feeling that this world, a world she loved dearly, was coming to an end...

The next morning, Richard, Terry and Kevin – the other members of Near Zero, joined Mary, Razor and the children for breakfast on the Jones' veranda.

As Razor walked out to greet everyone, Terry was reading an article to the rest of the group. He'd found it in Music Today International:

> *"The manager of Near Zero, Judith Wells, the so-called sixth member of the band, has indicated that the group may well tour again, in the near future. This statement came as a result of an MTI (Music Today International) Poll indicating that some fans have become disillusioned with just seeing holographic images of the band.*
>
> *The band was formed seven years ago and at that time they found it impossible to get a recording contract. In the first two years nearly all the major labels passed them up. Eventually, Bill Evans of ElectricAudio signed a three-album-all-media deal with them, appointing Judy Wells as their manager. They never looked back.*

They became a worldwide phenomenon and broke all records when their first album, Cold Fusion, *was released. It not only topped the download charts for eight weeks but also resulted in every single track becoming a number one, as they released them individually over the following 12 months.*

The songwriting duo of Michael Jones (Razor) their main vocalist and Richard O'Shea (FourLeaf) their bass player, seems to be the real key to their success. These ruggedly-handsome men—"

Terry paused, and cheers and wolf whistles went up from the gathered party!

"These ruggedly-handsome men were both in the SAS during the 'Terror-Wars', and some of the horror of those days can be heard in the lyrics of their songs.

The other members of the band are: Terry Jones, Razor's younger brother, on drums (nicknamed 'Sticks', what else?); Kevin Dubois on lead guitar and nicknamed 'Dubious'. I am reliably informed that this has nothing to do with his guitar playing."

More cheers went up!

"And Mary Donaldson on keyboards, nicknamed 'Queenie', derived I suppose, from the antiquated idea that anyone from Scotland called Mary should be nicknamed 'Mary, Queen of Scots' or the shortened version, 'Queenie'.

"Mary now lives with Michael and has two children by him; Daniel who is five years old and Abigail, who is three years old. Unusually sensible names for rock-star children."

With this, everyone looked at Mary who just smiled. Terry continued:

"The band earned considerable sums of money over the next three years and some of that money went into the development of their now legendary holographic recording studio and projection system.

The story is, that Judy Wells had heard about the system being developed at Bell Laboratories and having had a demo, and knowing the group was unhappy with the constant demands on them whilst on tour, and coupled with a worry that the pressure could eventually lead to the break-up of the band, she agreed to inject billions of dollars into the project in return for 'first use' of the system and a 30% share in the project as a whole. The rumour is that the 'first use' part of the contract is about to lapse sometime in the new year.

From that day on, the group have not left their private island, preferring to record their gigs on their holographic recording system and then transmit them simultaneously to as many as 30 different countries at the same time. It is estimated with this process, their earnings rocketed and they are now estimated to be the richest rock group ever.

It's now three years since the band have been seen in public and there are all sorts of rumours doing the rounds. For example some say that their last album Stone Cold *is a metaphor for the death of Razor's brother, Terry Jones."*

"Terry, how can you be reading this? You're dead!" said Razor.

Everyone laughed!

"Judith Wells simply laughed when I put the rumours to her and said there would be some sort of announcement in the next few weeks.

We wait with baited breath, Judith—

Anyway, enough of the banter – what do I think of the album?

*Product ***** – As usual the group have included lots of extras in the product pack. Besides the ROM album itself, they've included an old-fashioned Blu-ray disk, for us old folk who have not yet upgraded their video/ sound systems. They've also included a holographic key ring with a picture of the group on one side and the native flag of the country the ROM album was bought in on the other – amazing!*

*Music and lyrics ***** – The words and music have a resonance that only Near Zero can produce. The harmonies are superb, the themes are superb and the musicianship is superb. I'm still a fan—"*

"Well, there you have it, lads."

Terry put the paper down and poured a cup of coffee.

"Look, all you who are not yet deceased," said Razor. "I've called this meeting because, like the article says, the fans, and to be truthful *me, a*re getting a little tired of us not being there when we play.

"The songwriting is suffering. The music is suffering. The playing is suffering and our enthusiasm for the band is beginning to wane. I think we should get back to playing for real. What do you lads think? Terry?"

"Hey, I'm the young one here. I'd rather gig any day than stay here and sunbathe."

"Richard?"

"I must admit it doesn't feel right not getting out there and experiencing real life, and there's no doubt that the songwriting is just starting to get a little bland and irrelevant because of it."

"Kevin?"

"I'm afraid I agree. What's the point of being famous if you never see anyone who actually wants your autograph?"

Everyone laughed.

"OK. That just leaves Mary?" Razor turned to look at her.

"It's not the gigging that's the problem – it's the children. I won't leave them behind," said Mary.

"Well, in that case, we take Nanny and the kids on tour with us," said Razor.

"But is life on the road going to be alright for them?"

"We make sure it is. We plan their itinerary, as carefully as we plan the group's itinerary. They don't need to be with us *all* the time. If you think about it, touring the world and seeing all the great sites can't do their education any harm. If we plan it carefully, it would only be the actual gig nights we wouldn't be tucking them up in bed."

"OK!" said Mary, "but if it doesn't work out that way, I reserve the right to come back here and forget touring, permanently.

"Deal!" said Razor.

"Who's calling Lenny then?" asked Terry.

Lenny Appleton was Near Zero's road crew chief, when last they were on the road. He'd been with them through thick and thin, right from the off and was a good friend of the band.

"I think it best we talk to Judy first. She'll talk to Lenny. I get the feeling there'll be a press conference or two before the week is out," said Razor. "I have one more question, though, that I need to put to all of you?"

"What's that?" asked Kevin.

"Are we happy with this decision, or is there still a reluctance to go back on the road?"

"On balance I think it's a good idea, so I'll say happy!" said Kevin.

All the others, except Mary who shrugged her shoulders, nodded in agreement.

"I'll phone Judy straight away," said Razor.

Judith Wells is considered to be one of the best A&R executives in the music business. She is a fiercely independent manager of some of the world's top artists. This includes artists like The Satellite Misfits, Paul Bruce, Garry the Demoniac, not to mention Near Zero.

A close friend of Bill and Cathy Evans, she was present when the first demos of Near Zero were being played in

Evans's office suite, at ElectricAudio's central office in Los Angeles.

It's reported that she was so impressed with their sound and repertoire, that she actually paid Bill Evans an undisclosed amount to manage the group. They both deny the rumour, but Judith Wells said that even if the rumour had been true, she would have been in profit within eight days of the release of their first album.

Judith was ecstatic at the news that the band wanted to return to live work and she relished the challenge of getting the band back on the road.

At the forefront of her mind was the sale of their legendary holographic suite. What better way to sell it, than by dragging it all around the world, filming live gigs for the most famous rock band in history?

She knew, almost instinctively, that she needed the right personnel deployed if this was going to be a success. Razor had already told her about Mary's misgivings, and as far as she was concerned, that was the key issue here. There was only one woman she knew that was capable of minding the nanny and the children, and that was her personal assistant, Cheryl Green.

"Oh! Come on, Judy, I don't want to be a nursemaid to two nappies and a nanny," said Cheryl.

"You can't look at it like that, Cheryl. You need to think of the bigger picture. At the moment I direct you and you organise my time so that I can function well.

"With this task, *you* will be doing the directing. Whatever happens, the buck will stop with you. This means, besides tripling your wage, if you succeed your reputation will increase dramatically because you'll have been seen to stand on your own feet and make your own decisions. Well?" For a short time there was silence.

After some soul searching, Cheryl said, "OK!"

"A wise decision, Cheryl. You'll not regret it!"

One down, one to go, Judith thought as she left the office.

Lenny Appleton was sorting out the gain structure, by adjusting the faders and input channels of an enormous mixing desk, as Judy Wells walked into the theatre control box. On the mixer head, the name 'Paul Bruce' was displayed in big bold type.

"Lenny! How are you?"

"*Judy!* I didn't expect to see you here today?"

Lenny immediately dropped what he was doing and gave Judy a hug.

"What brings the great Judith Wells out of her office?"

"Near Zero are going live again. The boys want you as their road crew chief!"

Lenny was overjoyed to hear the news and was desperate to jump up and down and say yes he'd do it. He also knew if he had done, it would have reduced his pay packet considerably.

"As you can see, Judy, I am fully employed, and contracted, to look after Paul Bruce's set-up. He pays good money and I certainly couldn't cope with another group on top of this job."

Judy knew it was only money that was the problem – there was no way Lenny would prefer Paul over Near Zero.

"The group have authorised me to offer you double your current salary."

Lenny knew that this was totally untrue. Judith Wells didn't need authorisation from anyone. She was, and always was, totally in control of wages for the whole team.

"Triple?" Lenny said. He thought a bit of negotiation was due here and well, it was worth a stab in the dark

"OK! But you'll have to promise me personally that you'll learn all about the holographic systems, before the tour begins. I don't want the boys to be reliant on anyone else."

"We have a deal!" Lenny extended his hand and Judith Wells shook it.

"Nice to have you back on the team, Lenny."

Judith gave Lenny a hug and as she walked away she was feeling good.

With herself and her new PA dedicated to tour planning, her old PA, Cheryl, on child- and nanny-planning duties and Lenny on engineering, nothing could possibly go wrong.

Z-Day minus two days...

In total secrecy, Near Zero's private jet touched down at Heathrow and taxied to a halt in a private corner of the tarmac, especially reserved for VIPs.

As the band came off the plane, Judith Wells, Lenny Appleton and Cheryl Green met them. Bill Evans and his wife were also there to say hello.

Judith approached the children and their nanny.

"Wendy, this is Cheryl Green, she's the one who's going to try to keep you and the children happy over the next three months. Cheryl, this is Wendy Grafton, the children's nanny."

"Hi! Wendy." Cheryl extended her hand out to greet the nanny. "Did you get the planning notes I sent you?"

Wendy was carrying Abigail, who had clearly fallen asleep on the plane and had not yet woken up. Wendy smiled and said, "Sorry!" in response to not being able to shake her hand. They both smiled at each other. Wendy said in a quiet voice, "This is Abigail," as she looked down at the lump in her arms. "And holding onto my left leg, is Daniel." Daniel gripped Wendy's left leg even more tightly and moved closer to her.

"Say hello to Cheryl, Daniel."

Daniel said very quietly, "Hello," and then promptly hid his face behind Wendy's leg.

"Yes, Mary and I got the notes, Cheryl, but we only had time to look at the first three days. The rest hasn't been digested yet."

"Oh! So you know we're going up to Manchester, early?"

"Yes, on the train?"

"Well, I thought it would be exciting for the children."

"Perfect choice, Cheryl. Daniel's been telling me he's never been on a train before – he's quite excited."

"We should have time to look at next week's agenda,

whilst we're travelling. I thought we'd go through it a week at a time."

"Yes," said Wendy. "But don't forget to leave plenty of down time and play space, in your agenda. Overall we need a much calmer experience, than the group are going to have over the next three months."

"Yes, Mary has already talked to me about it!"

As Cheryl and Wendy were discussing their itinerary, Judith walked over to where Near Zero were and pulled Mary to one side.

"Mary. I've booked a couple of adjacent suites at the Savoy. One for you and Razor and the other for Wendy and the children – here are the keys. The rest of the group are spread over another five suites on the same floor."

"Thanks, Judy. Wendy and I have looked at the plans for the children, it looks good so far, but can you keep that standard up for the next three months?"

"It's all Cheryl's work," Judith said, as she glanced over to look at Cheryl, Wendy and the children. "I'm sure she can pull it off, Mary."

After saying hello and goodbye to Bill Evans and his wife, the five black limousines carried the band and their entourage to the Savoy.

Night was falling. Tomorrow night the band would be playing Wembley Arena, and Near Zero fans would be watching the first live performance by them, in over four years.

Razor was with Mary, Wendy and the children, in one of the blacked-out limousines.

"We have a team meeting at eight o'clock tonight, Mary. You don't have to be there. It's just to check that everything's going OK for the dress rehearsal, tomorrow afternoon. Why don't you, Wendy and the kids have a night out, maybe go to the London Eye?"

"No, Michael. The children have to be up early tomorrow, to catch the train up to Manchester. We'll dine in the hotel restaurant and have an early night."

"OK!"

"We're going to the Science Museum in Manchester tomorrow, Daddy," said Daniel.

"And we're going on a train," said Abigail.

"So, Wendy says we have to have an early night."

Abigail carried on.

"So we're not too tired to employ ourselves."

"Enjoy ourselves, Abigail. Not employ ourselves," said Wendy.

The adults smiled at one another.

"What time's the train?" asked Razor.

"We're leaving on the ten o'clock Euston to Piccadilly train. We'll be there for dinner. Cheryl's doing the journey with us, so we can go over the plans for the children for the next couple of weeks," said Wendy.

The limousines pulled onto the Savoy front entrance and the whole team went into the hotel.

"Lenny, how are you doing with learning the ins and outs of the holographic system?"

"More or less finished now, Judith. Just need some real-world experience and I'll be fine."

"Good. OK! See you at eight."

The pre-rehearsal meeting went fine. In fact the main concern from the road crew was packing up after the London gig.

Would they have enough time to pack up everything, go north to Manchester and set-up the gear ready for the next gig? After much discussion, it was decided that they would have to hit the road north to Manchester as soon after the London gig as possible.

Z-Day minus one day...

Next day, once Mary and Razor had waved goodbye to Wendy and the children, at Euston, they made their way to the stage and rehearsals. Everything went well. The holographic array worked like a dream and was tested over the main links to Paris, Copenhagen, Reykjavik, Madrid and Berlin.

By the time all the testing had been completed and they'd checked the opening sequence, it was getting close to the time for the show itself.

Mary came dashing into Michael's dressing room.

"I've got Daniel and Abigail on the phone. Quick!"

Mary shoved the mobile into Razor's hand.

"Which one?" he whispered.

"Daniel."

"Hello, Daniel. So what have you been up to today?"

Daniel said excitedly, "We've been on a train, Daddy, and in tunnels and we went to the museum."

"And are you and Abigail ready for bed yet?"

"Yes, but Wendy promised that we could watch you on the telly? How do you get *that* small, Daddy?"

"Well, it's a little bit of magic; I'll tell you all about it when you're older."

"Wendy says we can only watch the beginning."

"Well, it's on until very late and you and Abigail need your sleep. Where is she?"

"She's sat on Wendy's knee."

"Is she going to talk to Daddy tonight?"

"Abigail, are you talking to Daddy?"

Abigail just sat there sucking her thumb and saying nothing.

"Don't think so, Daddy."

"Well, OK! I have to go now. You just give Abigail a kiss from me and Mummy, and tell her we'll see her tomorrow."

Razor was just about to ring off when Mary snatched the phone back.

"Are you still there, Daniel?"

And as Mary continued the conversation with Daniel she walked out the room.

"Michael! Stop pacing up and down," said Terry.

"You're not going to believe this little bro', but I'm as nervous as hell!"

"Not one shred of nervousness over the last three years and now you're like this?" said Terry.

"You should know. He's always like this before a live gig," chipped in Richard.

The stage monitor system sprung into life, "Would Near Zero, please make their way to the stage entrance, thank you!"

As the band walked towards the stage entrance, the noise of the assembled crowd became louder and louder, and as they walked on stage, there wasn't a single member who was regretting going live again.

Initially the stage was dark, but the crowd could see that there was increased activity near the instruments, which led to part of the crowd cheering. Then the crowd hesitated, it was obvious that they were unsure whether it was the actual band on stage, so the initial cheers started to subside.

Suddenly Kevin (Dubious) hit the first chord and the audience went wild. The stage burst into life with smoke and flashes.

The first song was one of their many hits and as the chorus started, the whole crowd could be heard singing the words along with Razor. It was a magic moment. Razor stopped singing and offered the microphone to the crowd who duly sang the song for him, word perfect.

He raised his hands over his head and started clapping, the crowd joined in. Mary looked at Terry and they both just smiled – it was a terrific night to be a member of Near Zero.

There were three encores before the audience were willing to let the band go.

After the gig they signed autographs and chatted to their fans for over an hour at the stage door.

Now, Mary was showering off in the ladies dressing room and looking forward to getting on the tour bus for a relaxing trip north. It was in her mind to sit at the rear of the coach and just be quiet. She was far too pumped-up with adrenalin to sleep. Anyway, the Manchester gig itself was not for another two days, so she knew she would have plenty of time to recuperate and see the kids, before the adrenalin rush started all over again. Michael had been right, though. For all the pain travelling around the world gives you, having sleepless nights, booking into anonymous, cold-hearted hotel rooms and more – you can't beat playing to a live audience.

There was a hell of a lot of noise coming from the men's dressing room, as the team unwound from their performance. But that wasn't for her. She had Mum duties tomorrow and she wouldn't miss them for the world.

Z-Day...

Within two hours of the gig ending, everyone was on the tour bus, heading north to Manchester. The tour bus was accompanied by four articulated lorries carrying the group's musical instruments, amplifier stacks, the line arrays, the stage lighting, the stage construction kit, light and sound mixers, and the new holographic recording and transmitting equipment. The convoy was quite an impressive sight and attracted a lot of car horn noise as it passed through the streets of London.

– Chapter Two –

Gorizon Prime

Z-Day minus 18 years...

The sun shone like gold that morning, as little winged creatures, on their way to dance with the flowers in the meadow, meandered between the trees. A rush of water, brought on by a winged creature bathing in the pool, disturbed a skimmer on the tense, mirror-like surface of the pond. On the banks, leaves fell on the dew-covered grass, as the ivy-like fauna climbed the trunk it had been clinging to for such a long time.

No, there was no doubt about it; Gorizon Prime *was* paradise, before the radiant bomb awoke and fried everything.

The loss was so profound that there could be no forgiveness for the evil brought upon this land. Once the trigger had been pulled there was no ability to undo what had been done and as for the one who pulled the trigger? There was no remorse. It was just the flip of a switch!

* * *

"There are no life readings, emanating from this planet, Shezar!"

Rial and Shezar, both shape-shifters from the planet Calron, were on a routine visit to the Gorizon System.

The second planet from the sun, Gorizon Prime, was a life-bearing planet that had been discovered three years prior. The Galactic Archivists had asked the Enforcement Brigade, who were the ones that initially reported life on the planet, to revisit, when convenient, to perform a preliminary survey. This would allow the Galactic Database to be updated with a more detailed synopsis of the planet. Rial and Shezar were not expecting a lifeless piece of rock.

"But that's impossible. I was here, only three years ago, when we discovered the planet, it was thriving," said Shezar.

Rial could tell she was upset and disturbed by the instrument's reading.

"OK! Rial, send a probe to check the southern continent."

Rial entered the co-ordinates for the centre of the southern landmass and launched the bio-probe.

"Probe launched, Shezar."

Both Shezar and Rial were glued to the video link on the probe as it flew over the southern ocean. The telemetry was already confirming that the planet was devoid of life but the two Galactic Enforcement Officers were still finding it difficult to take this fact in.

As the probe came upon the southern land mass they could tell, almost immediately, that there was a problem. From far away the landmass looked brown and desert like. As the probe neared the edge of what was once a verdant, green forest, it could detect no life signs. The only clue that there had been life here in the past was a huge stand of grey, bare, tree trunks with not a leaf on them.

"Whatever happened here, Rial, it happened quite recently."

"Yes, I agree, Shezar. I don't think there's any doubt about it. It's as if the planet has been sterilised."

"If we're looking at sterilisation then we need to check the archives. Rial, see if there have been any gamma ray bursts in this sector since we last visited."

Rial called up the Galactic Database, Stellar Mapping Section and entered the Events Diary. "No, not within

100,000 light years of this system. Certainly nothing close enough to sterilise Gorizon Prime."

"Then what happened, Rial?"

Their spaceship slowly circled the globe, with both of them sat in silence, looking for some sign of life or at least a clue as to what may have happened.

"What about a large solar flare?" asked Rial.

"Possibly, but you'd expect one side to be more affected than the other, and anyway, the magnetic field is really strong, and from what I can see, in good health. So any solar flare would have been redirected to the poles. There would just have been a damn good aurora that night."

"Magnetic field reversal?"

"Yes, but again, Rial, you'd expect some pocket of the surface to survive a simple change of the poles."

"Are there any residuals that will give us a handle on the problem?"

"Well, the ozone layer's gone. Damn! There are radioactive nuclei all over the planet. In fact, I would say this planet isn't going to be habitable again for a few thousand years, depending on the half-life of those nuclei."

"I'll see if there are any residual energy readings – there may be anomalies?"

Rial took a wide-sweep energy reading of the planet. The result surprised him. "There is, what looks like, a residual energy signature coming from the other side of the planet."

"Is it lethal?" asked Shezar – mindful of what had happened to the rest of the planet.

"I can't tell from this distance. We need to get closer."

"OK! But whilst I get the ship closer, keep an eye on the energy readings. We don't want to end up fried or sterilised."

"I'm on it!" said Rial.

As the ship zeroed in on the energy source, the energy readings inexorably rose.

"Whatever it is, Rial, it's now directly below us."

Rial was looking at the energy readings on a monitor screen, which was also showing the detailed structure of the land below.

"It's in a cave; it's only about 50 metres below the surface. We'll need protective suits to go in there. The radiation on the surface won't fry us, but in the cave it may make us infertile, if we stay there more than a few hours."

"OK! Let's land, take a look and then get out of here as quickly as possible."

"Sounds like a plan!"

Shezar landed the ship on a smooth piece of ground that was as close to the cave entrance as she dare go. Even so, the cave was quite a distance away from the landing site.

After suiting up with their protective clothing, designed specifically to reduce radiation exposure in high-energy environments, they walked and then climbed up to the cave entrance.

Rial sensed that Shezar was reluctant to go in.

"Are you sure it's safe? Rial."

Rial smiled, "Of course, but we only stay for 90 minutes. Yes?"

Shezar nodded in agreement and they both clambered into the cave system.

Rial brushed his gloved hand over the cave wall.

"These surfaces are far too smooth to be natural. I see the mark of intelligence here, Shezar."

"I think you're right—" Just at that moment, they reached a point where the tunnel branched off. "Go left, the readings are much stronger in that direction."

Less than 100 metres further in, Shezar saw the source of the radiation.

"Oh! My God! Rial. You were right. It's a machine!"

As Shezar walked cautiously over to the device she monitored the energy readings at every step.

"It's cylindrical in shape," she said.

"Can you make out those markings on the side?"

Shezar was standing, looking amazed at what she had just found. "I can read every syllable, Rial. It's from Zindor. I worked on the planet for 16 months. Got to know some of the population quite well—this large plaque here just has the word 'Scorch' on it—there's a date here—hell! It's only one year old. This sign here indicates radiation danger."

"They seem to have been right about the radiation. But Zindor's nearly two light years from here! What's their technology doing on a primitive planet like this?"

"Judging from the radiation readings and the fact that the moon and the two nearer planets have also been irradiated, I'd say that this thing has somehow generated a burst of energy strong enough to irradiate the entire system."

"But you'd expect the machine to be destroyed, along with half the damn planet, if that were the case."

"Maybe it generates small bursts. Pulses that destroy life but not property – neutron bomb style."

Shezar looked at Rial. "What are we witnessing here, Rial? Is this a genocide event?"

"I don't think there's any question about it, Shezar. This planet has been murdered!"

"There seems to be more offshoots from this cave. They all seem to be dead ends. We just need to see what's contained in at least one of them, before we depart. What are we like for exposure, Rial?"

"We're fine for another 30 minutes."

"Let's try this way." Shezar started to walk down another branching tunnel, further into the cave system. Only a few hundred metres in, they found another cylinder.

"This one's dated eight years earlier."

"It looks like a failed attempt to initiate the same event."

"I think you were lucky to see a live planet, Shezar."

"What do you mean?"

"When were you last on this planet?"

"Hell! You're right! If this one had worked we wouldn't have known the planet was ever alive."

Rial looked at his exposure meter.

"I think it's time to get out of here or we'll not be having children in the near future!"

Rial and Shezar made their way out of the cave system and back to their ship.

The strict protocols in situations as grave as genocide, dictate that they must report into headquarters immediately the opportunity arises. Thus, before take off, Rial transmitted their co-ordinates; the code for a genocide event and whom they thought may well be responsible for the atrocity to Brigade HQ.

"I think it may be wise to visit Zindor, Rial. See if we can find out what's going on."

"Have we no one nearer?"

"We're the only ones in this sector."

"Then I can't see any alternative. Let's program the flight and get into stasis. Contact Brigade HQ, let them know what we're doing."

Shezar switched on the vox-line.

"This is Shezar Tine calling from Gorizon Prime. Are you there, Commander?"

"Yes, Shezar. We have your communiqué, can you follow it up?"

"That's exactly what we intended to do, Sir. We're going into stasis now; we'll contact you when we get to Zindor."

"Give our regards to Rial, and good hunting."

Absolutely the worst thing about being in the Enforcement Brigade was the amount of time one had to spend in stasis.

The hope, in times gone by, that there would be quick ways to fly around the universe, using worm holes for example, never came to fruition. Wormholes were used for communications but they were tiny. You wouldn't even get an insect through. Larger wormholes were considered, but the power to generate a large one was of an order of magnitude bigger than it was possible to supply.

So moving from star system to star system was a time consuming business. Currently the Galactic Enforcement Fleet had ships that could travel to velocities nearly 65% of the speed of light.

Thus, in practice, to travel to a star some two light years away, would mean a journey time of around three years.

So even though their communications with the Galactic Enforcement Brigade were almost instantaneous, sometimes just moving to the next planet could take years.

The powers that be, tackled this dilemma in two main ways:

First, they invented the stasis pod. This allows their men and women to enter suspended animation for the period of their flight. During stasis the average age loss is one hour a year. So travelling for four years in stasis means, at the other end, you're only four hours older.

This remarkable invention resulted in an elite brigade that, to the general population of the worlds they visited, never seemed to age. Take Rial, for example. He joined the force when he was 19 but to date has logged 164 stasis hours in less than a year of real time. He is thus currently logged as nearly 184 years old. His body, however, is truly only 20 years old.

When the enforcement officer goes into stasis and comes out again he, or she, feels the time pass to the same degree as the body clock.

Because of this, when the individual comes out of stasis, they generally suffer from stasis lag. It normally takes a few days to shake off the feeling and re-adjust to the new reality.

It's during this recovery period that officers try to reconnect with their past, if they still can. As a minimum, they are advised to catch up with the news snippets that get collected the moment the stasis pod is activated, and stored ready to be regurgitated when the stasis pod is opened.

Second, they established an enforcement team, where practicable, on nearly every inhabited planet in the galaxy. Thus, because the communications from star to star is almost instantaneous, then so long as enforcement officers are on many planets, leads can be followed up more readily. The diversity of life in the galaxy meant that if the enforcement teams could not be recruited locally, shape-shifters would be recruited.

In this sector of the galaxy most civilisations were young and thus had no inkling that the Galactic Enforcement Brigade even existed. Therefore, it was impossible to recruit locals and so a large number of shape-shifters were employed in this neck of the woods.

Some three years later the starship that was carrying Shezar Tine and Rial Azuth detected it was approaching the Zindorian System and began to slow down. The stasis pods began to warm, and as soon as the flight computer detected movement in the stasis pods, it opened the airtight stasis capsules. The rush of air announced the awakening of the crew. The ship's automated announcement hailed the arrival of the ship at its programmed destination:

"Please unfasten your safety harness and do your re-animation exercises. You have been in STASIS for three years, sixteen days, three hours and twelve minutes. It is possible that you will suffer from nausea and dizziness for the first hour. Before embarking on your mission you should eat your first meal. This should be small and you should take your time eating it. Tomorrow you may eat, as normal but do not have a large meal for at least five days.

"The ship is now in the Zindorian System and we are currently on time for orbiting over the main population centre. The ship will be there in seven hours and eight minutes. The ship is in stealth mode. It will not be detected."

Z-Day minus 16 years...

"Well, that's another three years gone, Rial."

"It's what we signed up for, Shezar. It doesn't bother me any more. It did bother me once upon a time – especially when my mum and dad passed away whilst I was in stasis. In fact, I visited my little sister who had never travelled. She was 86 and looking very frail when I saw her. She told me that they were very proud of their son being recruited into the Galactic Enforcement Brigade. She said she was also very proud. 'It's like looking back into my youth seeing you there still so young and handsome,' she said."

"Handsome? Was she also going a little blind, Rial?" Rial smiled.

Whilst Rial ordered up two small meals from the replicator, Shezar contacted Brigade HQ.

"Hi! Shezar, we've been expecting your call. Nothing more has transpired whilst you've been in stasis, so your mission is the same – try to find out more about Scorch and any plans they may have for its further use."

"OK, Commander, we'll be in touch."

"We really need to get down there, Shezar."

"Yes, I know. Did you look at the downloads you were sent whilst you were in stasis?"

"Yes, why?"

"Then you know what the Deepfall is?"

"Yes."

"Well, when we enter the atmosphere we must avoid the Deepfall, otherwise the shuttle will be spotted. We need to stay on the hot side, away from the city."

"No problem," said Rial.

"Last time I was here they were working on plans to improve their colonies. They were building a huge ship. They called it an ark. The idea was to shift thousands of their people off Zindor to uninhabited worlds in nearby star systems."

"Like Gorizon Prime!"

"Exactly. Why would you do such a thing to a planet you could live on?"

"How many did the ark hold?"

"The archives said up to 500,000 at any one time. But even though the main skeleton had got off the drawing board, the rest of the design was sheer conjecture. I thought the way they were going to fill the central canal with water was interesting."

"Why's that?"

"They'd already intercepted a comet fragment. They were going to haul it to the ship, chop it up and melt it."

"How the hell do you know all that?"

"I was working as an archivist for the central museum."

"Boring!"

"Well, it was the best way to quickly find out the history of the planet's inhabitants.

One thing I did find out was that everything the government did was archived there. So one of us needs to get a job there. Then we need to check back in time, say the last five years for anything named Scorch."

"I think you should write me a letter of recommendation, Shezar. If you go back they'll wonder why you look so young."

"Once I'm in Zinden shape, I can age myself slightly."

"No, a fresh face will be less complicated."

Shezar and Rial proceeded to change shape. They took their shuttle down to the planet's surface, travelling behind the Deepfall to ensure they remained undetected.

* * *

The entrance to the museum was via the great hall. The Zinden were enormously proud of their history and culture and nowhere was this more apparent than in the lavishness of the central museum.

Shezar and Rial had entered the building together but remained separate in their actions. No one would guess that they were working together.

As Rial approached one of the many archive terminals, Shezar watched surreptitiously to ensure no one was watching or following him.

Rial placed a small rectangular device next to the keyboard. It had been pre-programmed to search out the archivist database and to display the list of current entrants on the screen. As the device probed the central computer system there were several flashes of red, saying incorrect password, on Rial's screen. Even though the correct passwords were never given, the device sailed through all the security levels and eventually listed the members. Rial inserted his name and archivist number into the database and set the display back to the original page. He placed the small rectangular device back in his pocket.

Rial then left the building, followed some five minutes later, by Shezar.

"Did you implant your name?"

"Yes, no problem – according to the database it's been there for years."

"When are you going in?"

"Now! There's no time like the present. See you later."

Rial headed for the great hall once more.

"You come highly recommended, Rial," said Radolfin Dax, the chief archivist for the Zindorean museum. "My word! Yes! Shezar was an excellent archivist. How is she, these days?"

"She's in good health, Sir. She sends her regards to you and the team."

"I heard she was off world on one of the new starships?" Radolfin hadn't heard this – he was probing for an incorrect response, just to be on the safe side. He certainly didn't want just anyone looking at sensitive archives. He needed people whom he could trust, who would be discrete, just like Shezar was when she was at the museum.

"No, Sir! You must have heard wrong. She's in Eifen, on the southern rim." Rial knew that was where Radolfin thought Shezar was.

"Ha! Yes, now I remember." There was a long pause, "So what do you think the most important characteristic of an archivist is, Rial?"

"To be low-profile and discreet at all times, Sir."

"Do you think you could be as discreet as Shezar was?"

"I would expect so. Shezar would not have recommended me if *she* did not think so."

"But I'm asking *you*, Rial!"

"Yes, I will be very discreet."

"Good," Radolfin carried on reading Shezar's letter of introduction.

"It says here you have experience with the Primax Sixty-Four."

"Yes."

Radolfin thought he'd throw a small technical question in to see if the facts in Shezar's letter were accurate.

"So how can you tell the difference between prime and sub-prime artefacts?"

"A sub-prime artefact has the double entic symbol prior to its proper name."

"And if I have a sub-prime object in my hand. What is the easiest and quickest way of finding the prime object?"

"Simply through Primax Sixty-Four's, database."

"What if I have no access to the Primax Sixty-Four?"

"Then you would log on to GlobeNet and key into their search engine – a double entic, followed by the first five digits of the sub-prime's label, followed by another double entic."

"And this would give you a result, would it?" asked Radolfin.

"Well, it would ask you for your National Archive Number, but yes, so long as you were an archivist, you would get a result."

That was a good enough reply for Radolfin. "OK, you're hired, Rial."

Because of the shortage of staff, it was only a matter of a few days before Rial was alone and able to interrogate the Primax Sixty-Four. He knew that his login name would be stored against every search he made and against every page he read. If he were lucky, they wouldn't review his account details until Shezar and he had left the planet. Regardless, he had to take the risk. The Galactic Enforcement Brigade would never know the truth of the matter, if he didn't access those files.

He searched for the proper noun, Scorch. A very long list of results ran down and off the screen. He filtered on 'results', the list shortened. He noticed that near the top of the shortened list was a listing named, 'initial results from Gorizon Prime'. He called the paper up and scanned the text.

—Gorizon Prime was chosen as a test site, since only primitive life forms existed on—

—Measurements taken, on the target planet (second from the star) and the third planet, were by remote sensors. The fourth planet had a small science team on it, to capture further data. Encasement shielding protected this team from the expected radiation bursts. The main science team

stayed on the starship Queron, which remained beyond the outer planet, Sidor – the tenth in the system—

—Even though the science team on the fourth planet were well protected, they did not survive the bursts. The main science team were admonished for—

—There was an unexpected visual result reported by observers on the fourth planet before they succumbed. They said that Gorizon Prime glowed for a short time and—

Rial knew that this was the evidence he needed for the report to the Galactic Council. He set his mass storage device to 'copy', and carried on reading the text whilst his finger-sized device recorded the terabytes he needed as proof that the Zinden were responsible for mass murder.

—On returning to the target planet, radioactive nuclei with half lives of over 6,000 years were present—

—Conclusions: Unless Scorch is used thousands of years before occupancy is envisaged; the device is of little use—

—Science teams should know that remaining in the Stellar System during the detonation phase is not an option and is likely to prove fatal—

The 'ping' signified that his mass storage device had finished doing its job. This was Rial's cue to get out of the building and back to Shezar.

He switched off the Primax Sixty-Four and pocketed the mass storage device and walked out of the central archive room. He called the elevator, and as he stepped in and pressed the button for the ground floor, his pulse was racing. He knew if he were to be caught now, it would be curtains for his mission and himself.

He left the main elevator and headed for the main exit doors, at the front of the building.

"Rial! Hello there, I'm pleased to see you again. How is your new job?" It was Radolfin Dax, chief archivist, accompanied by someone he had never seen before.

"Absolutely wonderful. I must thank you for giving me my position, Sir."

"What's it like working for the great Radolfin, my boy?" asked the stranger.

Radolfin realised, by the questioning look on Rail's face, that he didn't know who his friend was.

"This is Slevin Binx, Rial, chief of security for the whole of Zindor."

"A great honour, Sir," Rial tried his best to look calm and not at all in a hurry to escape the building.

"And what do they have you working on at the moment, Rial," asked Slevin Binx.

"Collating accident statistics, in preparation for the annual listing."

"So is there anything that stands out this year, Rial?"

Rial had absolutely no idea. Yes, it was the job he was given. But no, he hadn't done any of the work. He'd been far too busy looking how to get hold of the Scorch results without initially being detected.

"From what I can see, so far, we've had an unusual number of accidents and incidents regarding the Deepfall winds." Even as this totally made up information was leaving his lips, he just knew he would regret saying it. Why couldn't he just have said, no, nothing stands out as yet. In his head, he was kicking himself.

The chief of security suddenly took an interest. "Yes? Is that so? You will have to show me these results, Rial."

Oh! Shit, thought Rial. "Are you available later, Sir?"

"Why! I'm available now," said Slevin.

Rial knew if he couldn't get out of this, he was sunk.

"I have promised my girlfriend I'd meet her for dinner. I can come back early, if you wish?"

"Ha! No, no – we don't want to stand in the way of true love, do we, Radolfin? I will come and see you later today."

"Thank you, Sir."

As Rial walked away and through the doors of the museum, he could feel himself sweating profusely. Boy, that was a narrow escape, he thought.

By the time he'd got back to the ship and Shezar, he had calmed down, although to Shezar's ears he didn't sound calm.

"We need to get out of here now, this minute!"

As Shezar activated the cloaking device and started the shuttle's engines, she asked, "Why?"

"I've got all the proof I need in here!" Rial held up the mass storage device as he strapped himself into his flight chair. "But I'm guessing that what I've been doing whilst in the archive offices is being looked at right now." He watched as Shezar strapped in. "And they will not like what I've been looking at."

"Who's they? What are you talking about?" asked Shezar.

"Slevin Binx!"

Unlike Rial, Shezar knew exactly who Slevin Binx was.

"How the hell did the Supreme Enforcer get involved with a mere employee of the central museum?"

"He's a friend of Radolfin. You know, the guy that employed me. I was just coming out of the building after capturing the data, when I bumped into the two of them. He started asking awkward questions. I'm not convinced I gave the right answers."

Shezar suddenly treated the incident more seriously.

"Give us your data store."

Rial handed the mass storage device over to Shezar. Shezar placed it into the data transfer conduit and pressed the emergency transfer button.

"That's a bit premature, isn't it?" said Rial.

"Probably," said Shezar, "but we need to be sure that the data gets to Brigade HQ, whether we survive or not. We can't let the Zinden get away with this crime."

The unmistakable voice of Slevin Binx came on the shuttle's communications link.

"This message is for whoever is piloting the ascending spacecraft on the hot side of the Deepfall. If you do not abort your ascent, you will be shot down."

"Have they the technology, Shezar?"

"Yes!"

"Then—"

Rial paused and looked over to the green light on the data transfer module. It had not yet illuminated.

The computer said, "Emergency data transfer complete!" The green LED illuminated. Rial finished his sentence.

"—it's time to see our gods!" said Rial. "We cannot be captured."

"It's been a pleasure working with you, Rial!"

"And you, Shezar."

Shezar pressed the self-destruct button.

Both the shuttle and the mother ship exploded. The detonation was designed to ensure that no fragment, greater than a millimetre, would survive the blasts.

– Chapter Three –

The Journey North

Z-Day...

Razor hadn't driven an articulated truck for some time. In the past he'd always enjoyed the experience. Like Mary, he knew he was far too pumped up with adrenalin to sleep, so he'd talked to Mary about driving one of the trucks. She had no problem with the idea since she knew exactly how he felt. She'd even thought of joining him in the truck but decided against the idea. She wanted to be as fresh as possible for the children the following morning.

Razor opted for driving truck one. The trucks were all numbered so that the right equipment went in the right truck. The main reason for this was to ensure that the holographic recording suite was kept as a separate entity, for demonstration purposes, between the tour dates.

Besides the tour coach itself, truck number one was of significant value. It was the actual truck carrying the holographic systems.

When Judith Wells heard that Razor was to drive, she opted to get in with him to discuss next week's planned schedule. She was particularly worried about the radio interview lists and whether the group could also attend some of the holographic demonstrations.

As the convoy moved out of London and onto the M1 super toll, Judith called the Wilmslow office.

“Phil, nice to here your voice! Did you watch it?”

Razor could hear Phil’s voice but couldn’t make out the exact words he was saying. However, he could tell from Judith’s reaction that he had seen the gig, and that he’d enjoyed it.

“Yes, they are amazing, aren’t they?” Judith smiled at Razor.

“Sorry, say that again, Phil!”

Even though Razor couldn’t hear Phil’s words, he could detect excitement, or was it panic, in his voice?

“What’s wrong, Judy?”

Judy ignored Razor’s question, “What do you mean, fireworks?”

Suddenly a large buzzing sound was heard and the phone went dead.

“Phil? Are you there? Phil?”

There was no answer.

“What was he saying, Judy?”

“That there were fireworks in the sky. Big ones!”

“Weird. Tune into Radio Manchester, there may be some news about the display on the channel.”

Judy turned on the truck radio and tuned into Radio Manchester’s frequency band. There was just static.

Razor and Judy just looked at each other.

“Try Radio Merseyside, they may have noticed something in the skies above Manchester.”

“Good idea!” said Judy.

She tuned into Radio Merseyside and music invaded the cab. They listened for quite some time. There was news of their gig in London, and the DJ played a number of their big hits, but there was no news, at all, of any lights over Manchester.

“Judy, call everyone. Tell them to follow me into the services.”

Five more miles down the road, they pulled into the lorry parking bays, at Newport Pagnell services, just south of the turn off for the M6 to Birmingham and Manchester.

“What’s wrong, Razor?” shouted Lenny, as he jumped down from truck two’s cab.

"Probably nothing. Judy and I got a little spooked that's all. Thought we'd tell you about it."

As Razor explained the night's events so far, Lenny pushed the events to the back of everyone's minds reminding them why they were travelling overnight anyway.

"OK! It's a bit spooky, the radio station being down and all, but I don't think we've any choice. We need to get up there and set this gear up or the concert will not happen on time."

Like everyone else, Razor immediately accepted Lenny's logic, but still he felt uneasy.

"Who's been driving the coach?" asked Razor.

"I have," said Barry Sharp, one of the senior roadies in the crew.

"Where's Mary?"

"Fast asleep at the back of the coach," said, Barry.

"OK! Lenny you take over from me in truck one. Barry, you're driving truck two. Judy and I will be in the coach the rest of the way to Manchester."

Razor got his oPad out and called up the road maps around Manchester. He looked up to address everyone.

"Look, let's all agree to stop at the services just south of the Thelwall Viaduct. According to this map that's the Knutsford services. We'll have supper there and then carry on into Manchester. Agreed?"

Everyone agreed.

Just as the team were getting back into their transport, a bunch of teenagers, who obviously attended the gig, roared past in their mini-coach, chanting, "Near Zero! Near Zero!"

The incident lifted the spirits of the whole group.

As the coach and the trucks got underway, Razor was feeling better, both because of the teenagers' chanting and the fact that he was on the coach. At least if something was awry, he was with Mary.

As time passed, and they branched off from the M1 to the M6, nerves were beginning to settle down again. The journey through Birmingham brightened his spirits. The motorway was lit up like a Christmas tree and for a change there were no traffic jams. Ah! The joy of motoring when driving late at night, it's lovely, he thought.

This temporary change in mood was short-lived, however, since as they were coming out of Birmingham, suddenly the lights on the motorway system went out completely.

Razor looked at Judy, they both knew instantly that something serious was afoot, but what, neither could possibly guess.

"There's no harm trying Radio Manchester and Radio Merseyside again, Judy, whilst we're travelling. Just keep the volume down, there's a lot of them asleep back there."

Judy started to call up the stations. As she was doing so, the four trucks started to overtake the coach.

"What the hell are they doing?" she said. "What's your speed, Razor?"

Razor looked down at his speedometer.

"Damn! I've slowed down."

After the last truck passed him he put his foot down to keep in-touch with its tail-lights.

As Judy set the radio frequency to Radio Manchester again, only static could be heard. She immediately tried Radio Merseyside. Again there was music from the DJ and some chat but nothing that was out of the ordinary.

"Leave it on Radio Merseyside and on low, Judy. If there is something going on it's likely that Merseyside will know about it before any other station."

As their journey continued, and to calm nerves, Razor thought it would be a good idea to talk about the more mundane items on their joint agenda.

"How are the sales of the holographic equipment going?"

Judy was glad of the switch in focus.

"There's been an enormous interest in the gear and we have pre-release orders already, but as you know, I'm not allowed to start selling them until next month."

"Since the band have a stake in those sales I don't think any of us would mind if you started selling early. Especially since we're gigging again."

"No, Razor. We need to keep everything strictly by the book. Another month won't harm."

"How's Mary?" asked Judith.

"OK for now, but in the end, if your team don't do a good job with the kids, I think she'll quit the band."

"Then what happens?"

"If she quits, so do I. It'll be more a wrench for me, but I ain't loosing Mary and the kids, for anything."

Judith wouldn't have expected anything less from Razor.

"It'll be fine. I've got my best girl on the case – what can go wrong?"

Razor was quiet for a while, looking at the road conditions and the lack of traffic.

"Have you noticed something, Judy?"

"What?"

"We haven't seen any traffic coming south for a good 15 minutes – now that's not normal."

Suddenly that irrational fear had come back with a vengeance. She had a bad feeling in the pit of her stomach.

"There's probably been an accident or something?" said Judy, hoping that was a reasonable explanation for something so unreasonable.

"We're travelling at around 80 miles per hour. That means we haven't seen any traffic for 20 miles. Now that's a worry," although Razor didn't know what he was worried about.

"You would expect a lot of traffic on a Saturday night, wouldn't you?" Judy mused.

"Well, there's plenty of traffic going north." Razor said, as a number of vehicles overtook them.

"Sandbach Services is only three miles ahead. We'll stop there and go and have a word with the services staff on the southbound carriageway. They may have heard something. I know we said we'd pull over at Knutsford, but radio the trucks to see if they want to pull over early, at Sandbach."

Judy radioed ahead.

"Tour coach to truck one. Lenny, Can you hear me?"

"Loud and clear, Judith."

"We've noticed a lack of traffic coming south. We thought we'd stop at Sandbach and have a word with the southbound services staff. Can you see if anyone wants to pull over early, with us?"

"Barry and I will, Judy, we're just coming up to the turning now. The other two trucks have already driven past."

"Oh well, no harm. Let the other trucks know what we're doing though, and tell them we'll meet them at Knutsford as planned. Tell them we'll give them a call if we find anything out."

As Judy signed off, the 'one mile to the next services' sign was passed.

A few minutes later they turned into the services and pulled alongside trucks one and two. Lenny and Barry were stood around discussing possibilities for the lack of traffic on the southbound carriageway.

"Well, let's go and have some supper and then we'll walk over to the services on the other carriageway and see if the staff there know what's going on."

Razor moved to the back of the coach, sat beside Mary and nudged her. Mary slowly opened her eyes.

"Hello, sleepy head. Fancy some supper?"

The mention of food did the trick. "Absolutely, I'm famished!" Mary added, "Where are we?"

"Sandbach Services."

They climbed off the coach, very quietly, not wishing to wake the rest of the team. As Mary walked past Terry, he woke.

"I need to go to the loo," he said.

"Shush!" said Mary and Razor, in unison.

After visiting the toilet and getting a paper and a couple of chocolate bars from the shop – Terry joined the others who were raiding the food counters at the café.

They all helped themselves to large amounts of food then pulled a few tables together and gathered around Razor and Judy.

Razor, sitting behind his 'Full English' and looking at Mary, said, "There's been a bit of excitement whilst you've been asleep, young lady."

"Tell me, tell me!" Mary replied excitedly.

Razor informed Mary and Terry of what had been happening.

"Michael, our children are in Manchester!" said a worried Mary.

"It does seem a little on the sinister side," said Judy.

Because of the noise coming from the end of the table, the conversation paused and everyone turned to look at Terry who was eating his meal, at a tremendous rate.

"Whoa there, little brother. Slow down."

Terry looked up from his meal and around at everyone staring at him, "What?"

"You'll get indigestion," said Mary.

"I'm not like you old folk. I need sustenance to grow and develop."

"Old folk!" said Razor, as three of them jumped on him and pretended to beat him.

Supper over, Mary, Judy and Razor walked over the footbridge spanning the two carriageways and strolled into the southbound restaurant, approaching a young girl on the till.

"Have you any idea why there's no traffic going south?"

"No, we've not been told of any problems. But you're right, it's not normally this quiet on a Saturday night."

Even though there were no customers in the restaurant, everything seemed so normal. The three of them started walking back over the footbridge. When they were about two thirds across, there was a huge flash of light, coming from the sky above Manchester. They stood rigid to the spot, looking over to where the flash had come from.

"There was no thunder," said Judy.

"Sheet lightning?" said Razor.

"No way was that sheet lightning," said Judy.

"What time is it?" asked Mary.

"Razor looked at his watch. Ten past two," he said.

Judy and Razor, who had been noticing these isolated incidents from the start, were really quite concerned now. Mary was beginning to pick up their concern.

"Razor, our babies!"
"I know love, that's the main reason we're definitely not going back."

As they rounded up the stragglers, still in the northbound carriageway café, everyone was talking about how bright the flash was in the sky.

They eventually managed to get everyone back into the tour coach.

"Barry, Lenny – we keep together this time. We'll put the coach between the two trucks and both of you have to keep it in your sight. That'll make sure we don't separate.

They both nodded.

The coach headed back onto the northbound carriageway. Richard, who'd slept through everything so far, woke up and joined the others in the front of the coach.

"Where are we?"

"Just south of Knutsford Services," said Mary.

"Boring journey then?"

They all laughed, and Razor told Richard of the night's events.

"Ah! It'll be nothing to worry abou—what's that?"

Coming down the southbound carriageway was a truck, the trailer clearly on fire, and moving at enormous speed. The truck didn't stop.

Up ahead, they could see flickering lights on the northbound carriageway. As they got closer they realised they were looking at more burning trucks and cars.

* * *

Razor's memories were invading the present. To most people the terror wars may have been lost in the mist of history, but they were as clear as daylight to all those that were involved. It was impossible to forget the brutality of the Tong-Hu. God! This can't be happening again! He thought.

Then he was in the past, fighting in the streets of Ashgabat, Richard and the Russian by his side. He was driving the truck when the missile hit. The truck was thrown on its side. The Russian died instantly. The Russian's body lying between the road and him was the only thing that saved his life. Now he was trapped. Then Richard climbed in the cab, dodging the bullets that were making quiet thuds and pinging noises all about them.

"Come on, Michael. It's not your turn to die yet, we've some songs to write."

* * *

Suddenly he was back in the present.

Lenny, who was in the truck ahead of the coach, had slowed down and then stopped. Razor got out of the coach and went to his cab.

"Why've you stopped, Lenny?"

Lenny nodded his head in the direction of two of the burning trucks.

"They're ours, mate!"

"God! Who was driving?"

"Jimmy and Colin were in truck four. Tom Price was in truck three. I'm afraid, from what I can see, Tom's still in truck three!"

Shocked, Razor went around to look into the inferno that was the cab of truck three. He too could also see the outline of a man in the midst of the flames – he felt quite sick.

He rushed back to Mary and the others and told them to stay near the coach. He then climbed the grass bank to the side of the carriageway.

As he climbed the steep embankment, about half a mile away, a car's fuel tank exploded. With flickering light from the burning trucks and cars illuminating the grass slope, he could clearly see that there was no one else on the bank. As he got to the top he started shouting Jimmy and Colin's names. There was no response.

To his left he could see a small wooded area. A perfect hiding place if one was under attack, he thought. He headed into it still shouting their names.

There was a rustle of leaves just off to his right. "Jimmy? Colin?" he repeated, not saying the names quite as loud this time. Again there was no reply.

He suddenly realised that he would be quite defenceless if this was one of the attackers. He grabbed hold of a broken branch and slipped behind a tree trunk. The rustling was much closer now. He was just about to pounce on the noise when he heard, Lenny whisper, "Razor, is that you?"

"Yes," Razor replied.

Lenny jumped! "You frightened me to death!"

"Snap!" Razor said. "There's no one here. We'd better get back to the others."

As they scrambled down the embankment, Razor took out his mobile and called 999. All he could raise was a 'line busy' tone.

"Well, that's a first for a 999 call."

"What is?" asked Mary.

"An engaged tone on the emergency line."

Razor handed over his mobile to Mary.

"Keep trying to raise the emergency services, Mary."

He turned to Lenny.

"Look, Lenny. Knutsford is only a few miles ahead. Let's get there, we'll have a meeting with everyone, and decide what to do. That way if anyone wants to go back south they can take the service road and get on the southbound carriageway from there. I'll take the lead!"

They could probably see Knutsford Services from a good three miles away. Initially they didn't realise what the conflagration was, but as they approached the services it became all too apparent that the whole of the complex was on fire.

It was also apparent why there had been no traffic south. The whole of the southern carriageway was littered with cars and trucks that had been abandoned. The weirdest thing was that most of the cars were undamaged except their bonnets were up. All of their bonnets were up.

"Radio the two trucks, Judy. Tell them to follow me."

Razor took the slip road and carried on round to the service road. He didn't attempt to cross the southbound carriageway. Instead he turned in the opposite direction and moved the tour coach and the other two trucks to a small wooded area, off the main route. By this time everyone in the coach was wide awake. As soon as it came to a halt, Razor shouted, “Right! Everybody out!”

Lenny and Barry jumped out of their trucks and everyone gathered around Razor.

“Look everyone, the first thing we need to do is hide truck one. We can’t afford to lose the holographic systems, regardless of anything else that is happening.”

Razor turned to Lenny and pointed to the small wooded area.

“Lenny, take the truck along that dirt track and back it under that canopy of leaves, it’ll help hide the truck from the air. If we lock it up and leave it here then there’s a chance it won’t get spotted.”

He turned back to face the gathered crew.

“OK! It must be obvious to everyone that something very bad is going down north of here. We may not know what it is, but we do know it’s organised around the Manchester area. We’ve just travelled all the way up from London without any incident and we’ve seen for ourselves that everything south of here is still good.

“In situations like this you have to think with a clear head, so here we go.

“First of all, forget the group and the gigs – they’re history. They’re both completely at an end, until status quo is resumed.

“Second, as you already know, I am ex-special forces and my kids are probably in the middle of what’s going on up there. So I will be travelling north to find my children. My advice to the rest of you is to get on the tour coach and go back south whilst you still can.”

“I’ll be coming along with you, Razor,” said FourLeaf.

A small group, led by Mary and consisting of Lenny, Barry, Sticks, Judith, Dubious and a couple of roadies, gathered beside FourLeaf.

“And so will we,” said Mary.

“Mary—” Razor said.

“Our kids are in Manchester, there’s no way I’m getting on that coach.”

Razor knew immediately there was no changing her mind.

"Make no mistake, anyone coming with me will be putting their life on the line."

There was no response.

"OK! The rest of you, on the coach."

As the crowd split, there was little discussion or indecision and all the others opted for the coach and the safety of getting away from whatever was happening in the area.

Razor was glad to see that most people were heading back south.

"Barry, I want you to drive the coach back south. I know you'd like to stay with the group but they—" Razor nodded towards the coach, "—are going to need a leader on the way back south.

"As soon as it's safe to pull over and contact the authorities, then do so. Tell them what you've seen. Tell them you have a coach full of people that will corroborate your story."

"OK, Razor. Good luck!"

"You too, Barry, you're not out of danger yet. You need to get south as quickly as possible. Probably best to drive without lights. We know there's nothing in front of you, for at least 50 miles."

"OK, Razor – see you at the next gig!"

"Yeah! See you at the next gig, Barry."

With that, Barry climbed into the tour coach's driving seat, started the engine and headed for the southbound carriageway.

Razor opened the back of the remaining truck and let the doors hang loose. "Jump on everyone, we're going to dump this back at the services or it'll lead whoever's creating this mayhem, to the one truck we can't afford to lose. Mary, Judy, you two are in the cab with me."

Razor drove the truck back to the blazing services, driving quickly past and keeping well away from the refuelling area – just in case the fuel tanks blew.

The crew assembled around the truck once more.

"We need to look for transport that's small and nimble. Trucks and four by fours are no good for what we need."

As they spread out to look for the preferred transport, the tour coach was starting to go down the slip road on the southbound carriageway. Everyone paused and ran over to the edge of the carriageway to wave them off.

"Look there's something on fire, travelling on the southbound," said Judy.

The assembled crew could see flashes in the sky, above the fire.

"It's a truck! He needs to slow down. He'll never make it through those stationary vehicles!" said Mary, who was stood next to Judy.

"He isn't going to slow down, Mary. Those flashes are from an aircraft behind him – he's in trouble," said Razor.

"That's no aircraft, Razor," said Judy.

As they watched, the truck started to swerve from side to side. The craft above the truck could now be seen and nothing on planet Earth looked like that.

"My God. It's extraterrestrial!"

The truck took one last swerve, then jack-knifed, rolled over and slid into the stationary vehicles. It kept on sliding and stopped just before it came level with the overpass. The spaceship didn't slow down. It flew past them. It had obviously seen the tour coach and was targeting it. The coach had cleared the slip road and was going full speed in the direction of Birmingham.

It didn't stand a chance. Two flashes came from the spaceship. The tour coach exploded in a huge ball of fire.

"Oh! My God!" exclaimed Mary.

Everyone just looked on in silence as the spaceship flew over the edge of the motorway and disappeared.

Mary threw her arms around Razor, buried her head in his chest and started weeping.

This was the second time Razor had lost members of his crew and this time some of them were his friends, as far as Razor was concerned, the fight just got very personal.

"Look," said Judy. She was pointing to the overturned cab of the truck that had just crashed – someone was climbing out of it.

"Come on! Let's help him," shouted Lenny.

Dubious and Sticks were the closest to the crash. They rushed over and helped to pull the man out.

"Thanks!"

"You OK?" asked Terry.

"A little worse for wear, but OK!" said the stranger.

The three of them ran from the blazing truck, jumped over the central barrier, and ran over to the car park where the rest of the team were.

"That was mighty close," said Razor.

"Far too close for me," said the stranger.

"What the hell was that chasing you?"

"It was an extraterrestrial. They're all over Manchester and the surrounding area. I was going north, trying to get over the Thelwall Viaduct. A huge spaceship and a fleet of smaller ships blocked the road. I managed to pull over and dive into the grass and bushes, on the edge of the motorway. I watched for a while. They were killing everything that moved.

I left my car and jumped over to the southbound carriageway and started walking south. I picked up the truck a few miles down the road. I thought I'd got away from them. Obviously I didn't."

"What do they look like?" asked Judy

"I got a glimpse of some of them on the bridge. They're slightly bigger than us," he said. "Craggy, slightly orange faces. Everything in proportion though, very humanoid in appearance."

"Enough! What's your name, stranger?" said Razor.

"Alan Smith."

"Well, Alan. I'm guessing that we're heading in different directions. I have children in Manchester. I'm not running away – I'm going in to get my children out."

He turned to address the others.

"OK, guys! There are ten of us altogether. We'll travel in pairs from now on. Is there anyone beside Richard and I that has experience of riding motorbikes?"

The stranger and Lenny raised their hands.

"Then let's find some motorbikes if possible, small cars if not. Make sure they'll start. They're no good if they can't move."

"It might be that none of them will work?" shouted Alan.

"What do you mean, how do you know?"

"Did you not see the flash earlier tonight?" he looked at his watch. "At 2:10am?"

"Yes," said Razor.

"That was the EMP pulse – they'll have deployed that to stop any communications getting out from Manchester to the surrounding districts. It would also have paralysed any remaining transport within the Manchester area. They're trying to keep everything local."

"How the hell do you know all that?"

"I'm interested in science; I've read about these things."

"Do you know how to start any of these engines?"

"Funnily enough we are in the right place to find any unaffected vehicles. If the vehicle wasn't moving at the time of the pulse it stands a better chance of being unharmed. An older motorbike would stand a better chance of having survived, than a modern car. Look for bikes or cars that were not moving when the pulse occurred. Even better look for any old or vintage models."

"I think were in luck," said Lenny, as he walked over to a row of some 12 motorbikes.

Lenny, Terry and Kevin started hot-wiring them to see if they could get them going. Four of the bikes started straight away. "Do we need more, Razor?"

"No, but it's worth seeing if more will start, then choose the quietest runners. Fill the chosen four to the top with petrol, but siphon the petrol from other vehicles. Whatever you do, don't go near the garage area, it could blow at any moment."

As they continued to search, Alan Smith and Razor found themselves together.

"I think we need at least one small van in case we have to carry supplies," said Razor.

"What's your plan?" asked Alan.

"Plan? Our children are in Manchester, a few friends also. If they're still alive, I intend to rescue them, then go back down south. What are you going to do?"

"I need to go north, to the Lake District, that's were I live!"

"Are you sure it's safe up there?"

"From what I've seen it's only Manchester that has been hit so far. Things will be fine further north, just like they are down south. In fact, I would suggest that once you have your family, it would be safer if you travel further north than go back down south."

"Why's that?"

"If you're invading somewhere, it's no use capturing fields and lakes. Its population centres you need to attack first. The fields and lakes can wait until later."

"Damn good logic," said Razor.

As they were chatting they were searching amongst the remaining vehicles, in the services car park.

"This is a nice little van," said Razor, as he bent down to hot-wire the starter button. The van sprung into life.

"Would you have space for a few others at your place?"

"How could I refuse," said Alan with a smile.

"Well, why don't you tag along with our group and we'll go north together?"

"What and get shot to pieces, trying to rescue people I don't know?"

Razor gave him a questioning glance.

"Yes!" Razor said.

"It would be my pleasure."

Razor instantly took a liking to the man.

"Thanks!" he said.

– Chapter Four –

Alan Smith

Z-Day minus two weeks...

Alan Smith is an alien shape-shifter, one of many shape-shifters working for the Galactic Enforcement Brigade in this sector of the galaxy. His real name is Uban Drix and he's from the planet Calron, a mind numbing 27 light years from Earth. He chose Alan Smith as a name because it was thought to be one that would allow him to easily integrate into the local population of England, specifically the Lake District – his base whilst on planet Earth.

He chose England on his first trip to Earth, some 50 years ago, because English was the Earth's most common language. So he thought that England would be a good place to check out his linguistic skills.

Once England was chosen as the country to settle in, the Lake District was a certainty as regards where in the country to have his base camp. Fifty years ago, it was not only lightly populated but also seldom visited. To his chagrin, on this trip he has found a huge change, with visitor levels dramatically higher than they used to be. A lake is still a damn good place to hide a spacecraft though.

The reason he is currently on planet Earth is because the Galactic Federation of Planets monitors closely all planets with indigenous, intelligent life forms. This is simply a routine visit for Alan, from which he has to compile a report on the human race and its advances over the last 50 years.

One of the Galactic Federation's basic problems is the sheer number of life-bearing planets in the galaxy. Coping on such a large-scale can sometimes make the Federation seem remote and out of touch.

For example, out of the millions of planets that support intelligent life in this sector of the galaxy, only a few hundred were expected to survive and go on to become successful members of the Galactic Federation. This is because there is a tendency towards extinction on most planets that give birth to the more intelligent life forms.

Why is this? Well, there are so many reasons why these extinction events take place.

Over the last century alone, over 23 worlds have been lost to the Federation in this way. The guestimate, and it is just that – a guess, not an estimate, for the total number of lives lost, is more than 300 billion. This does not include microbial life or insect life.

On the one hand, some losses are due to natural causes, for example: four out of the twenty-three losses were due to unexpected collisions with newly-discovered comets. Three were lost due to sterilisation by gamma ray bursts and would you believe that seven were lost due to short-lived suns engulfing their inhabited worlds.

On the other hand, some problems are self-generated: the leaders of five worlds were unable to understand the disastrous consequences of full-blown nuclear war and were lost due to nuclear annihilation. That's not quite the whole story since the actual extinction event tends to occur some 12 months after the wars have taken place.

Three worlds wandered blissfully unaware into the runaway greenhouse effect. On one world, their scientists successfully engineered a virus that wiped out the whole population of the planet.

In this particular case, the Federation had to step in, but not to save the population. No! Once the virus had done its worst, and the Federation monitored this extinction event, the planet had to be completely sterilised in order to ensure life was safe in the rest of the galaxy.

Don't be fooled by what appears to be callous neglect of dying worlds. If the Federation could help, it would. But because of the sheer numbers involved it knows that, in most cases, this is just not possible.

Almost all of the worlds in the Federation, when they hear about the death-throws of planets such as these, wish they could help. In fact, there are times when consideration is given to that possibility. Maybe one day a situation will occur where other worlds can help, but at present the Federation has decided that to stand apart is the only option.

This conscious decision led the Council of the Federation of Planets to issue a number of directives, laws to you and me, that must be adhered to at all times by its citizens. They are:

The Prime Directive: No planet will knowingly interfere in the development of another planet, either to enhance or retard its development.

This directive was enacted to ensure that planets did not come to dominate one another, or interfere in each other's progress or politics.

The Second Directive: The future well-being of a planet's inhabitants is inextricably linked to the planet's fate!

There are good reasons for this. For example, just imagine trying to relocate 60 billion people from a planet, say on average over three to four light years distant – it's just not possible.

This actually resulted in the making of the third directive also.

The Third Directive: The Federation does not make itself known to fledgling worlds until it is statistically confident that the world will survive its birth pangs.

Just imagine the situation where the population of a doomed planet knew of the existence of the Galactic Federation. This would fill them with false hopes of rescue.

Many lifeboats would be launched into space with no hope of ever being found.

The Fourth Galactic Directive: The Federation will not knowingly stand by and let a civilisation perish that can be helped, so long as the first three directives are upheld.

The fourth directive was agreed some 240 years ago.

This came about because the civilisation known as Brion mounted a successful attempt to alter the trajectory of a fast-moving comet that was going to impact the world known as Asrual in the Tas-Viron system. The collision was due to occur some 76 years in the future and the population of Asrual were completely unaware of their impending doom. It was estimated that the scientists on Brion saved a staggering 67 billion people that year. The Federation praised the planet Brion for their selfless action and awarded the planet their highest honour, The Galactic Medal of Honour.

Under normal circumstances this medal would only be awarded to an individual. Brion is the only planet in the galaxy to have ever been honoured in this manner.

The Fifth Directive: The Federation will not knowingly stand by and let peaceful civilisations perish at the hands of war-like races.

The fifth and final directive gained acceptance only after a bloody conflict between the traders on Scipal and the indigenous population of Dracken. It is estimated that as many as 320 billion people perished in the Dracken wars, mostly on innocent planets, before the conflict was eventually resolved.

This last directive resulted in the formation of the Galactic Enforcement Brigade and Alan Smith was at the sharp end of this outfit.

Field Officers normally work in pairs, generally male and female who bond for life. Alan had not yet selected a partner and it didn't much concern him, he was in no rush. In fact, he was beginning to enjoy his freedom. It was quite common for shape-shifters to pair with individuals outside their actual species. In these circumstances though, offspring were forbidden.

When visiting other planets, Alan always makes a point of buying an address. On Earth, his address is a little holiday cottage on the outskirts of the village of Gosforth near Wastwater in the Lake District National Park. He'd bought it for cash from a local farmer on his first visit.

Being a holiday cottage, he can ensure that when he is away, and he is away a lot of the time, it is let to other holidaymakers. This keeps the cottage dry and warm. He chose his solicitor, banker and letting agent very carefully and made arrangements with them such that the building, more or less, ran itself.

Any payments made to the agent are passed, on a monthly basis, to his solicitor. His solicitor has full access to his bank accounts and deposits all monies earned from the holiday letting.

He'd arranged for the agent to inspect the property once a year and send a detailed report of the maintenance required to his solicitor. His solicitor then reviews the report and employs the necessary tradesmen to make the repairs. The solicitor pays the tradesmen by withdrawing the necessary funds from the account he has access to. The arrangement works very well.

In this regard the internet is a godsend, since even if he is at the other side of the galaxy, Alan can easily communicate with all of his accounts and agents within a very short time.

It may be difficult to actually move from planet to planet, but communications from any planet to anywhere else in the galaxy is easy and more or less instantaneous because of the microscopic wormhole technology.

Another one of Uban Drix's basic philosophies is to use, where practicable, local transport. By doing this he learns much more about what the actual population of the planet think, and sometimes this diverges quite significantly from the rhetoric of their leaders.

He also makes a point of knowing at least one of the languages so fluently that he could easily be regarded as a local. He ensures that he also has cursory knowledge of at least two or three of the other main languages of the planet.

Another trick he uses when away from the spaceship is to only ever use indigenous systems. For example, a company called Orange Computing manufactured his computer pad, the oPad. A manufacturer that was indigenous to the planet Earth. Of course, some of the software and a few hidden scanning devices are from Calron, but these would be completely undetectable, even by the best scientific brains on Earth, if something went wrong and the computing pad fell into local hands.

He knows that, in his line of work, anything could happen. He isn't indestructible. If a building fell on him during a seismic event here on Earth, he would perish just like any local inhabitant would. But no alien devices would be found. Yes, his suit was designed to rapidly decompose his body, if his life was extinguished. But other artefacts, such as the oPad, would remain. It is thus imperative that these items blend in so that when they are subsequently discovered there is no sign of extraterrestrial life.

Z-Day...

This is the back end of Uban's second week here on Earth. The first week had been spent visiting NASA and other locations in the United States. The itinerary for the third week took in Russia and China, but he was on the border with France and Switzerland looking at the CERN facility, when one of the detectors in his oPad registered the impending presence of the Zinden.

The detector was saying that it was only a small force and that they were still beyond the orbit of Saturn. Nevertheless, he knew he had to change his plans immediately. The Zinden were not exactly a peaceful race and it was imperative that he got back to his ship before the Zinden landed.

His ship was near the cottage he'd purchased. It was lying in a body of water called Wastwater in the Wasdale Valley. He used this particular 'parking spot' quite often, simply because he liked the scenery. It also helped that it was sufficiently isolated from the general population – well, it was when he bought it.

The ship was cloaked, of course, and rigged for silent running at low speeds. It was a remarkable craft and not just because it could go at 65% the speed of light. It could actually go super slow also. For example, the speed of exit and entry to the lake can be so slow that humans would find it almost impossible to detect movement, even if they were looking directly at it during take off or landing. The parking spot itself was 200 feet below the surface, so he was quite confident that the ship would not be detected.

As he hurried to book his flight back to England, he couldn't help wondering why the hell the Zinden were here? The planet Zindor was not in the immediate vicinity. Although he vaguely remembered that the two planets were about to come fairly close together, on the galactic scale that is, as they passed each other on the same spiral arm of the galaxy, but if his memory was accurate that wasn't for at least 11,000 years.

The population of Earth had called the Zinden sun the Barnard star and even though they knew about its closest approach, he wasn't aware that they knew of the presence of Zindor itself.

Alan had spent several weeks on Zindor during his training and was not at all impressed with their aggressive attitude.

The Galactic Council does not consider war-like races to be enemies of the Galactic Empire, so long as they keep their war-like nature on their own planet.

This stems from the fact that nearly every species in the Galactic Empire started life by being war-like. This is an early survival strategy for most species. However, nearly all of the planets that survive their early existence become less war-like as they develop. In general, by the time they start on the road to colonisation of their surrounding space, their war-like nature has all but disappeared.

Worryingly, the Zinden are not following the normal pattern. It is possible that one day they may well have to be exterminated to prevent serious loss of life on other worlds.

Being isolated, Alan could only observe what was about to happen. There was very little he could do to help the local population of Earth. Assuming his ship is still intact, then if he could get back to it, he could contact his enforcement team.

It's the usual story, though. The distance between stars makes it nigh impossible to help planets in distress.

He'd got on a KLM flight from Geneva to Manchester with a view to hiring a car to take him the short journey from Manchester Airport to the Lake District. His detector wasn't giving him good news, however. He'd been viewing it ever since getting on the KLM flight and he was beginning to get quite nervous since the detector was implying that the aircraft that he was on would land at Manchester Airport, just as the Zinden would land south west of it.

What the hell were they up to? He thought.

He didn't like the fact that he would be so close to the Zinden ships when they landed. If his true genus were detected, he would be hunted down like a dog. He was thinking that they wouldn't expect other alien life on the planet and any detection systems they had wouldn't be switched on. On the other hand, he might well end up needing help, just like he imagined the local inhabitants of this planet would need help in a few hours' time.

The aeroplane landed without incident, but he knew he had very little time to get on the move. Quickly hiring a rental car, he drove out of the airport and onto the M56, heading towards the M56/M6 interchange, so that he could journey north to the Lakes.

As he joined the M6 northbound carriageway, his detector was telling him that the Zinden mother ship was on the ground, directly ahead. He slowed down to a crawl, everything looked quite normal so far.

The car that was immediately behind him sounded its horn and he could hear swearing from the passengers as they overtook him. They didn't have long to be angry. As the car swept round the curve in front of him, a death ray came out from a spaceship, which had just appeared above them. The car suddenly erupted in flame.

Alan pulled over, jumped out of the hire car and headed for the bushes on the side of the road. Immediately his car was engulfed in flame.

He could hear and see the panic in the indigenous species; it was obvious that they hadn't seen anything like this before.

As he peered through the undergrowth he could see the enormous mother ship that had already landed and was sprawled across the two carriageways on the top of the viaduct he'd been heading for. There was little point in trying to carry on driving up the M6. Absolutely nothing he had could get him passed that.

For a time he just watched, both wondering what the Zinden were doing, and how to get around them, so he could reach his own ship.

It was obvious they were securing the motorways around Manchester. He could see further flashes behind the Thelwall Viaduct, probably along the M62 – he thought.

Alan knew the Zinden language and there were Zinden actually standing on the bridge, but he just couldn't get close enough to hear what they were saying.

It was time to get out of here. He'd learnt all that could be learnt from his current situation and now he needed to find some way around them. Keeping low, he crawled over to the central barrier. After jumping the barrier and carefully crossing over the south-bound carriageway, he moved south on foot, assessing the cars and trucks that weren't on fire, to see if there was one he could salvage, in order to move south more quickly. After about two miles he noticed a dark shape amongst the trees ahead.

It was a truck, untouched! The driver had obviously driven it into cover, but had then fled, or worse. The cab door was open the keys still in the ignition, sandwiches still on the passenger seat. He carefully angled the wing mirrors so that he could see a little of the sky as well as the road. As he turned the ignition key, Alan was praying to his god that the damn thing would start up. It did. He set off very slowly, keeping on the hard shoulder and as near as possible to the banking. He kept the lights off all the way and was only illuminated by the fires from the cars and trucks that had been destroyed in an earlier bombardment. His only thought was what may come from the skies, not what may be on the road. He was so busy looking at the sky that at times he clipped other cars and trucks as he drove south.

With every mile gained between him and the bridge, he drove faster and faster and felt safer and safer. He decided to head for the services. He had it in his head, that would be a good place to pick up another vehicle for travelling back north, but this time off the motorway system altogether. He knew Knutsford Services were fairly close by, so he headed for them. He was probably only a few miles away from Knutsford when he saw the high-altitude electromagnetic pulse in his wing mirrors. Instantly the lights for miles around went out. He was expecting the truck to stop but then he realised the truck was old, old technology, no microchips. Thank God for old technology, he thought.

His elation was short-lived, however. The pulse flair must have highlighted his movement and suddenly a Zinden fighter was upon him. The first few shots went wide but the third shot hit the rear of the articulated truck. He was now driving along in a truck that was on fire, a Zinden fighter still attacking him and he still hadn't reached the services.

As he swerved to avoid being hit again by the fighter's death rays, he could see the services come into view. Just another mile would do it—!

– Chapter Five –

Dave's Brother

Z-Day...

Dave Singleton lived in Blackburn some 30 miles north of Manchester. It was his baby brother Simon's birthday and the lads had gone into Manchester to celebrate. He felt guilty as hell not being there, but he just couldn't leave the business on this particular night.

The business was a bar in the centre of town. The owner of the bar was on holiday for two weeks and Dave had the responsibility of keeping it operational during that time.

For a Saturday night it had been relatively quiet, a lot of the town were on holiday just like the bar owners, so by one o'clock the place was nearly deserted.

Still, it was around quarter past two in the morning when he'd finally cashed up, and got the place ready for the next day. The chef and the kitchen staff had long gone.

He stepped outside and was surprised to see it was a clear, dry night, yet he was sure he'd seen lightning just before he came out.

As he locked the door his mobile phone rang. It was Simon.

"Dave, something very strange is going on here."

"Simon, is that you – why are you whispering?"

Dave could hear screaming in the background, getting louder then quieter as if the person who was screaming had just run past Simon's mobile.

"Dave, I'm in this huge underground car park near the G-Mex Centre. I was inside the car when I saw a brilliant flash of light. It could be terrorism. The car won't start, there are lots of people here but my phone is the only one that is working – phone the cops! – can't stop – got to go – phone the cops!"

"Is this a joke?"

"Not this time, Dave. Tell them there's a big group of people in this underground car park – got to go!"

There was something in Simon's voice that made it seem very real. It didn't feel like one of Simon's jokes and then there was the screaming in the background.

Dave dialled the local police station, and as he was doing so, he unlocked the door he'd just locked and re-entered the bar. He walked over to a small monitor and switched it on. If anything was happening in Manchester, especially anything to do with terrorism, there surely would be something about it on Sky News.

The desk sergeant answered the phone.

"Blackburn Police Station."

"Hi there, my name is Dave Singleton, I've just had a phone call from my brother, who is in Manchester, he's told me to phone the police. He says there's a terrorist attack taking place."

"Do you think he may be drunk, Sir?"

"No! He's not a heavy drinker."

"Well, in that case, you tell him to phone the police station in Manchester, Mr Singleton. They're quite capable of handling such an emergency."

Dave switched his phone off in disgust and threw it on the bar.

"Coppers!"

There was nothing on Sky News to indicate anything unusual. Just Alistair McGovern talking about United losing their fourth game in a row. So he went to turn off the monitor. He was just about to press the standby button when the newscast was interrupted.

"We're just getting reports coming in of an unusual occurrence in the skies above Manchester. Our Sarah Brandon is in Macclesfield, following the Home Secretary's visit to the north west. She's on air now, live from Macclesfield—"

The screen changed to a shot of a slim, blonde woman looking directly at the camera.

"Sarah, what can you tell us?"

"Well, nothing concrete at the moment, Alistair, but just a few minutes ago there was a huge flash of light that came from the direction of Manchester. The crew and I actually saw it. It only lasted for a very short time. There's been real speculation here as to what it was. We've had suggestions ranging from an asteroid exploding high in the atmosphere, to a nuclear explosion. None of us really know. We've decided to go up to Manchester and talk to the people up there. So we may have more to report to you in about an hour's time."

"OK, Sarah, speak to you then."

Dave didn't need any more prodding. He realised the thing he thought was lightning was probably the flash that everyone saw above Manchester. If his little brother was in trouble, he needed to be there. He grabbed his mobile and set off for Manchester in his beat-up and very old Mini.

Dave was on the A666 on the high side of Darwen. It was a stunningly beautiful, moonlit night. The pinprick of light from each and every star was as sharp as he had ever seen. The moors were illuminated with the light from the full moon and away in the distance were the red, vertical lights from the mast on Winter Hill.

He couldn't have been more than a few minutes out of Darwen, when he saw his first glimpse of the alien craft. It was hovering above the Winter Hill transmitters and shooting at the base of the towers.

The scene he was witnessing was far enough away for the sound to have not yet arrived. So he was seeing what was happening, but it didn't register as being real, until the sound did eventually arrive. Then there was no doubt whatsoever – it was real, alright.

He parked his Mini to the side of a dry stone wall and watched the firework display, fascinated by what was unfolding before him. Suddenly, a car sounded its horn as it fled past him, then another.

The sound of the horns seemed to mingle with another sound that was getting louder and louder. Then he realised that whatever was making that sound was near, he glanced to his left "Holy shit!" he remarked as a spaceship attacked the cars that had just passed him. There was an almighty double-bang as the two cars erupted into balls of fire. He jumped over the dry stone wall hoping to God that the aliens hadn't spotted him.

He crouched behind the wall for some time until he was convinced he hadn't been seen. The spacecraft was hovering over the A666 as if blockading the road to Bolton. In the distance, coming up from Bolton, Dave could see headlights. The spacecraft turned and headed away from Dave's position as if to intercept the traffic.

This was his chance – he was thinking he might not have another. He climbed over the dry stone wall and quietly got into the Mini. The noise of the driver's door closing seemed like thunder.

He waited, poised with his hand on the ignition key, to start the engine. He knew that the ship would attack the cars heading his way and the moment the attack started would be a good time to move.

The ship fired on the oncoming traffic. One of the cars instantly exploded. At that precise moment he turned the key, the Mini sprung into life. He immediately did a u-turn and headed back to Darwen.

He was looking in his rear-view mirror, seeing the headlights turning into balls of fire as the spacecraft did its murderous work and thanking God that he was in his Mini. No other car he knew could have done a u-turn on that road. To him, the situation was obvious. Whilst the aliens were busy attacking the cars coming out from Bolton, they wouldn't be attacking him.

As he drove back into Darwen he couldn't help but notice how normal everything was. Just over the hill people were dying. Just here, nothing untoward was happening. A stop at the local police station would do no good since it would not be manned now, anyway there was no time to waste, and judging from the reaction he got when he last phoned the police, he was not sure they would believe him anyway.

He drove to the M65 and headed for the M6, deciding that the M61 ran too close to Winter Hill so it was no use taking that route.

He removed his mobile phone from his jacket pocket. Yes, it was illegal to use it whilst driving, but what the hell! This was one night where the rulebook just didn't apply.

As he turned onto the M6 he tried Simon's number. Simon answered in a whisper, "Dave, can't talk. Dangerous situation."

"Simon, don't hang up! You don't need to talk, just listen. I've just seen what's causing the mayhem. They look like alien ships. They seem to be running a cordon around the Manchester area; there's no sign of them moving any further north, as yet. I'm going to try to come in and get you. I know roughly where you are, I'll contact you later when I'm nearer your position. Put your phone on silent and vibrate, and keep it close to your body. Meanwhile don't do anything rash. Keep safe and sit tight.

It was good to hear Simon's voice. Now he knew that at least his baby brother was still alive.

As he went south he turned the radio on and tuned to Radio Manchester – there was just static. He tried Radio Lancashire, the local station based in Blackburn. He knew Blackburn was untouched; he'd just driven through it.

The sound of Fred Starkey coming over the airwaves was comforting – just at that moment the program was interrupted.

"We're just getting news of a serious accident at the junction of the M62 and the M6. It is expected to cause severe delays. You are advised to use alternative routes."

That had to be the aliens, Dave thought. There's no way I'm going to get into Manchester using the main roads. Then it struck him – the canal, doesn't that go all the way into the centre? Surely the aliens wouldn't think of that.

He knew he would have to turn off the M6 before the M62 junction and he'd used junction 24 in the past, when he'd gone to the Haydock Racecourse to watch the horses.

He turned off, drove passed the turn-off for the Haydock Racecourse, and headed for the Runcorn Bridge that spanned the Mersey and the Manchester Ship Canal.

As he drove through Widnes and over the bridge he looked for some sort of transport up the canal but he couldn't see a boat or ship anywhere.

He parked the Mini on the quayside and wandered towards what looked like a party still going on at the local pub. A small group of people were stood outside smoking.

"It's nearly 2:30 in the morning, what's going on?"

"A wedding mate! The coppers turn a blind-eye when it's a wedding. So long as we keep the noise down."

As he wandered into the pub, he was again struck by how normal everything was, yet he knew that just a few miles down the M56, there were aliens invading the planet. After ordering a pint of beer, he sat down to collect his thoughts.

A local rushed into the bar and shouted, "Something's going on in Manchester. It's on the news."

The bartender immediately switched on the TV and turned to Sky News.

It was Sarah somebody or other? The reporter he had seen earlier. She was crouched down and whispering, as if hiding from something.

"We've just driven through Stockport and we're now on the outskirts of Manchester – just past a roundabout that has the Apollo Theatre on it. As we took the roundabout we heard several explosions just north of here.

"There's definitely something going on here but we still don't know quite what it is. We're hearing lots of explosions

and seeing numerous flashes of lights in the sky. It's almost as if the city is under attack."

The wedding party started to crowd around the TV.

"The crew and I are going to try to get nearer, but we dare not use the van. We are going in on foot."

There was a large explosion a couple of hundred metres away, at the end of the street. The camera caught a large pawl of black smoke rising into the air, followed by a billowing cloud of grey ash that swept across the street.

The local crowd were stunned into silence. Dave spoke up.

"It's an alien invasion you know, I've seen their ships."

Some of the assembled group weren't for believing Dave, and he wasn't surprised. He could hardly believe it himself. Still, he could tell there was a few that did. He suddenly realised that one of this lot might have a boat.

"Look my kid brother is in Manchester. I've tried to get in by road but the aliens have all the roads blocked. The only way I can think of getting to the centre without using the roads is via the ship canal. I don't think the aliens would be looking there. But I can't find a damn boat anywhere round here. Has anyone got one?"

Well over half the people he was talking to, just ignored him. They were too intent on seeing the news coverage.

A short, old man with a white beard, moustache and hardly any hair on his head, turned and said, "I 'ave one lad, but it comes with a skipper and it's moored at Ellesmere Port's Boat Museum."

Another local, Jack, chirped in, "They're all narrow boats, Bill."

"Best type. Don't have to worry about the swing bridges. Anyway the problem isn't the boat but the locks, Jack." He turned to Dave, "You see, young man, there are four sets of locks twixt 'ere and the centre of Manchester: Latchford, Irlam, Barton and Mode Wheel. We'd 'ave to get through every one of them without being caught."

"Do you know how to get us through those locks?" asked Dave.

"We'd 'ave to break into the lock-keeper cabins. The locks aren't the type you can work by hand – but yes, I know what to do!"

"Bill! Are you up for it?" asked, Dave.

Bill smiled, "Too right, I am lad."

"You seem awful keen to put yourself in danger, Bill."

"Old soldiers, never die," he said. "Besides I worked on the canal all my working life. Loved it! It'll be like going back in time for me. Where's your brother?"

"He was supposed to be in the G-Mex, but when the aliens struck he was in what he describes as a huge underground car park. How far does the canal go into the centre of Manchester?"

"All the way, lad, and from what your telling me, damn close to the place your brother is."

"How long would it take to get in there, once we're on the boat?"

"That's going to be another problem. Let's put it this way, it'll definitely be daylight by the time we get there."

"Then let's get out of here, we haven't a minute to lose."

Dave and Bill left the pub.

The others remained glued to the newscast as the anchorman talked over the live feed.

"Sarah, what do you see? Can you see what's caused the explosions?"

"Not yet, Alistair. There's a huge amount of noise coming from the end of the street. We're going to try to get that far."

The live feed was showing the devastation in the street, with masonry, glass and dust all over the tarmac road. There was a definite rise in background noise, as the camera was taken further down the street.

After a short time, the camera finally reached the end of the street and panned around.

The live feed showed an extraterrestrial spacecraft hovering about 20 feet off the ground. The crowd in the pub gasped! Everyone in the pub believed the stranger now.

"Oh, my God! Alistair. It appears to be a spacecraft," Sarah's voice was just a whisper now. The live feed showed the death ray coming out now and again, as the alien craft detected movement or sound.

Suddenly the death ray flashed towards the camera. Static appeared on the screen, where just a second ago was the picture. After a few more seconds the screen was once again filled with the image of Alistair McGovern, clearly worried for the safety of the camera team.

"Well, we seem to have lost our live feed from Manchester. Let's hope Sarah and her team are OK."

He regained his composure.

"It's obvious now that there is some sort of attack taking place in Manchester."

A small 'picture in picture' box appeared showing the scene outside the Prime Minister's residence.

"Let's go over to Cameron Draper, who's outside Number 10 Downing Street. Cameron, have you heard anything from Number 10?"

"Yes, Number 10 have issued a statement saying that, and I quote: 'There is something unusual going on in the city of Manchester.' *It also states that the Prime Minister will come out and speak to us, as soon as he has some clarity on the situation."*

"OK, Cameron—we'll take a short break. We'll see you after the adverts – don't go away."

The crowd's silence was replaced by a cacophony of noise as everyone discussed what they had just seen.

Just as the second commercial was about to appear on the screen, pictures coming from the live feed outside Number 10, interrupted it.

"Shush! Everyone. There's something happening!" shouted the barman.

The noise abated and Alistair McGovern's voice could again be heard.

"We're told that the Prime Minister is to address the nation—Yes, the door of Number 10 is opening—"

The PM walked up to the podium that had been set up in front of the press.

"Good evening, everyone. I have some grave news to impart to all our citizens. It appears that Manchester is under attack from an alien force, of which we know very little.

"It is clear that this attack is isolated. There have been no other attacks that we know of anywhere else in the world. We are currently trying to communicate with the aliens but we have not been able to do so, as yet. We have had reports that they are also removing large quantities of artefacts and materials from Manchester.

"I have instructed our armed services to surround the affected area, and repel any effort by the aliens to expand their territorial gains. The commander in chief, Major General Sir John Dowding, has informed me that currently, the aliens are staying where they are and they are not expanding their boundaries. In fact, the aliens who invaded the area south west of Manchester have actually retreated back to their central location.

"Well, that's all I have for you at this moment in time. Are there any questions?"

"Have you any advice for the people in Manchester?"

"Yes, stay in your homes and don't panic. We have had no reports of the aliens attacking homes – just cars, trucks and large structures, especially motorways and anything moving on them."

"Have you any idea why we didn't detect them before they landed?"

"Not at the moment."

"Don't you feel this is a somewhat peculiar invasion?"

"In what sense?"

"Well, surely if you're going to invade a planet you'd want to have multiple points of entry. It seems more like a robbery to me, targeting one area and removing artefacts."

"I understand your point but we have nothing to base any assumptions on at present. That's all, ladies and gentlemen." The PM didn't wait for further questions. *"When we have any further news, we will let you know."*

With that the PM went inside Number 10, ignoring further questions from the press core.

– Chapter Six –

A Way In

Z-Day...

Razor gathered everyone together in front of the little van. His oPad was in his hand. He'd been using it to map out their next move. The flickering light from the services' café, which was off to the right and still totally engulfed in flames, made the scene look almost primitive.

"OK, everyone! Everything's fuelled up and ready to go. I suggest that we get off the motorway system altogether and head up to Warrington. See if we can take the M62 into Manchester."

"I don't think that's a good idea," said Alan Smith.

"Why not?"

"I think all the roads into Manchester will be blocked."

At this point Razor had no other suggestions as to how to proceed.

"Have you a better idea, Alan?"

"I've been looking on the oMap. There seems to be a way that the aliens may have completely overlooked."

"And what's that?"

"The ship canal."

Razor typed the words into his oPad and the ship canal was overlaid onto his map in bright blue. He looked at it intensely.

"That's not a bad idea, Alan," said Razor, "and it seems to go all the way into the centre?"

"From what I can see on my oPad, it does. There appears to be one major problem, however."

"What's that?" asked Razor.

"If I view oEarth, I can't find any small ships on the canal, until I go out as far as Ellesmere Port. There's a boat museum there, which houses what looks like small boats. Whether they would be suitable or not, I can't say?"

"That's a long way out, Alan."

"There's nothing else. Have a look."

Some time was spent following the canal on oEarth. Alan was right, nothing until the museum, then a load of them clustered around that site.

"It looks like we've no choice but to head up there, if we're going with Alan's idea," said Razor.

"It sounds good to me," said Lenny.

"I agree," said Judith.

"OK! We'll avoid the M56 by following the A roads through Northwich, then Chester, then get on the M53 to Ellesmere Port. Let's hope the aliens aren't looking to move that far west.

"Mary, you're with me, on the Triumph.

"Alan and Judy on the Harley.

"Kevin, you and the lads take the van.

"Richard and Terry on the Honda.

"Lenny, you bring up the rear on the other Harley. If we get separated, we meet at the boat museum. If the aliens stop any of us, then the rest keep going. No going back for anyone – is that clear?"

There were nods all round.

Judith was quite pleased that she was riding with the stranger, she'd taken a shine to him straight away, and this would be a good way of getting to know him.

As the little convoy set off, they had no choice but to go past the garage, which was by now an inferno. The road past the garage was close to the conflagration, far too close for comfort.

Each vehicle drove past the hot spot at speed, and turned onto the A5033, heading towards the A556.

Lenny's vehicle must have only been three or four hundred yards past it when the garage finally blew. The blast and heat radiation from the explosion nearly toppled him.

To make things worse, as they moved along the A556 through Northwich, the sound of the alien invasion fleet attacking the citizens of Earth, seemed to be getting closer and closer.

"I don't think they're staying in Manchester, Michael," Mary shouted to Razor over the noise of the wind.

"I feel like we're being followed," said Razor.

The two of them carried on in silence as the motorbikes roared through the countryside towards Chester.

As the mini convoy joined the A54, an enormous explosion was heard in the direction of Winsford.

"I'm surprised they're bothering to invade this area. It doesn't appear to be heavily populated," said Alan.

"Maybe they need a supply of salt for their spaceships," Judy said jokingly.

"Why, are there salt mines around here?"

"Yes!"

Judy was feeling very comfortable behind Alan. Maybe it was the close proximity or just having to hang on to his waist as they sped through the night.

This was a romantic moment for her. She'd had very few romantic moments over the last few years and so she'd decided that she was going to enjoy this one.

Suddenly a death ray shot just wide of them. She looked behind her and saw that the van was under attack.

"What's happening, Judy?" asked Alan.

"They're attacking the van, I don't think they've even seen us!"

"Then I think we'd better—" Alan stopped talking mid sentence and slid the bike, himself and Judy into a field at the side of the road. As all three of them came to a halt he added, "Sorry, Judy, had to act in a hurry!"

That was fine with her. For a moment she lay on top of him wondering whether to kiss him.

They both rolled over to see whether or not the van had got away. There was a mighty explosion, as the van's fuel tank was ripped apart. Judy immediately threw her head into Alan's chest and started to cry. She was losing the only people she cared about and it hurt like hell.

Alan stroked her hair.

"Judy, you need to hold it together, there's nothing we can do for them now. We have to be strong if we're going to get our own back on these monsters."

Judy stayed nestled in his arms, still crying.

It had been a long time since he had felt warmth and affection from someone. Alan was thinking that it was good to be needed.

He thought it best to just leave her there for a moment.

Judith didn't want to lift her head, or go anywhere else. She just wanted to stay safe in these arms that were wrapped around her.

They remained there for a few more minutes, and then a voice broke the silence.

"You OK, you two?"

It was Lenny.

"That was a hell of a good manoeuvre, Alan. It damn well saved your life."

"Thanks, Lenny. I'd have preferred not to do it, though." He stood up and bent his back forward as if he'd hurt his spine."

"Are you alright?" asked Judy, tears still running down her face.

"Fine." He smiled at Judy and looked at Lenny. "I was following the front two bikes, Lenny. I don't actually know the way to the museum, do you?"

"No problem, Alan. Just follow me."

Lenny was ready to go. Alan stopped him.

"I think we should just wait here for 30 minutes, Lenny. We'll go over and hide under those trees, just in case the spaceship returns."

They rolled their bikes under the tree cover.

"Of all the places on Earth to choose, who would have thought Manchester was worth the effort?" Lenny said in exasperation.

"It's not just Manchester, Lenny. Why are they attacking this area, also? What is this little town called, Judy?"

"Winsford! You don't know this area, do you Alan?" asked Judy.

"No, not really. I once visited Jodrell Bank. That's somewhere around here isn't it?"

"Maybe that's why they're here," said Lenny.

"Maybe," said Alan in a most unconvincing manner.

The spacecraft's engines could be heard getting louder and louder. Everyone crouched down and remained silent.

The ship hovered for a while and then moved down the road in the direction of Northwich. After two or three minutes they began to talk again, but in a whisper.

"Should we get going?" asked Lenny.

"Yes, but let's keep everything low-key, nice and slow, no lights. Use your mirrors to look up and back, rather than just back. If you spot anything, just run off the road if you can – I'll follow."

They mounted their bikes and slowly but surely rode towards Chester, the M53 and the boat museum.

Mary and Razor had no idea who may have survived the last attack. They knew there was an explosion but they weren't sure whether any or all had been hit by the death ray.

Razor wouldn't stop to find out.

"We must press on," he said.

Mary was wondering, after the last attack, whether or not she had many friends left. She was feeling tearful, but not having any of it. This wasn't the time to let her emotions get the better of her.

"I wonder if anyone has been able to get word out about what's going on?" she said, "You'd think that with all the mobile phones and internet connections in Manchester, someone, somewhere should be getting a message by now."

"You heard what Alan said. If that electromagnetic pulse did its job, everyone's phone and computer would be out of action!"

"So you don't think the rest of the country knows what's going on?" asked Mary.

"I don't think they know yet. I think they will know by dawn, no matter how much containment the aliens think they can conjure up. Reports of their activities will be out there by then."

"Why would they want to keep a lid on it anyway?"

"Time, they need time to get a foothold. Maybe they're digging in for the long haul. It's obvious their intentions are not peaceful so maybe they need time to put in place a defensive mechanism."

As Razor and Mary talked, they progressed onto the M53. Richard and Terry's bike was still behind them.

"We've not far to go now," said Razor.

It wasn't long after joining the M53 that the brown signs for the boat museum came into view. The two bikes pulled off at the next exit, turned under the motorway and then immediately left into the museum car park. As the two bikes parked up, the four of them gathered together.

"I don't think Kevin or the lads could possibly have survived that strike," said Terry.

"It was the van that exploded?" asked Razor.

"Yes."

"Did anyone see what happened to Alan and Judy?" asked Mary.

"I saw them come off their bike, just as the van blew," said Richard. "Lenny was following way back in the rear, so I'm guessing he'll be OK."

"Maybe we should give the lads a little time to get here before we launch ourselves on that canal. Terry, you and Mary stay here, wait for them. Richard and I will go and see what lies beyond that entrance."

Richard and Razor quickly disappeared from view as Mary and Terry waited in the car park.

"I can't believe that the aliens in that spacecraft didn't see the bikes," said Terry.

"Thank God, they didn't," Mary said, "but I don't think Alan and Judy could have been hit. If that spacecraft didn't see us, then it didn't see them either."

Some 15 minutes had passed by the time Richard and Razor returned.

"We've just been—shush!" said Razor.

The sound of motorbikes could be heard coming along the M53. The bikes turned onto the road that led to the car park and museum.

Mary rushed towards the second bike's, pillion passenger.

"You made it!" She threw her arms around Judy.

"Thanks to Alan's quick thinking."

Razor came up and shook Alan's hand, "Well done, mate. Lenny tells me you saved our Judy's skin."

"A purely selfish act, Razor. I was on the bike with her, remember."

Judy hit Alan on the back, "Alan! And I thought you cared!"

Alan smiled and turned to Judy, "I do, Judy – but we've only just met."

"Shush—" said Razor.

This time the sound was of a small car's engine being pushed to its limits, accompanied by the screeching of tyres as it rounded the roundabout under the motorway flyover.

It was a Mini with two occupants. It tore into the car park and came to a halt, across from the gathered cyclists.

The driver of the Mini jumped out and walked over to the assembled bikers. "Are you lot anything to do with the boat museum?"

"No! Sorry, what's the problem?" asked Razor.

"Look I know this may sound silly but there are aliens in Manchester—" Dave paused, expecting to be given short shrift by the people he'd just met.

"And you want to go in via the canal because all the roads are blocked?" said Razor.

Dave was stunned, "My kid brother's in there, I need to rescue him."

"Where exactly is he?" asked Razor

"In a car park under the G-Mex Centre. I've been talking to him by phone," said Dave.

"His phone is working?" asked Alan.

"Yes, he's waiting for news from me – on a rescue plan."

"What's your name?" asked Mary.

"Oh! Sorry, it's Dave, and my friend here is called Bill. He has a boat and is an expert on the ship canal."

"Dave you've made my day, my name's Razor."

Dave laughed, "You don't need to tell me who you are. Everyone on Earth knows you."

"Well, my children are in Manchester, Dave. So I'm also on a rescue mission."

"Whereabouts are they?" asked Bill who had wandered over from the Mini.

"They're staying at the Lowry Hotel. It's in central Manchester," said Mary.

"That couldn't be better placed, it's actually on the canal," said Bill.

"Can you help us?" said Mary.

"Yes," said Bill.

"We were about to do exactly what you were planning to do. My kid brother's in there and we plan to get him out," said Dave.

"It's obvious we'll need a big boat if we're going to try to take lots of people out," said Razor.

"No, the smaller the boat, the better. That way we won't have to bother about any of the swing bridges. The best bet is a flotilla of narrow boats," said Bill.

"OK! Let's get the boats moored on the side of the canal," said Razor. "Bill, you're in charge. What do we do?"

"First of all, you lot all need to understand that in order to get into the centre of Manchester we will have to break a few laws. The police may come after us."

"Explain yourself, Bill."

"Well, the canal is monitored and controlled by Shipping Control at Eastham, so once we proceed down the canal we'll be seen. Now they won't bother about us until we break into the first lock-control building at Latchford."

"Why do we need to break into the place?"

"The clue's in the name of the canal. It's a *ship* canal, not a boat canal. The lock gates are massive and they can't be moved by hand. We will have to operate them from the control building and even though the building won't be manned, it will be locked."

"Do you know how to do that?"

"I've worked on the canal all my life, of course I do."

"So, what's the problem, Bill? They'll not be able to do anything about it. We'll be through the lock gates and long gone before the police arrive," said Alan.

"Yes, but then we have to do the same at Irlam, Barton and Mode Wheel. They're going to get very angry."

"Yes, but you have to remember, Bill, once we get under the Thelwall viaduct, it doesn't matter. We'll be in alien territory by then. Just as long as they can't stop us prior to that, we'll be fine," said Razor.

"OK! Another thing to get in your heads is that this trip is going to be a long one. It'll take at least six hours, possibly eight, to get in and the same to get back out. These boats aren't fast and that canal is very long!"

"I think the slowness of the boats works in our favour, Bill. I think that's why the aliens have so far, and will continue to, ignore them. So, in my opinion going slow isn't an option, it's a necessity, if we're going to survive the trip," said Alan.

"OK, so long as you understand," added Bill, who busied himself checking the fuel levels on the few narrow boats he could easily get into the ship canal. There were only two with enough fuel for the round trip. He thought of towing more behind the two working boats, but rejected the idea. He didn't want to slow the journey down even more. It would be long enough as it is.

He demonstrated to Razor how to negotiate the smaller locks and in very short time he had the two boats in the ship canal.

– Chapter Seven –

The Children

Z-Day (earlier in the day)...

"I'm looking for feedback so I can give you the perfect 12 weeks. You've seen the itinerary for the first two weeks. Do you think it's too busy, Wendy?"

"Not at all. All the visits you've planned are excellent, but you mustn't keep that pace up. You see, for a few weeks the children will lap it up, but if the pace is too fast it'll all become a blur and they'll stop enjoying it. I think one of the keys is to try to stay in one place for, say, each four-week period. And you need to think like a homely person. If you think like that, we'll be stopping in cottages and villas rather than hotel rooms. These are the things that are important to children – stability is the key."

Cheryl was slightly worried now. She'd never thought of the homely aspect until Wendy had said those words. She'd just been thinking of what they would like to see. "So do you think I've started off badly, with booking into the Lowry?"

"Not at all, because the children have never stayed in a hotel. So for the first week they'll enjoy their time there. After the first week I would move us to more homely residences and calm it down a little. But don't get me wrong, Cheryl, I think for the first week, hotel rooms are just fine."

There was a whoosh, then outside only blackness. Seamlessly, the carriage lights switched on. For a few minutes, whilst the train was in the tunnel, neither spoke, with Wendy checking the children and Cheryl thinking of how to reorganise things a little. She needed to fit into Wendy's view of what should really be happening over what would be an extended period.

She was beginning to like Wendy. The girl knew what she was talking about when it came to children. No wonder Mary and Razor spoke so highly of her.

The view outside returned once more as the train exited the tunnel.

"So you're disappearing once we get up to Manchester?"

"Yes, I just want to make sure you settle in OK, then I'm straight back down to London for an important meeting with one of Judy's team."

"I really don't know how you cope with that pace of life, Cheryl."

"Each to her own, Wendy. I don't know how you manage to be with kids twenty-four seven. It would drive me daft."

The children were absolutely fascinated with their time on the train. Tunnels were really exciting, and the children jumped out of their skins when other trains, travelling in the other direction, passed them.

After her eleven o'clock snack, Abigail fell fast asleep whilst appropriately counting sheep in the fields passing by. Daniel was fascinated by how different the scenery was from the island they'd been on for the past three years. He couldn't take his eyes off the vistas that were opening up in front of him. What a big world, he thought.

On arrival in Manchester, Wendy had to wake Abigail.

A car was waiting for them at the station, to take them to their hotel. Then, after saying goodbye to Cheryl, they embarked on their trip to the Science Museum.

They arrived in front of what looked like a very old railway station with a big 'MOSI' sign posted over the entrance door. Apparently MOSI stood for Museum of

Science and Industry. Initially, they went to eat dinner at the museum café after which they toured the museum buildings.

By the end of the tour Wendy was pleased that the children had enjoyed themselves and learned something at the same time. She especially liked the fact that the exhibitions were dramatic, but also down to Earth. Daniel was well impressed with the transport halls showing everything from motorbikes to aeroplanes. Abigail was much more interested in the part of the museum that showed various household appliances. This riled Wendy a little, she didn't approve of stereotyping so the children conforming to stereotypes annoyed her slightly.

On the way back from the museum, Mary had phoned to see how the children were. Dad had spoken briefly to Daniel but Abigail was far too tired to speak to anyone.

By the time they returned to the hotel once more, they were completely exhausted. The trip from the Science Museum was very short, but still Abigail managed to fall asleep again. Wendy asked Robert, their driver, to carry her up to their rooms, rather than wake her up again.

Abigail was put straight to bed whilst Wendy ordered a light dinner for Daniel and herself.

"Can I stay up and watch Daddy and Mummy on TV?" asked Daniel.

"Afraid not, Daniel. I've had strict instructions from Mummy and Daddy that you have to go to bed on time tonight because they are taking us all out tomorrow. So you have to get your sleep."

"Where are we going?"

"The Peak District National Park."

"Have we been there?"

"No, *none* of us have ever been there, Daniel."

After eating dinner, Wendy put Daniel to bed and settled down in front of the TV, to watch Near Zero's concert. Slowly her eyes closed and she drifted off to sleep.

It was a very long time ago since Wendy had such a vivid dream; she was in a sand-cruiser riding across the desert, with her boyfriend. They were under fire from some mercenaries, when an explosion hit the underside of the vehicle. She was knocked out by the force of the impact and was lying on the ground. Her boyfriend was trying to wake her, but try as she might, she couldn't move. No matter how hard she tried, she couldn't move.

Suddenly she was awake and it wasn't her boyfriend that was trying to wake her, it was little Daniel. "Wendy, Wendy, hurry. You'll miss it!"

There were flashes of light coming from outside their windows, and a noise – no *noises*! They appeared to be explosions.

"My God!" She suddenly realised that the explosions were real. "What's happening?"

"It's a big fireworks display," said Daniel. "It woke me up!"

"Where's Abigail?"

"She's asleep."

"No, I'm not. I'm frightened," said Abigail, tearfully, standing in the doorway of the lounge.

"Come here, sweetheart. There's nothing to be frightened of. It's just a firework display."

Just as the words left her lips, there was a tremendous explosion and flash of light. Wendy could tell immediately that it was much closer than the other explosions had been. The building shook. Glass objects rattled. Everyone jumped, including Wendy, and Abigail ran crying into Wendy's arms.

"That doesn't sound like fireworks to me, Daniel."

She sat Abigail and Daniel down, next to each other and said, "Don't move, either of you, until I've had a look."

She opened the curtains and looked out on a scene that could only have come from a page of science fiction. There was a large spaceship hovering above central Manchester with lots of smaller ships flying around below it, shooting at what looked like random targets on the ground. As she looked down at the ground she could see people scattering in all directions trying to get away from the explosions that were happening all around them.

She turned to the children who were looking bemused rather than frightened. "Get yours and Abigail's coat,

Daniel. We're getting out of here."

"But we've only got our pyjamas on, Wendy."

"That's fine, Daniel. We're not going far – but I want you to have your coats and shoes on in case it gets cold."

Wendy busied herself getting Abigail's shoes on whilst Daniel went to the hall cupboard for their coats.

"Can I take Rory?" asked Daniel.

Rory was Daniel's comfort toy. He always had it in bed with him. Abigail also had one, called Emily.

"Yes and we'll let Abigail bring Emily as well."

Abigail nodded.

Once they were all dressed, Wendy opened the door that led from the suite to the rest of the hotel, and led the children into mayhem.

The noise immediately frightened Abigail so Wendy picked her up in her arms and carried her. People were scurrying all over the hotel, some heading to their rooms, and some hurrying out of the hotel altogether. She even heard people at the desk asking the staff what was going on. As if they would know, she thought.

Wendy grabbed one of the waiter's arms as he rushed past her, away from the restaurant. "Has the hotel got a basement, a cellar?"

"Yes! Through the double doors, over there." He pointed over to the rear left corner of the large entrance hallway. Wendy grabbed Daniel's hand and went through the double doors. She looked around. Just to her left there was a door marked 'Staff Only'. She went through the door and down the steps carrying Abigail and still holding on to Daniel's hand. The cellar was dimly lit. There were wine racks all along most of the walls. From what she could see there looked to be several more rooms. There were people looking and smiling at her but making no noise. There were quite a few people down in the cellar but, even so, she was surprised that the rooms weren't more crowded.

Seeing some up-ended coopered barrels on the floor in one corner, she sat Daniel and Abigail on one barrel and herself on another. She'd decided it would be prudent to wait for the noise above to subside, before they would again venture out of the cellar.

Suddenly there was a huge explosion above, accompanied by the sound of glass breaking and women and children screaming. Then the lights went out. She grabbed the children and held them close to her and tried to comfort them as best she could.

* * *

Simon could feel his mobile vibrating in his pocket. He moved away from the small crowd that surrounded him and retrieved it.

"Dave, is that you?" he said in a whisper.

"Yes, Simon. All the roads are blocked coming in and out of Manchester. We can't get you out by road. We think we can get you out via the ship canal. Do you know where that is?"

"Yes, it's due south of me."

"It is! Simon, we need you to see if you can find someone on your way to the canal."

"*Dave!* I'm not even sure I can make the canal, never mind look for someone as well?"

"You know that concert you were going to tonight."

"Yeah! I don't think it'll be on now though," said Simon, sarcastically.

"Well, it's Razor's children that we need you to find."

"You're joking?"

"No, I'm not. We think they're trapped in the Lowry Hotel. It's directly between your current position and the canal."

"OK, but I want an autograph if I manage to rescue them," Simon said jokingly.

"Simon, you'll be a friend of the family for life if you succeed."

"That'll do me."

"OK, seriously. I'll contact you as soon as we get near your position. How's the phone for battery life?"

"It's fine at the moment, but I didn't charge it yesterday."

"OK. Speak to you soon, take care."

Simon carefully put what had become the only way of

communicating with the outside world away, before he returned to the crowd he was with. He was convinced that if everyone new his mobile was working it would be lost in an instant. Everyone has someone they want to talk to before they die, he thought.

He crawled up to the two mates he was with, Gary and Jimmy. "Look lads, I'm going to try to get out of here."

"How the hell are you going to do that, Simon?"

"I'm going down to the canal. If I can find something that floats, I'm going to give it a try."

"Well, it's better than sitting here doing nothing at all," said Gary.

"I'm staying here, Simon," said Jimmy.

"Jimmy, the situation's not going to improve here – come on." Simon tried to pull Jimmy up.

Jimmy shrugged off Simon's hand, "No! I'm staying here!"

He patted Jimmy on the shoulder.

"I'm sorry, mate. I have to go! Are you coming, Gary?"

"Sorry, Jimmy," Gary said, as he stood up and went with Simon.

Even though the sun couldn't yet be seen, the dawning light was slowly breaking through the early morning mist. Simon assumed that it was the numerous explosions that had caused the haze. A bit like after bonfire night, he thought.

Regardless, he was thankful for anything that obscured him from the alien craft above. The mist wasn't much, but it was cover.

The streets were absolutely deserted. He'd never seen Manchester like this before. There was no traffic, although there were plenty of abandoned cars. There were no people, in fact he just realised, there were no birds either. He would normally have expected to see some pigeons. There wasn't a single one to be seen.

He was terrified of venturing out onto the street but he was absolutely sure that it needed to be done. For God's sake, there were children involved here – it had to be done, he told himself.

"No talking, Gary. Hand signals only. If either of us see aliens, then signal like so!" He held both his thumbs upside down.

"OK."

Simon took the lead. He crossed the first junction, the canyon-like streets of central Manchester, amplifying, and echoing the sound of his footsteps. The aliens *had* to hear that, he thought, but there was no way of making progress without making that noise. He was at the other side of the street now. He signalled for Gary to join him.

As they hugged the wall, down to the next junction, they could hear rustling around the corner from their position.

Simon slowly peeped round the corner. It was an alien, engrossed in rummaging through some dustbins and litter, piled up at the rear of a shop.

Simon gave Gary the two-thumbs-down signal. Gary nodded. Simon quietly crossed the junction behind the alien. When he reached the far side he turned and signalled for Gary to cross.

Gary was just about to cross when there was a noise from inside one of the buildings, near to Simon's position. The alien heard the noise and stopped what he was doing. Gary stopped himself from crossing the junction. The alien walked towards Simon's position. Simon pressed himself further into the wall so that the alien wouldn't see him. Another few feet and he would be discovered. Again the noise they'd heard earlier came from inside the building. The alien stopped and turned to face the door from where the noise emanated, just a few feet from where Simon was pressed against the wall. The alien went through the door, missing Simon by inches.

Simon and Gary breathed a sigh of relief and Gary crossed the junction to join Simon.

"That was too close, Gary. Look, if anything happens to me, I want you to carry on with the plan."

"What plan?" said Gary.

Then Simon explained about the mobile phone and the conversation he'd had about Razor's children.

Their progress to the Lowry was slow. Every now and again a spacecraft would fly over the top of them, but fingers crossed – up to yet, they hadn't been seen.

As they moved down King Street they could see the footbridge that led over the canal to the Lowry, just behind some small trees. Gary was the first to the footbridge and the first to look across the canal to the Lowry.

"Shit!" he muttered, and just stood there as if he'd been pole-axed.

"What's wrong?" Simon came from under the trees and saw the building, or what was left of it. It was just a mound of concrete, steel and glass. No resemblance of a hotel could be seen.

"There ain't *nothing* surviving that!" said Gary.

"No, Gary. We can't just give up like that. We have to have a closer look. Give them a chance of life. You never know, it is possible someone survived."

"Damn unlikely, if you ask me."

In his heart, Simon agreed. But in his head, he wasn't for giving up.

"OK. We need to get across that bridge," said Gary.

"No time like the present!" and Simon just went for it. He may have been running for only a short time, but running over such exposed ground in these circumstances, felt like an age. He ran behind the rubble to what looked like the back of the hotel. Gary joined him. They were both breathing hard.

As they circled the base of the hotel, Simon's initial optimism began to fade.

In frustration, Simon ran onto the side of the rubble field, and started to dig though the mess with his bare hands. Gary didn't join in.

"There are no survivors, Simon."

Simon just knelt there for a moment.

"OK! Gary, OK!" He got up and dusted himself off.

Simon pointed to the canal.

"There's a bridge over there, let's just wait under the span for the boats to arrive."

Gary was just about to say yes when he heard a faint noise.

"What was that?"

"What?"

"Shush—" they both fell silent. This time both of them heard something.

"Over there!" said Gary. They ran over to a small corner of the building that stood a little taller than the surrounding rubble pile. Beneath, there was a small gap, big enough to crawl into. They could hear the sound of crying coming out from the blackness.

"Is there anybody in there?" shouted Gary.

The crying continued but there was no reply. They both cupped their mouths and shouted again, in unison, "Is there anybody in there?" A man's voice replied.

"Hello! There are eight survivors down here, five men, one woman and two children. But we are trapped."

"The opening up here is wide enough for you to crawl through," said Simon.

"The problem's down here. We can't get a foothold. It seems to be a vent of some kind. It may be clear to the top, but we simply can't climb it."

"I'm going to throw a small stone down to see if it's clear all the way down."

"OK, go ahead."

"Stand clear," then Simon threw the stone.

It rattled and bounced off the metal sides of the shaft.

"Yes, it landed, no problem."

"OK. It looks like we just need something to pull you out of there," said Simon.

Simon turned to Gary

"Let's split up. You go that way, I'll go this – no more than 30 minutes, and then we meet back here. Agreed?"

"Yes," said Gary.

Simon shouted into the cellar.

"We're just going to have a look for some rope so we can pull you out of there. Keep calm, we'll be back."

They went their separate ways. Gary was the first to return; he couldn't find rope or anything similar that would do the job. He'd got back after the agreed 30 minutes but that was nearly an hour ago. He was getting worried that Simon had been caught, or worse. Then he saw him coming down the middle of the street carrying orange netting and some scaffolding poles. There was a load more netting dragging behind him. How he'd not been spotted from above, Gary had no idea.

"I think they must use this stuff when they're scaffolding. It was tied around the bottom of a tower. There should be enough length, but whether they can climb up it is anyone's guess. There sure isn't any rope around these parts."

"No, I couldn't find any, either."

The noise of a spaceship could be heard.

"Drop it, Simon. Get under cover."

They both took shelter in a doorway. The craft passed overhead.

When they got back to the hotel, they noticed that the crying had stopped.

"Hello, are you still there!"

"Silly question," came the reply.

"Yes! Sorry, we've been looking for rope so that you can climb out. We couldn't find any but we did find some orange mesh that might do the trick."

"Yes, I know the type you mean. That should do the trick!" said the voice.

"OK. We'll secure this end, then we'll lower the rest down to you. You'll need to stand back away from the shaft. I'm going to weight the end of the mesh so that it will drop all the way down."

Simon pushed the scaffolding posts through the mesh and wedged them at each side of the entrance. He grabbed a chunk of masonry from the fallen hotel and tied it into the bottom part of the netting. "Coming down," he shouted.

He lowered the mesh gently into the hole. Even so, the masonry occasionally banged onto the side of the ducting. Everyone fell silent each time this happened, wondering whether the aliens would respond to the noise. There was no response.

The netting went slack.

"Has it reached you?" asked Gary.

"Yes. I'm going to send the woman up first then the children. You may well have to pull these up. They may not be able to climb."

"OK, no problem! Send her up."

Wendy had no problem in climbing up the netting. As she appeared in the crack in front of them, Simon held his hand out.

"Hi there, let me give you a hand."

Simon pulled her out and she dusted herself off.

"Are you Daniel and Abigail's Nanny?"

Wendy was taken aback by the question.

"How did you know that?"

Simon smiled at Gary.

"We were sent here to rescue you."

"Well, you're sure doing a good job so far, lads."

"Wendy!" said the voice.

"Yes?"

"I'm going to take the stone out of the bottom of the netting and tie the netting around Abigail. I'll shout when she's ready to be hauled up."

"OK, Rob!"

"Who's the guy?" said Simon.

"He was our chauffeur when we arrived in Manchester; I think he's employed by the hotel."

"Ready when you are!"

"OK! Pulling her up now," said Simon.

Abigail was brought to the surface and immediately she was untied from the netting she jumped into Wendy's arms.

"Clear the base again, I'll have to tie some masonry on it to weight it down again."

Simon lowered the netting once more.

"We'll do the same with Daniel. Even though he says he can climb it," shouted Robert.

"Let us know when you're ready," shouted Simon.

There was a slight pause.

"Ready!"

Daniel was pulled to the surface and just like Abigail, when he was released from the netting he immediately ran to Wendy.

"You three need to get under cover. Gary, get them over there under the footbridge. It's deep enough to hide them whilst we get the others out."

Gary nodded, "This way, folks!" Wendy, Daniel and Abigail followed Gary to the footbridge.

Simon again weighted down the netting with fresh masonry and lowered it.

"You five OK for climbing out, unaided?" asked Simon.

"Think so," said Robert. "We'll let you know."

"One at a time, mind. The netting isn't strong enough to carry you all at the same time."

Slowly but surely the five men climbed out of the hotel cellar and one by one made their way over to the shelter of the footbridge.

Simon was still very wary of letting anyone know he had a working mobile. As far as he was concerned it was their lifeline out of this mess, so once the men had joined Gary, Wendy and the children and he was alone, he sent a text message to Dave:

"We have the children and the nanny safe and sound, Dave. We await your instructions."

Dave's phone buzzed in his pocket. It was the distinct sound of a text message. He read the message out to Razor and Mary.

"Marvellous!" Razor shouted, and both Razor's fists and Mary's fists punched the air in celebration.

Gary and Simon led Wendy, the children and the others along the canal and under the first wide bridge they could find.

"We'll have a rest here for a while," said Gary.

Simon sat beside Wendy and the children.

"That was a clever move going into the cellar."

"It wasn't that clever, there were hundreds in that cellar before the collapse. As you can see only eight of us got out. We were just lucky."

"Luck had nothing to do with it. If you hadn't have moved down there you and the kids would be dead by now."

"I know," Wendy replied quietly. "Thanks for coming to rescue us, that was very brave of you. How did you get into Manchester?"

"Gary and me – we were already here!"
"Then how did you know about us?"
"My brother met, Razor. They were both trying to get into Manchester the same way – along the canal. They knew they couldn't get in by road so they thought the canal was worth a go. Razor was coming in to rescue you and the kids. Dave was coming in to rescue me."
"But how did you know?"
Simon whispered so the children couldn't hear, "I have a mobile that works!"
Wendy lowered her voice, "Well, can the children phone Razor and Mary?"
"No!" Simon said emphatically. "The battery indicator now says low. I can't be sure how long the battery will last and it's our lifeline out of here. If we let the children have a go the others will want a go, also. Sorry!"
"No, that's fine. Very sensible," said Wendy.
"What's it like working for someone so famous?"
"It has its moments, and you see the world, but to be honest I'm more interested in making sure the kids are brought up as normal as possible than I am in the celebrity side of the job."
"You must have met some interesting people, though."
"Yes, but discretion is part of the job, so I can't talk about them."
"Oh!"
Simon let the conversation end naturally and leant back against the wall.

– Chapter Eight –

Retrieval

Z-Day…

It was getting on for five o'clock in the morning by the time the two canal boats were ready for the trip into Manchester. The sun was just appearing on the horizon and the bird song from the morning chorus, had just died away. The waters were calm and lapped gently against the canal side. The only other activity on the canal was the occasional squawk of a seagull.

Razor and Mary had, as usual, opted to take the lead and together with Bill and Dave had immediately started down the canal towards the first set of locks. Judy, Alan, Terry, Lenny and Richard were in the second boat. Lenny, having had a number of holidays on narrow boats, had taken control of it.

By going in via the boat museum, the two boats had already circumvented the entry locks at Eastham, but another four locks lay ahead and negotiating them would not be easy.

As the boats moved down the canal, running parallel with the River Mersey, Razor was struck by the incongruity of the seagulls squawking, and the lack of a salty smell one would normally associate with the close proximity of a tidal river.

Judging from the speed they were travelling, Razor was beginning to form the opinion that their journey was about to be slow going.

"Is this the fastest we can go, Bill?"

"Afraid so, lad."

"This may be a blessing in disguise, Razor," said Dave.

"Why's that?"

"Well, the aliens won't be thinking that anything travelling this slow is a threat, would they?"

"You may have a point, Dave."

"What's that water-way coming in on the right there, Bill?" shouted Alan, from the other boat.

"That's the River Weaver, Alan. It's used for shipping salt from the salt mines in Cheshire."

"Is it still used?"

"Yes."

"You two stop shouting at each other. We're supposed to be keeping a low profile here," said Razor.

"I'm surprised at how low these banks are, Bill. I'd have expected them to be a lot taller than they are. Being that the canal is a *ship* canal, not a narrow boat canal."

"Don't worry, Razor. The size of the lock walls will reflect the fact that it's a ship canal."

In the distance could be seen the first set of locks and as Bill had predicted, when the boats eventually glided into them the sheer size of the walls was overpowering.

"Razor, keep the boat to the left side and go slowly. You'll see a ladder rack, set in the wall. You need to pull up against it. We'll have to climb up it to get to the control housing."

Razor manoeuvred the boat, to lie against the ladder rack.

"Are you sure you can climb that, Bill?"

"Yes, I'll be fine, but you're going to have to carry the bolt cutters and when we're up there, you'll have to do the cutting."

"I'm with you, Bill."

Bill started to climb the ladder rack; as he did so he turned and called to Razor.

“Razor, be careful as you start the climb. The rungs that have been submerged are covered in slime and are very slippy.”

As the two climbed the ladder rack, Bill had to pause several times to get his breath.

“Sorry, Razor. Not as fit as I used to be.”

“You’re a lot fitter than I’d be at 73.”

On reaching the top of the ladder rack, Bill sat down to get his breath back, whilst Razor looked around the control building.

The building was probably only as big as the back of a container truck, but getting inside was definitely going to be a problem. It was obvious that the authorities had problems with vandals. The steel, shuttered door of the building was padlocked. A large, galvanised metal fence also surrounded the building. Further, the gate through the fence was also padlocked.

“Cut them open, Razor. We’ve no time to lose.”

Razor used the bolt cutters to cut through the locks and levered the metal door ajar. Bill entered and closed the lock gates, to the rear. Once they were closed tight he flooded the lock. The whole of the rescue team were astonished at how quickly the water level rose. Once the water level was at the same height as the rest of the canal, Bill opened the lock gates.

They both clambered back onto the front canal boat and they headed further up the canal.

‘The Latchford Locks are next,” said Bill. “Normally we’d have to bother about a load of swing bridges but these narrow boats are small enough to go under all of them.

The two boats moved slowly but steadily towards the Latchford Locks. There was still no sign of the alien invaders. They could not see any flashes in the sky or hear any noise from explosions. In fact, the whole scene was so normal, and except for the noise of the two engines, so peaceful.

On reaching Latchford, Bill and Razor followed the same procedure and were quickly into the control building. This time Lenny joined them.

“How are we doing, you two? Is everything going OK?”

"Yes, Lenny. Fine!" said Bill. "But the next three locks are controlled from Latchford, so I'm going to have to stay at Latchford whilst you two travel in."

"Damn! Won't I make a mess of this without you?" said Lenny.

"No! There's not much to remember. Just keep to your right when sailing the canal but pull into the left when entering the locks, and you can't go wrong. I'll be able to see you on the monitors at each lock, so once the two boats are in, I'll know to operate the gates.

"Your main problem will be after Mode Wheel Lock, because after that you'll truly be in hostile territory and you'll still have a distance to go before you reach the Lowry Hotel. Lenny, I suggest *your* boat stays at Salford Quays, while Razor's boat does the final run in. It'll be less noisy with one boat and a lot less conspicuous."

"OK! Let's do it! You take care now, Bill – we'll pick you up on the way out."

"Yeah! See you in a few hours. Remember, no shouting between boats from now on – low profile time!"

Lenny, then Razor, climbed down the ladder racks to the two boats.

Irlam Lock and Barton Lock were easy to get through. As promised, Bill did all the hard work remotely.

As the boats neared Mode Wheel Lock, Razor heard the distinctive noise of helicopter rotor blades, getting louder and louder. He turned to see a Police Helicopter flying directly towards them, following the line of the canal.

As the helicopter came above the leading boat, their loud hailer sprang into life:

"This is Greater Manchester Police. We have reports that the two boats you are travelling in are stolen."

"Damn, don't they realise they're putting us all in danger?" said Razor.

He tried to wave them away.

"You will proceed to the next locks and disembark from the boats. We will meet you there."

Razor gave them the thumbs-up sign in order that they would quickly move away from the two canal boats.

At that, the helicopter flew forward of the boats and hovered over Mode Wheel, waiting for the boats to follow.

"One can only imagine they're hovering there to ensure that we do what they say," said Mary.

"They're in great danger—"

Razor didn't even have time to complete his sentence. A death ray, from God knows where, shot into the helicopter and blew the thing apart.

Everyone immediately went below decks, except Razor and Lenny who slowed the boats down.

"Damn those aliens!" shouted Lenny.

With Bill still pulling the strings, Mode Wheel Lock was as easy to get through as Irlam and Barton but as the two boats cleared the lock, the mood on the boats changed completely.

Smoke from the recent attacks blanketed the city, with many fires still burning. Some of the larger buildings had been struck part way up, but had not completely collapsed. The lower half of the buildings looking almost normal but the upper half completely wrecked. Other buildings had collapsed completely.

Hanging in the sky to the north east, probably over the centre of the city, was a huge cigar-shaped object. Smaller extraterrestrial craft were darting in and out of it. It looked like there was some form of pattern in the sky. Razor thought that it could be the pattern of major road routes in and out of the city. Now and again there was a dart of a death ray from one of the gnats in the sky, followed by a huge explosion.

Everything else was so quiet that each explosion echoed around the city, as one would imagine it would in an old Roman amphitheatre.

Now and again one of the alien craft would pass overhead and there was many a time they thought they would be attacked, but they were completely ignored. The aliens' concentration was entirely fixed on the roads and their airspace.

As previously arranged, Lenny's canal boat pulled up alongside one of the quays, off to the side of the Lowry Outlet Centre.

Razor's boat continued in.

"Time to check Simon on the mobile, Dave!" said Razor.

Dave accessed his mobile.

"Ask him for his exact position."

Simon's phone vibrated in his pocket.

"Thought you'd never ring. Where are you?"

"Very close, Simon. We have a couple of canal boats. We're heading to your position in one of them. We haven't experienced any problems getting in. We need you to give us your exact location."

"I'm not sure I can do that, Dave. While we've been waiting for you we've been moving away from the centre, along the canal, towards the Salford Quays area. We're currently resting under a railway bridge."

"Is it the first railway bridge you've come to, since leaving the hotel area?"

"Yes."

"Hang on, Simon. Razor's just checking it on his oPad. Are you on the same side of the river, as the hotel?"

"Yes, but the hotel is no more."

"Blimey!"

Razor had finished checking. "I can see which bridge he means, Dave. Tell him to try to get the group as far as the next road bridge and we'll pick them up from there."

"Did you hear that, Simon?"

"Yes, the next road bridge. Looks easy from here. See you there."

"They're only around the next bend in the canal, Dave," Razor said excitedly.

As the boat came into view of the waiting group, the children started jumping up and down, with the anticipation of seeing Mum and Dad. Wendy had to quickly remind them that they must remain silent or they would be in danger.

As the boat drew alongside, the bridge provided the perfect cover whilst everyone climbed aboard.

"Daddy, Mummy!" Both the children ran into the arms of their parents.

Wendy followed, with a huge hug from both Mum and Dad.

"Well done, Wendy. That must have been some ordeal?"

"I'm not convinced it's over with yet, Mary," she said nervously.

"Razor, this is Robert, our driver whilst we were here in Manchester," said Wendy.

"Hi there, Robert. Who are the other chaps?"

"No idea! We're a collection of the lucky ones who made it to the cellar of the Lowry before the aliens dropped the thing to the ground."

"Well, we're glad you made it."

"We wouldn't have, if it hadn't have been for Simon and Gary. They pulled us out of the rubble," said Robert, as he looked up at the two young men, filing onto the boat behind him.

"Simon, Gary! Well done, lads. Robert tells me I have you two to thank for saving my kids lives."

"Dave mentioned free tickets to your next concert, what else could we do?" Simon said jokingly.

"I think we can do a lot better than that, Simon. Come on everybody into the belly of the beast. You'll all have to keep very quiet, while we get out of here."

Razor manoeuvred the boat around under the bridge, and headed back along the canal, keeping to the right as Bill had told him. As he passed boat number two, nothing was said. He just lifted both thumbs in the air and waved at Lenny to follow.

They re-entered Mode Wheel Lock. Razor was praying that nothing had happened to Bill, to prevent him from operating the lock gates. He needn't have worried. As the two boats entered the lock the gates immediately closed and the level of the water started to subside.

Barton Lock was the next on the list and Razor was not going to feel comfortable until they were through it.

As the two boats neared the lock they were buzzed by a low flying, single prop airplane. Neither Razor, nor Lenny could believe their eyes.

"What the hell is that joker doing?" Razor muttered to himself.

Just as he'd finished his sentence he saw a death ray just miss the plane. The extraterrestrial craft wasn't far behind and was clearly intent on destroying the light aircraft. It didn't take long before the inevitable happened and a direct hit was scored.

"Kill the engines!" Razor shouted across to Lenny.

Both engines died almost immediately and both craft carried on cutting lazily through the water. The alien craft came back for a look but took no action against the two boats.

Even without the engines running, the two canal boats lazily moved into the lock. The lock gates closed behind them. Thank God, Bill's still alright, thought Razor.

Once the water levels had been equalised and the lock gates opened, it was time to re-start the engines. With some trepidation, Razor started his engine first and moved out towards Irlam. Lenny quickly followed.

Again, to Razor's surprise they weren't attacked as they made their way steadily back to Latchford.

As far as Razor was concerned, reaching Latchford Locks was like reaching home.

"Bill. It's good to see you! That was one hell of a journey."

"I'm really glad to see the children are alright, Razor."

"You and me both, Bill – you and me both."

"So what's the next move?"

"Get back to the boat museum and head north. Alan's got a place in the Lakes; he's going to put us all up until we know what's going on down here."

"Do you mind if I tag along?"

"Not at all, Bill – not at all."

The journey back felt a good deal shorter than the journey in. It was near closing time at the boat museum as they arrived back.

The chief engineer, Dan Boswell recognised the missing boats as they came alongside and was about to go into a rage, when he saw Bill.

"Bill, it's you. Where the hell have you been with my boats? I've got the police out looking for them."

"Yes, I know, poor sods," Bill said under his breath. He thought it best to change the subject.

"Have you heard the news about what's happening in Manchester?"

"Yes, it's all over Sky and the rest of the TV channels. They think it's an invasion of Earth by extraterrestrials. I think that's aliens to you and me."

"We've just been into Manchester on your boats, to pick the children up." He nodded towards Wendy and the children, who were just disembarking.

"It's been a full day of a job. They could do with a drink and a bite to eat, Dan."

"Come into the cafeteria and we'll find something."

The group walked into the museum's cafeteria.

"You look exhausted, Bill. I think *you* could do with a drink, never mind the kids."

Bill told Dan all about what had happened, whilst the children had their sandwiches and a drink.

– Chapter Nine –

The Lakes

Z-Day...

After experiencing the mayhem in the city avoiding the Zinden, travelling north towards the lakes on a nearly-deserted road, with nothing chasing them, was a real breath of fresh air for everyone.

On returning to the boat museum, nearly everyone opted to stay together. Only a few went their separate ways – some of the guys in the cellar and Gary, who headed back to Blackburn, to check his family were OK.

When Wendy saw the transport choices, she immediately confiscated Dave's Mini, for the children, Mary and herself – Terry also managed to squeeze in. Razor was left giving Richard a lift on his bike. Dave and Simon were allocated Terry's bike and so this meant that Judy had been lucky enough to ride with Alan once more. Lenny had ended up at the rear carrying Bill.

Since it was Alan's hideaway they were going to, Alan and Judy were at the front of this mini convoy. As they travelled, Judy was in a mind to find out a little more about this handsome man, whose waist she had her arms around.

"So home, Alan. Where exactly is that?"

"We're off to Wastwater. It's near Gosforth. It's a small cottage on the side of the lake."

"Are we to meet your family?" she said. At this point she had her fingers firmly crossed. She did not want to hear that he had a wife and kids.

"Mum and Dad are long gone, I'm afraid."

"Oh! Sorry to hear that, Alan. No, I meant Mrs Smith."

"There isn't one, I'm a bit of a loner you see."

That was good enough for her. She hugged him a little closer, "Well! You've got *me* now."

He felt the increased pressure around his waist as she said the words. Again, he liked the feeling of being wanted. He could get used to being wanted. Besides that, she was a hell of a good-looking woman – for a human that is.

"What's Razor doing?" Alan said.

Razor and Richard had overtaken them and Richard was signalling for them to pull over.

"I think they just want us to go to the services. We've just passed a sign saying Burton-in-Kendal Services. He's probably short on fuel."

The mini convoy pulled into the services car park. Everyone crowded around Razor.

"I need some petrol, so I thought it best we all fill up, whilst we're here. As you all probably know I have a rather large platinum credit facility, so let's use it."

"And I need the loo," said Bill.

"It would also be a good idea if the children had a break, before we hit the A roads," said Mary.

"OK, let's take some time out," said Razor.

The group got their refreshments and gathered around a large 3D screen, whilst they ate. Sky news was on.

"After the initial reports of strange happenings in the Manchester area, as you may know, we lost a film crew early this morning. We now have confirmed reports of alien craft targeting transport links, all around the city.

"The government say that the aliens are not present in sufficient numbers to pose a serious risk to Earth. Nevertheless, they are trying to open a dialogue with the invaders, to see exactly what they are doing on our planet."

"I know what they're doing. They're invading it, that's what they're doing!" Simon said in anger.

"Simon! The children," said Wendy.

"Sorry."

"Something doesn't smell right here," said Razor.

"I agree with Razor," said Lenny. "Why are they here in such small numbers? Why are they attacking us? In fact, why Manchester? Why not London or Washington? They don't appear to have a specific objective in mind, as yet."

"What do you think, Alan?" asked Judy.

"Maybe they do have an objective, but it's not yet clear to us."

Razor broke up the discussions.

"Well, let's worry about that later. We need to get into the Lakes, and get some R & R."

"And make sure the children are safe," said Mary.

"Exactly. Then we can decide what our next move may be, after we've assessed the news reports coming out of Manchester."

After refuelling, the group set off north again, turning onto the A590 and heading for Newby Bridge.

It was early evening now and everyone was feeling the chill of the night. The street lights came on and the moon rose in the night sky. Razor realised that not one of the riders was wearing the right clothes for travelling on a motorbike late at night.

After passing Grizebeck, they joined the A595 to Ravenglass and eventually arrived in Gosforth.

Alan pulled into the car park of the Westlake Hotel and waited for everyone to catch up.

"OK, folks, I know you're all tired but we've only one more road to tackle. We should be there shortly – is everyone OK?"

"A little chilled, but yeah! Let's finish it," shouted Lenny.

Alan led the convoy onto the Wasdale Road and headed for his cottage.

By the time they got to the cottage everyone just wanted to crash out.

"Just bed down where you can find space. Upstairs is reserved for women and children – that includes toileting and bathrooms. There's a toilet and shower downstairs at the back of the cottage."

Alan was too uptight to go to sleep straight away. He made his way into the kitchen – turning the central heating on as he walked by the control unit. He filled the kettle and switched it on for a late night drink of tea. Judy followed him. On his first visit to Earth, he'd discovered that one of the characteristics of the English was their fondness for tea. On arrival he was keen to try this out. When he initially tried it he really couldn't understand what the fuss was all about, but being that his duty was to be perfectly disguised as an Englishman, he persisted with it. Now it was his staple drink and he thought he probably enjoyed it as much as any of the indigenous population.

He smiled, as Judy walked into the kitchen.

"Tea?"

Judy nodded "No sugar!"

Alan made the cuppas.

"You should be asleep, Judy."

"Too much adrenalin pumping round my system, I think?"

"Same here!"

"I enjoyed our time together today, Alan," she said as she arrested the cup of fresh tea from Alan's hand, she smiled and sipped her tea.

"I'll see you in the morning."

"See you in the morning, Judy."

Alan was thinking exactly the same. He liked Judy a lot.

As Judy ascended the stairs she met Wendy who had just been tucking the children into their great big double bed. She was switching their light off and coming out of the room.

"Hi, Judy. You're in the next bedroom with Mary and me. It's two single beds and a sleeping bag. I've volunteered for the sleeping bag."

"The way I feel, I am not going to argue."

The room was very small. The two beds were on opposite walls with only just enough room between them for Wendy's sleeping bag. Mary was already fast asleep. The two of them settled down for the night. If nothing else, it was cosy, warm and silent – well, except for the entire snoring community, sleeping downstairs.

* * *

"Daniel. Come away from the stairs."

There was masonry falling all around, just missing Daniel's head. Daniel wasn't listening.

"I can't find Rory."

"Never mind Rory. We'll find him later."

Daniel didn't stop searching. His head and shoulders were now full of dust and the masonry was falling closer and closer to him.

"I can't find Emily."

Wendy whipped her head around. It was Abigail. She was also covered in dust and the masonry was getting closer and closer to her, also.

She knew immediately that she couldn't save both of them. But how could she choose? Both of them were shouting her name.

"Forget the teddies, forget the teddies—" Slowly the scene in front of Wendy melted away and in its place was Mary's face saying her name. "Wendy—Wendy wake up!"

Wendy sat bolt upright "The children! Are the children alright?"

"Calm down, Wendy. They're fine. You were dreaming."

Slowly, Wendy remembered the rescue and the fact that they were now in the cottage, safe and sound. She settled back down. Mary stroked her hair.

"Everything's fine," said Mary quietly.

* * *

Even though it was only seven o'clock in the morning, as usual, Daniel and Abigail were already up and playing in their room, when Wendy looked in.

"We're going on a picnic today," said Wendy.

Abigail jumped up and said excitedly, "Can we take some bread to feed the ducks?"

Wendy smiled.

"I'm not sure there are any ducks around here, Abigail."

"But there's a big pond outside. All ponds have ducks!"

"It's a lake, Abby. It's a bit bigger than a pond, but we'll take some bread, just in case we see some ducks."

"Hooray!"

Both Daniel and Abigail were bouncing on the bed now.

"Right, you two, bath time."

Wendy went to run the bath, whilst Daniel and Abigail took off their pyjamas. Wendy heard Daniel say, "No! Abigail, you have to take your pull-ups off and give them to Wendy."

A few seconds later, Abigail brought her wet pull-ups into the bathroom and pushed them into Wendy's face.

"There!" she said.

Wendy quickly removed her nose from the close proximity of the sopping wet disposable and said, "Good girl, Abigail, that's what we do. We bring dirty pull-ups to Wendy. Well done."

Wendy sat Abigail on the toilet and held her under her arms to support her, there was a small dribble.

"Well done, Abigail – what a big girl," and she gave Abigail a hug.

Wendy tested the water to ensure that it wasn't too hot then she lifted Abigail into the bath. Abigail immediately started splashing the water with her hands. Wendy waited for Daniel to come in. Daniel dashed in and headed for the bath.

"No, Daniel." Daniel corrected himself and climbed on the toilet. There was a little dribble and then he launched himself off the toilet, eager to climb into the bath, to play with the water.

"Stop splashing now, Abigail. You'll get soap in Daniel's eyes." Abigail calmed down and Wendy bathed the two children.

After bathing them, and letting them play in the bathwater with the sponges and flannel for a few minutes, Wendy lifted them out of the bath and escorted them off the slippy bathroom floor and into their carpeted bedroom.

Wendy dried both of them and dressed Abigail, as Daniel dressed himself. Today he did well. Only his t-shirt was the wrong way round.

"What are you like, young man?" said Wendy as she re-adjusted it. Daniel smiled. He knew he'd done something wrong, with Wendy's choice of words, but he'd no idea what.

Wendy led the children downstairs, the children giggling as they saw everyone sleeping on the floor.

"So what are we having to eat this morning?" Wendy said, as she and the children climbed over everyone, in order to get to the kitchen.

"Jelly!" said Abigail. Knowing very well that her wish would not be granted.

"You can't have jelly for breakfast, Abigail. I'll give you some choices. Now what do we have here—" Wendy rummaged around in the kitchen cupboard but could find nothing for the children. "OK! We have—no cornflakes, no porridge, no chocolate ricicles—or you can have toast and butter."

"No chocolate ricicles—they both said in unison."

"So! You want toast and butter, do you?"

"OK," they both said glumly.

"You cannot, under any circumstances whatsoever, beat the smell of toast in the morning," Mary said as she walked into the kitchen.

"Mummy!" they both shouted, and the toast in front of them was completely forgotten, as they ran over to hug Mum.

Mary crouched down and gave them both a hug, then lifted Abigail into her arms. "C'mon you two, we can't miss breakfast, we've got a lot to do today. We've got to go shopping for better breakfasts and things, then after dinner we can go for a walk."

Just as she'd got them back to the table, Razor appeared. He wasn't fully awake. "Daddy!" and once again breakfast was immediately forgotten as the children ran over to him.

Razor grabbed both of them around the waist and carried them back to the dining table. "You'll never be big and strong if you don't eat your breakfasts," he said.

The children finally settled down to their breakfast.

Razor looked at Wendy, "Well, Wendy. I think the itinerary has changed somewhat. How are you?"

"I'm fine. A little shaken but I'll be OK now the children are safe and away from that evil."

Mary looked at Razor.

"Wendy and I, and the children, are going into the village for supplies. Judith says she's had a word with Alan. We can stay as long as we wish. She says he's enjoying having all of us around. I want Wendy and the kids to stay here until we know it's safe to move."

"Absolutely, Mary, but that needs to include you as well."

"Well, yes, we can both stay here also—"

"No, Mary. Someone has to fight those monsters down in Manchester and this small team have experience of what it's like in there."

Mary knew that this would be in his mind – she just didn't want to lose him.

"Just let the government take care of it now, Razor."

"No, Mary. It doesn't work like that. It's personal now. They killed three of our lads in the trucks, everyone on the bus. They killed Kevin and the other lads in the van. They nearly killed our kids and to be honest, if they could do it now, they would. These aliens are not going to stop at just playing God in Manchester. I don't know what they're up to but I do know that all of us are still in great danger. No, it has to be faced."

There was no arguing with Razor's statement.

"You just make sure you come back safe, if you're going back in there, for the sake of our children."

She gave him a hug and kiss.

The noise of the children had wakened everyone, and mayhem ensued as they all attempted to get toast and tea for breakfast. Needless to say, the supply of bread ran out well before the queue ended, but Mary, who had been the canteen staff whilst breakfast was on, promised everyone a good meal, later in the day.

* * *

Over the noise, Alan called to Judy, "Fancy a quiet stroll by the lakeside, Judy?"

"Good idea. I'll pack some drinks, no food left I'm afraid."

"That's OK."

Alan waited outside the front door for Judy to appear.

"OK! Let's go," said Judy as she came outside.

The early morning mist had already dissipated and Alan could feel the warmth of the sun on his back as they started along the road by the lake.

"It's a beautiful sight, isn't it?" said Alan.

"How the hell did you find such a wonderful place?" asked Judy.

"Just lucky, really. Happened upon it totally by chance."

Judy and Alan were walking the northwest edge of Wastwater and looking across to the other side, where the screed slope plummeted straight into the lakeside. They hadn't planned the walk at all. They both just wanted to get away from the mayhem in the cottage.

Alan continued.

"I came up walking one day and got talking to the old man who owned it. He told me he would sell it only on his deathbed and then only to raise money for his grandchildren's education.

I told him I wanted to buy it. I suggested he sell it to me early, for an agreed amount, and I would give him free tenancy for life. He agreed and it became mine."

"How long did he have the benefit of it after you'd signed up?"

"Eleven years. He got a good deal."

Part way along the lakeside they spotted a grassy bank above the road and scrambled up, to sit there.

"You know that Razor and I have decided to go back into Manchester."

"Yes, I know."

He looked deep into her eyes.

"Are you happy with that?"

"Whatever is happening down in Manchester needs looking at. Just take care; neither Mary nor I would like to lose either of you two."

"Well, that's a compliment. Thank you."

Judy blushed, slightly.

"Why do I get the feeling you asked me out here for a reason?"

"What? Besides liking your company, you mean?"

"Yes!"

"Well, there is something."

"What is it?"

"OK! Judy, take a deep breath."

"OK!" she took a deep breath.

"I'm an alien!"

Judith's jaw dropped. She felt more than a little faint. She shuffled away. Her instinct was to get up and run but she resisted the urge.

"You can't be one of them?"

"No! After what I've seen today, I'm their sworn enemy. Just like you and the rest of mankind are!"

"But you look so human."

"I look human because I'm a shape-shifter."

"What does that mean? How much shape can you shift? Is everything about you currently exactly the same as a human?"

"Everything."

Judy was beginning to calm down and to think straight again.

"What's your normal shape?"

"It doesn't work like that. I don't have a normal shape. The minute we are born we are constantly changing shape in response to our surroundings. It's a survival thing. Mum and Dad would always know who we were or what we were, no matter what shape we became. In the early days I used to take the shape of my food."

Judy laughed.

"OK, you'll have to show me."

"Alright."

Alan's arm morphed into a tennis racket.

"Anyone for tennis," he said.

Judy was horrified, her misgivings returned.

"As they say in the movies, are you friend or foe?"

Alan tried to reassure her.

"Definitely friend."

"But what are you doing here on Earth?"

"I'm a Galactic Police Officer, I was just on a routine visit. I was assigned to find out how the human race was developing and report back."

"You've been here before?"

"Yes."

As Alan's hand returned to what Judy would call 'its normal shape', Judy started to calm down again.

"So how are we doing?"

"Extremely well. It doesn't look like you're going to annihilate each other. You've recognised the potential threat of global warming and you're just about to colonise in a big way."

"We are?"

"Yes, you are."

Judith liked the reply but was still troubled.

"Why are you telling me all this?"

"I'm going to tell everybody tomorrow, but you and I hit it off yesterday and I thought you deserved to be told straight from the horse's mouth."

Judy smiled. "Now don't you go turning into a horse."

They both looked at each other and laughed.

"So do you get a lot of bad aliens out there?"

"Not really. You see, good predominates over evil in the universe, because in the end evil is destructive and those societies that follow the path of evil and aggression tend to annihilate each other."

Judith switched subjects.

"So if you can be any shape you want, why are you not female? You're not female are you?"

"No, I'm a male. But I can change into a female if you so wish."

"No, no. I was just wondering."

Over the next few hours Alan was grilled like he'd never been grilled before: What planet are you from? How did you get here? Where's your ship? Have you any family on your planet? How far away is it?

Likewise after dinner, or should we say 'liquid refreshment', since there was no food, it was Alan's turn. He was determined to ask nearly as many questions as Judy had asked.

By the time the day was coming to an end they had walked miles and talked for hours. They both felt they knew each other well and liked what they heard. As they returned they were holding hands and feeling an awful lot closer to each other.

It was dusk as the two wandered back to the cottage.

"Well, that was quite a walk, Alan. When are you going to tell the others?"

"It has to be tomorrow. I need to access the systems on my ship and I don't want to risk raising it, until everyone in our group knows."

"Hi, you two. We were thinking of sending a search party out for you," said Mary.

The two picnic benches to the side of the cottage had been moved to the front and were full of food. Everyone except Mary and Wendy were sat at the tables. Wendy was just sitting down, having done most of the cooking with Mary.

"Only three places left. You two come and sit down," said Mary.

"Alfresco then?" said Judith.

"Absolutely," said Mary.

As Alan sat down and looked around the tables, he could only think of the difference between the two races and the two planets. Here he was enjoying the company of people who celebrated life and freedom. Whilst just over the hills, was a race that wanted to dominate and exterminate.

As he looked around at the smiling faces, he couldn't help but wonder what future that evil might bring.

Once the meal had finished, Razor and Alan went into Alan's small study and Razor called up Sky News on his oPad. Alistair McGovern was back as the Anchorman.

"—It's been 39 hours since the EMP device was detonated over Manchester. The Armed Forces Minister has said that the city will be fully secured and quarantined within the next few days and no one should attempt to leave or enter the restricted zone."

"Damn," Razor said. "We'll end up fighting our own, as well as the aliens."

"If we stick to the canals we'll be OK," said Alan.

"—A number of our forces overseas have been recalled and we believe they are due to start arriving back as early as Tuesday morning.

"There have been no reports of further attacks by the aliens. We have Commander Jennings with us, one of Sir John Dowding's leading commanders. He's here in the studio, to talk about that precise point."

The camera panned back to show both Alistair and the commander.

"Commander, why do you think the aliens have stopped attacking us?"

"Well, it's always difficult to be precise about why an opposing force is doing what it's doing. My guess would be that they have reached their initial objective."

"And what do you think that would be?"

"Well, clearly to take control of Manchester and the surrounding area."

"Is there anything strategic in that area?"

"Well, that depends on the overall plans of the enemy. From our perspective we know of nothing strategic in that area. At first we thought they were heading for Jodrell Bank. But they stopped short of that target. In fact, they stopped just past Winsford but never went east of the M6. We, the military, are as perplexed as the rest of you as to why they would do that."

"Well, we have a camera somewhere up there in the northwest of England. Adrian, can you hear me?"

"Yes, Alistair, we are on a bridge looking over a deserted M6, just south of Knutsford. If you just come with me over here."

The camera panned around, staying focussed on Adrian as he walked over to the centre of the bridge and looked down. The camera panned down to follow Adrian's viewpoint. Under the bridge were four large tanks and to the sides, what looked like two large rocket launchers.

"This is what's keeping the traffic away. The carriageway is blocked in both directions and from here I can see the army moving in their heavy weaponry to each side of the motorway. I think next time the alien craft come out from Manchester, they're in for a fight."

The TV image switched back to Alistair in the studio.

Razor turned the sound down.

"Are you still OK for going back in and finding out what this is all about, Alan."

"Try to stop me, Razor. I don't like the look of this at all."

"Should we set off now?"

"No, I think we should sleep on it and we'll make better decisions in the morning."

"You're probably right."

"I'll see you in the morning, Razor, bright and early!"

Razor's head was full of what they might encounter on their next foray in.

As the girls put the children to bed, Judith looked out of one of the windows in the cottage that looked over the lake. It was a beautiful night. The moon shone on the lake and made Wastwater shimmer and glisten.

Judith looked up at the heavens and wondered if any of them had a future, and if they had, what life may be like out there amongst the stars.

– Chapter Ten –

Zindor

Z-Day minus 16 years...

Zindor is one of three planets that rotate around the star Ustulo. The name it has been given, on Earth, is the Barnard star. Some Earth scientists regard it as a runaway star but it's just that it's travelling faster around the hub of the Milky Way galaxy, than the Earth's sun.

Ustulo resides in the same spiral arm of the galaxy as the Earth's sun and is getting closer and closer to it. At the moment it's approximately six light years away, but in another 9,500 years, a very small amount of time to the Zinden, it will only be three point eight light years away.

The Zinden discovered Earth long ago. The colour alone convinced them it was a habitable, water-based planet. As years passed it was realised that the two systems were getting closer. Within a few years of its discovery, the Zindorean Supreme Council decided it would be an ideal world to move its peoples to. The arks were commissioned and an invasion plan was drawn up. The objective was to move the whole population of Zindor to the new planet, once the two systems were at closest approach.

"You've been keeping the development of Scorch, a secret for a long time, Ixes," said Baltire Adren.

Baltire Adren is the commander chosen to be in charge of the Pathfinder mission to Earth. He is addressing, Ixes Pen, Zindor's supreme leader.

"Yes we have, Commander, it's a rather scary weapon, is it not? We didn't want to scare the general population. Anyway, the scientific theory first had to be proved. If the theories couldn't be put into practice we would have raised hopes far too high as regards the loss of life during the invasion phase."

"Why weren't the military informed earlier of this discovery?"

"We thought you would have been impatient to invade," said Ixes.

"Well, of course! We would."

"That's exactly what we thought!" said Trelidin, Zindor's chief scientist. "So we decided that it would be prudent to withhold the information, at least until the scientific data had been collected collated and thoroughly studied. Anyway, you should know that lurking in that data, was some bad news."

"What do you mean?"

"Once the device is activated it will be at least 6,000 years before we can again set down on the planet, and even then, a further 1,000 years or so before we can settle."

There was silence.

The Supreme Council meeting was in the council chambers at the top of the Redus Tower, a three-mile-high citadel, on the outskirts of Zindax, the capital city of Zindor.

Baltire was pacing up and down and looking out through the high windows, at the swirling clouds of the Deepfall. An awe-inspiring sight he could never get used to. The Redus Tower was the only structure this close to the Deepfall that had retained its windows – specially reinforced to maintain the view. All other structures had long ago sealed off any opening that faced the Deepfall, turning their backs on the reality of living on such a vicious planet.

"Why don't we invade the way we planned to do, before you invented Scorch?"

"You know the answer to that, Baltire. We would lose an awful lot of good soldiers in a conventional invasion. These Earthlings are brave, resourceful people and even though their technology can't match ours, they would still give us a damn good fight.

"This way we lose hardly anyone and get rid of everything that lies in our way. OK, we have to wait a few thousand years. It's only our children's children that may benefit but this way most of our children will be alive to enjoy the experience."

"In the scheme of things, Baltire, spending a few thousand years waiting to get a pristine planet is well worth it," said Edaxin Randor, the supreme commander of the armed forces. He added, "This way the military are involved only as a diversionary tactic and we prevent a full scale war."

Invading Earth from Zindor, in the normal way, would not be an insignificant task. Transporting an invasion fleet over a six-light-year gap is a logistical nightmare. Zinden's current technology only allows them to travel up to 37% of the speed of light. At that speed, Earth is over 16 years away.

Zinden's science academy have calculated that by the time of closest approach, in 9,500 years, their technology would have advanced enough to travel at around 65% of the speed of light. This would reduce the time to travel to Earth to less than six years, a much more acceptable travel time.

"So what plans have been laid, Supreme Commander Edaxin?"

"The first part of the plan has you in Starship One, accompanied by the three new starfighter squadrons. You are to fly to Earth. You will then deploy Scorch and retreat to a safe distance before triggering the device.

The starfighter squadrons are to be used as a diversionary tactic so that the peoples of Earth think that they are under attack. You will make it look like a raid, rather than an invasion. You will steal artefacts and materials that they consider valuable. After you've left they will think they have been assaulted by thieves rather than by an invading army.

"When they retaliate, which they will do – they are a proud people, you are to make it look like you have been driven away."

Trelidin interjected. "You're objective at this time would be to place as much distance between you and the Earth as you possibly could, or you will not survive the radiation pulses. If you do not get beyond the planet they call Neptune before they start, you and all your subordinates will die."

"I'm informed that Scorch needs to be underground during detonation. How far do I drill down?" asked Baltire.

"You don't drill at all, Baltire," replied Trelidin.

"If you were to drill, the humans would detect what was happening and your cover would be blown. They may still not be able to protect themselves, even if they knew what was intended, but we do not want to take that chance.

"No! Your diversion will take place near a large mining complex. You will exterminate everyone involved in the mining operation and place Scorch in the most inaccessible part of the mine. Once it is in position and activated, you will make good your withdrawal from Earth. If the operation goes to plan, no one will even know it is there."

"There is a complication, Baltire," said Edaxin.

"What is that?"

"The humans have established a colony on one of the moons of Sol Four, or Mars, as they call it. They call this moon Phobos."

"And what difference does that make?" asked Baltire.

"Two things: One, we don't want you to be seen entering their system, so we need Phobos to be on the other side of Sol Four, when you pass. Two, we need to be sure the peoples of Phobos are fatally irradiated when Scorch is detonated. On both counts this means that you must adhere to the specific timeline set out in the plan."

"I would have done that anyway," said Baltire.

"Yes, but now you understand the true importance of the timing, in the plan."

Trelidin added, "A week after Scorch has detonated, you may return to Earth for a short time, an hour or so, to see if Scorch has been successful. By that time the whole system should be sterilised and completely free from contamination of Earth-based life forms.

"It will then be your job to get your team home – you must not stay there, since the gamma rays will produce photo dissociation of the nitrogen in the atmosphere, which will generate nitric oxide, which in turn will completely destroy the ozone layer. Further, the high-energy gamma rays will produce vast amounts of radioactive nuclei. These radioactive particles will be distributed by the winds, all over the planet.

"As we remarked earlier, because of the half-life of some of these particles, our 'new Earth', or 'new Zindor' as it will be called, will not be habitable for some 6,000 years."

Ixes added, "We will regularly visit the planet again, say every 2,000 years, to see how the biosphere is progressing.

"Around 6,000 years from detonation of Scorch, we will introduce life forms from Zinden and on closest approach we will migrate to our new home. By the time our population arrives, the planet will be a beautiful copy of the best parts of Zindor and in perfect condition."

"The plan is sound, but this is a 33-year round-trip, Edaxin. I only want to take volunteers."

Edaxin laughed, "I don't expect there'll be a shortage of volunteers, Baltire."

Zindor is by no means an easy planet to live on. Its star, Ustulo, is what is known as a Red Dwarf star. It is much smaller than the sun and a whole lot cooler. For Zindor to be habitable, it has to lie much closer to Ustulo, than Earth does to its sun.

To make things a whole lot worse, it is tidally locked to the star. This means that one side of the planet always faces Ustulo and the other always faces away from Ustulo. This combination of being close to the star and being tidally locked has a dramatic effect on the climate of the planet.

If you were to try to live on the face of the planet that permanently pointed towards Ustulo, you would be cooked alive – boiled and fried. The daytime temperature, and it's always daytime on this side of the planet, is well over the boiling point of water.

If you were to try to live on the face of the planet that always pointed away from Ustulo, you would freeze to death. The night-time temperature, and it's always night time on this side of the planet, is well below freezing.

Obviously there is a habitable zone on the planet or the Zinden wouldn't exist. This lies somewhere in between these two extremes. Not as you might imagine exactly on the margin of these two extremes, but partly on the dark side of the planet.

On the daytime side of the planet, in the centre, the sea boils, and superheated steam and hot gases rise and migrate outward from the centre, towards the rim of the planet.

On the dark side of the planet the superheated steam and hot gasses cool and fall. This results in a doughnut shaped cloud called the Deepfall, 160 miles from the rim.

Below the Deepfall and stretching to nearly the centre of the dark side, is the habitable zone of the planet.

The ocean currents lubricate the whole of the planet's weather system. The warm surface currents, coming from the daytime side of the planet, deliver warmth to the cooler side. Whilst this warm water is replaced from below by the deep cold water current, coming from the cold side of the planet.

It is impossible to get closer to the rim than the 160-mile barrier. It isn't just the speed of the winds, it's also the immense radiation belt and the radiation eddies that come over the rim, creating incredible lightning storms that never cease.

Billions of years ago the inhabitable zone was just jungle and swamp but as time passed, small areas of drier land developed, caused by the upheaval of portions of the land nearer the rim. In time, these drier spots enabled intelligent life to develop.

Tough, proud and resilient peoples emerged from the mists of Zindor but with only a small portion of the planet's surface available for life, Zindor's population has remained small. Even now, today, only 43.8 million people live on the surface of the planet.

The science on Zindor developed thousands of years before Earth's Industrial Revolution. The Zinden had discovered that Earth was a life-sustaining planet, some 3,000 years before man had discovered that the Barnard star even existed. You see, Ustulo is very old, much older than the sun and thus intelligent life has had millions more years to evolve and grow strong.

It's interesting to note that from Zindor, the sun is a very bright star and attracts a lot of attention from Zindor's astronomical fraternity.

About 900 years ago there was a gigantic flare-up from Ustulo. The scientists think these flare-ups have happened many times in the past and have, on occasion, resulted in mass extinction events. At that time, a large number of the Zinden race was annihilated. This resulted in changes to their building codes. Now each Zinden home must have a radiation shelter built below it. Other flare-ups have occurred since and many lives have been saved.

If one is caught outside the shelter during a flare-up, then usually death follows within a few days.

For people who have been exposed but are still alive they have two options: euthanasia or sterilisation. Everyone now sees this statute as an excellent solution to the real problem of radiation exposure since, over the last century, the number of deformed children has steadily declined.

Because of the difficulties of living on Zindor it was recommended by the Zindorian Supreme Council that the scientific community look into the possibility of transferring the whole of the population of Zindor to another world. It was always thought that Earth would be the obvious choice. It was agreed that the scientists would research that possibility and come up with a proposed solution. They were not given a deadline.

It took nearly 300 years to develop space flight to a level where 37% the speed of light was attainable. It took them even longer to develop Scorch. But as soon as Scorch had been tested and the scientists realised that the half-life of the radioactive nuclei was going to be in the order of 6,000 years, they knew it was time to act on their ideas.

Ixes continued, "Whilst Earth is recovering, during the 6,000-year interim, we will build arks – the design of which we now have. Cazein has suggested building 80, each capable of sustaining 500,000 Zinden. This means that the whole population of the planet will be transferred within a 22-year period."

Just as Ixes had finished speaking, the intercom sounded.

"Yes, Vanour?" said Ixes.

"I have Slevin Binx on line one. He says it's urgent!"

"Put him through, Vanour."

"Slevin, what can we do for you?"

"We've had an intruder looking through the archives at the museum, specifically the Scorch project."

"How did he get in?"

"He was employed by Radolfin Dax. He came highly recommended by an old employee of the museum."

"But if he's a trained archivist, what's the problem?" asked Trelidin.

"He lied to me about what he'd been doing. He suggested that we were having a large number of incidents in the Deepfall. I monitor that area very closely, so I knew that to be untrue. I was thus convinced that there was a problem."

"I see your point," said Trelidin.

"There's something else!"

"Yes," said Ixes.

"There's no record of the intruder, nor the one who recommended him to Radolfin, ever being born on this planet."

"My God, Binx, what are you implying?"

"There's one other thing you should know," said Binx.

"Get to the point!" said Ixes.

"After realising that our intruder may not be of this planet, I arranged for our mobile scanners to view the hot side of the Deepfall. That's where I would make my escape if I thought I might be detected. We immediately spotted a craft ascending just short of the top of the Deepfall. It was hard to spot, as if they were using some sort of cloaking device, but we detected an energy signature. None of us were sure it was a craft but I made the assumption that it was and called for them to surrender."

"You have them now, Binx?"

"No, they blew themselves up. A few seconds later a much larger craft blew up, far out in space. There was no trace left of either ship."

"Do you think the information about Scorch was retrieved," asked Trelidin.

"I'm absolutely sure of it! It is possible that what they discovered was lost with them. It is also possible that someone out there knows about Scorch."

"I can't believe a Zinden would betray their own world," said Baltire Adren.

"A fine sentiment, Baltire. Not one I recognise these days. Everyone seems to be after more wealth and power today and Zindor generally comes second in their thoughts, not first," said Edaxin.

"Well, there's one thing. It couldn't be anyone from Earth, they haven't got the technology," said Trelidin.

"We know of no other race, although we've all suspected that others must exist. Whoever they are, they have not interfered. Does anyone here suggest that we should forget our plans?"

He paused to see if there would be a reaction, there was none. "I thought not. We go ahead as planned."

Everyone nodded in agreement.

"Have Radolfin Dax executed for treason, he should have checked his employees more carefully," said Ixes Pen.

– Chapter Eleven –

Scorched Earth

Z-Day plus one day...

"Razor, Mary. Alan's called a meeting. He says he needs to talk to us all," said Judy.

"What's it about?" asked Mary.

"He wouldn't say."

Although Judy knew full well what it was about, she thought it better to let Alan tell the others in person, anyway it was too incredulous for her to want to bring it up, out the blue.

"On our way," said Razor, as he helped Mary up from where they had been sat – looking out over Wastwater. It was a warm, clear and beautiful day with not a cloud in the sky and the smell of breakfast still in the air.

As they got back to the cottage, the whole of the team were sat on the front lawn of the garden, in a semi-circle around Alan. Alan was sat on a tree stump to the side of the grassed area.

"OK! Now Razor and Mary are here, I can begin." There was a long pause.

"Look, there's no easy way of telling you this news. You all need to know that I myself am an alien."

There was a gasp from the gathering.

"But you were being chased by them, in the truck—" said Lenny.

"No! No, I'm not one of those aliens – they are as much my enemy as they are yours. But I *am* an alien."

"Are they after you, is that why they're here?"

"No! Look, I know you all have lots of questions. Let me tell you what I know and then I'll answer any questions you may have, afterwards.

"First, I know the invaders are from the planet Zindor. This is a planet that is vastly different from your planet, Earth. They are called the Zinden. I do not yet know why they are here.

"Zindor is not part of the Galactic Federation of Planets, partly because their whole culture is based on aggression. On Zindor it is considered a dishonour if you are not able to face down anyone who challenges your behaviour.

"This war-like race was confined to the planet's surface until about 500 years ago, when they discovered space flight. They spent the next century developing their spacecraft and populating the moons of their own star system. It looks like now they are exploring other systems with a view to populating those, also.

"Those of you who study astronomy would know their star as the Barnard star."

"OK! We now know who the invaders are. Who are you?" said Mary.

"My off-world name is Uban Drix. I am from the planet Calron. I am a Galactic Enforcement Officer. On Earth you would know me as a police officer."

"Then call in the troops, Alan!" said Lenny.

"That would do no good. The troops as you call them are too far away and at the moment they don't even know there is anything happening down here.

"I know that most of you want to go back to Manchester to fight these invaders but before we do, and I mean we, I need to access the systems on my spaceship and transmit an emergency message to the Galactic Council."

"Where *is* your ship?" Judy asked.

"It's in the lake, behind you. The reason it has not been raised so far is that, once above the water, it will be detectable by the Zinden. If they detect the craft they will attack it and anything surrounding it.

"I don't think they *will* detect it because they won't be looking for extraterrestrials, so I think it's worth the risk. However, I thought I'd give those of you who are nervous about the proposition a chance to leave the area."

He paused and looked around to see if anyone wished to leave.

"So, if anyone thinks they should move out, it's time to do so."

"I think a sensible precaution would be to have the women and children get in the Mini and drive a couple of miles away from here before you raise the ship," said Razor.

Judith insisted on staying put. Mary and Wendy, together with the children climbed into the Mini.

"We need to do a little more shopping in town anyway. We'll be back in a few hours if it's all clear on our return."

As the Mini set off, Razor said, "Raise it, Alan. Raise it now!"

Alan gave the signal, and the water in the centre of the lake started to churn. After a few minutes the spacecraft started to emerge slowly out of the lake. Hovering just above the surface of the lake, it then moved horizontally to the edge of the lake, just opposite the cottage garden.

Alan walked over to the craft—everyone followed.

With the sound of air being vented, the entry door to the craft opened up and Alan stepped in.

Alan tapped the emergency transmit button. The button glowed red. He turned on the real-time interpreter, which glowed green, and started to speak.

"This is Uban Drix, Galactic Ship C3012 – calling from Sol Three – Earth. There is a Zinden invasion force here. Much property and peoples destroyed – will call with further updates, as situation develops."

"What! Is that it?" said Razor. "Surely there's more can be done, than that?"

“I’m afraid not, Razor. It’s up to yourselves and the people of Earth to defeat the Zinden. Any galactic force would take many years to get here.”

“How long will it take for that message to reach the Galactic Council?” asked Lenny.

“Just a few minutes, but that’s because we use minute wormholes as a transmission medium—”

An alarm sounded within the cockpit of the spacecraft. A very robotic voice sounded:

“Automated Voice Response for key words: Zinden, Zindor and Gorizon Prime. Message Starts:

“It has come to our attention that the Zinden Race has developed a Weapon of Mass Destruction that has already been used on Gorizon Prime. They have a name for the device: Scorch. The detonation of this device resulted in the total extinction of all plant and animal life in that system. This has now been formally designated a ‘Genocide Event’. As you know, the punishment for such action, is death.

“If you are heading for Gorizon Prime you should not land there. The system itself is now designated a ‘Radiation Hazard’. Marker buoys have been dispatched. It is likely that the buoys will be resident for at least 6,000 years.

“If you are heading for Zindor you should note that the planet has been designated ‘Diseased’. Under normal circumstances the race would be sterilised within the next ten years. However, further investigations are ongoing since we have discovered that two more Scorch devices exist and we do not know where these devices are.

“It is unlikely that we will terminate until these devices are found and disposed of. When these devices are located, the planet and the Zinden colonies will be sterilised.

“The Galactic Council will announce the exact date and time for sterilisation, as soon as it has been determined.”

Everyone surrounding the spacecraft was stunned into silence, including Alan Smith.

“My God! Alan, what are we up against here?” asked Razor.

Alan quickly responded to the automated message:

"This is Uban Drix, Galactic Ship C3012 – please send details of Scorch's appearance and dimensions. Please also send details of deployment method."

Within a few minutes a diagram of the device and its dimensions became available for viewing, in the cockpit. The robotic voice returned:

"The Scorch device on Gorizon Prime was found in a cave system a few hundred feet underground. The caves were artificially drilled and the device lay on old sedimentary rocks, probably on an ancient seabed. Their prototypes were found in similar positions.

"It is presumed that to get the full effect, planet wide, the device needs to detonate underground. We are not sure whether the type of rock or geography is significant."

"There's an ancient seabed, within a cave system, down at Winsford," said Dave.

"Sorry?" said Alan.

"Of course, the salt mine at Winsford – we learnt about that at school," said Simon.

"And the military and I both thought they might be interested in Jodrell Bank," said Alan, "I knew something didn't stack up."

"And I was hoping that knowing why they were here, would make me feel a whole lot better – I certainly feel a whole lot worse now," said Razor.

"Move back, everybody. I'm going to send the ship back underwater again."

As the ship disappeared they all moved back to the front garden.

"Have you any guns or death rays on that ship to help us defeat them?" asked Richard.

"No, there are self-defence systems but nothing powerful enough to tackle an invasion force." Alan paused for a second. "There's something else you all need to know about me. I'm a shape shifter. I can take the form of any animal and plant I see. I can shift shape to nearly all types of objects."

"Can we have a demo?" Simon said, excitedly.

Alan turned into Simon.

"Wow!" Dave said.

He immediately turned into a Zinden. The audience lurched back. He turned back into Alan.

"I've found, in the past, that this ability to fool people is extremely useful, when working undercover. I suggest that a small group, maybe just Razor, Richard and I, go back in, to see if this Scorch device can be located."

"I think you'll need to take me along," said Bill.

"Explain yourself, Bill."

"I know the waterway connections to the salt mines and the museum has a small motor boat that will help us get in and out, more quickly than the canal boats."

"I must admit, the enemy do seem to ignore us if we travel by water. You're in," said Alan.

"Are you sure, Bill? It's going to be extremely dangerous," said Razor.

"No choice. You three won't find the best way to the mine without me."

"OK! Lets get packed and ready," said Razor. "We'll take two of the bikes. I feel a lot less of a target on those bikes than I would in that Mini."

The bikes were packed with food and drink. Alan handed Razor and Richard what looked like guns. "They're set to kill, so no pointing those things at me or Bill."

"Do you really have to go back in?" said Mary to Razor, reluctant to see her man head for danger once again.

"You know I do, Mary. The kids may not have a future unless we defeat these aliens!"

"I don't like the idea of losing the man I've just found," said Judith to Alan.

"We'll be back. Guaranteed!" Alan knew this was just bravado but he hoped the others couldn't see the nervousness in his eyes.

"Daddy's off to help get rid of those nasty aliens," said Razor to the children, who hugged Daddy tightly.

The four of them climbed on their bikes and set off for the boat museum. Alan and Richard took the lead on one bike, whilst Bill sat behind Razor on the other.

"You know, the museum will be open when we arrive," said Bill over the noise of the wind.

"Is that going to complicate matters?" shouted Razor.

"No, but we'll have to find Dan Boswell again – the chief engineer. He's the one that organised the food and drink when we came back out from Manchester with the children."

"I remember him," said Razor.

"We'll have no problem borrowing a boat so long as he's there."

"So where do we go once we have the boat, Bill?"

"You remember we passed the River Weaver on our way into Manchester?"

Razor nodded.

"Well, that's where we're going. The main salt mine at Winsford lies on that river."

The journey south, to the waterways museum, took much less time than any of them thought it would. Maybe the exhaustion everyone felt a few days ago, made the journey north seem much longer.

As they parked their bikes in the car park of the museum, they saw that the Navy had a destroyer on the canal.

They went into the museum and asked for Daniel Boswell. The girl in reception called him.

"It's Bill Symons, Dan. He says it's urgent."

Noise from the earpiece spilled over. The receptionist turned to Bill.

"He says he'll be here in a minute."

Bill headed for the cafeteria, off to the side of the reception area.

"Let's get a brew while we're waiting," said Bill, who promptly went over to the counter and ordered, "Five cups o' tea."

By the time, Dan arrived; the four were sat down sipping tea at one of the cafeteria tables.

"There's a brew for you here, Dan."

"Well done, Bill. It's absolute mayhem here at the moment. I haven't had time for a brew this morning."

Dan supped his tea.

"What's up, Bill?"

"Can we borrow the museum's motor boat?"

"This is not a good time to be asking that question, Bill. Anyway, I'm not having you take one of my prize boats into Manchester, only to have you and the boat blown to smithereens."

"Look, Dan. Alan here has an idea that these aliens are up to something more devious and a damn site more dangerous, than just a simple invasion. On our way up to the museum, before we went into Manchester to get the kids, there was a lot of activity around Winsford, so the plan is to go down the Weaver to the salt mine. See if we can find out what's going on. We've no intention of going into Manchester."

"I'll buy you two new boats, if yours gets damaged in any way," said Razor.

"He can afford it," said Bill.

"I know that. Even *I* know who Razor is."

"Well?"

"OK, old friend, but I'd rather have *you* back in one piece, than the boat."

"Thanks, Dan!" Bill shook Dan's hand.

Dan took them over to the boat and helped them through the locks and onto the ship canal. As Bill steered the boat onto the River Weaver, Alan and Razor had time to talk.

"So how come you make so much money from just playing music, Razor? I mean, there can't be much money in actually selling the track. There's too much downloading these days. Even if you made a film, that's as easy to steal as the audio in today's world, isn't it?" asked Alan.

"Yeah! We do get some money from honest sales, but you're right, it's not enough to become rich. No, haven't you heard about our holographic concert equipment?"

"No!"

"In the beginning we earned lots of money from media sales. The early money wasn't wasted; we invested in the development of some new holographic equipment. We'd noticed the revenues from the concerts were increasing all the time. With the new gear, we could be at 100 concerts at once – hey presto, money!"

“So most of your income is in that manner?”

“Well, it has been, but we’re about to go into the next phase. We’ve refined the equipment so that it’s much more portable and we feel it’s ready to sell to the world.”

Bill interrupted the conversation.

“Quiet, you two. No more chatting. Again, silent running from now on, we’re getting much closer. Razor, you take the helm. Keep the boat in the middle but move to the right if we encounter traffic. Although I don’t expect we’ll see any.”

As the journey progressed, the view started to change from the beautifully rich and green panorama of the English countryside, to scorched fields and burning buildings and dead people from the Zinden killing spree. There were lots of dead people; mothers, fathers, children, even babies. There were lots of dead animals too. There was nothing alive, that Razor or Richard could see, within a five-mile radius of the salt mine.

When they’d travelled into Manchester there had been much destruction, but very little carnage. This was different and you didn’t have to be a genius to figure out that the aliens didn’t want any witnesses to what happened, the night they visited this area. Alan Smith now knew exactly what he was going to find in that salt mine.

The relative calm of the trip down the Weaver was suddenly broken by Bill’s voice.

“Razor, turn the engine off. We’re getting close.”

Razor turned the engine off and the boat glided quietly towards a metal skeleton bridge.

“We won’t take the boat in any further than this bridge. We’re only a few hundred yards from number five shaft.” Bill said in a whisper.

“Right, it’s up to me now, fellas. I should be back in an hour or two. Meanwhile keep your heads down.”

To Bill, Richard and Razor’s horror, Alan Smith turned himself into an alien. After having seen the carnage, Razor had to fight back his instinct to kill the creature. Alan noticed the reaction and looked at him.

“We’ll have our revenge, Razor. They’re not getting away with this!”

After the transformation, he started down the riverbank on foot.

To Alan's surprise, the entrance to the shaft was not guarded. In fact, except for the dead humans that lay all around, there wasn't anyone there. He took the cage down to the deepest level.

As he entered the salt tunnels, he was struck by their size. He was surprised to find jeeps and trucks down at this level. He opted for taking a jeep as far into the tunnel as he could. Every so often he would come across a truck that had been stopped and the driver clearly executed.

At some intersections there were marks pointing in a particular direction. They looked sufficiently Zinden so he decided to follow them. As he progressed along the salt lanes there were more dead bodies. The aliens had clearly been this far into the tunnels.

All of the salt lanes were well lit, but as he turned to join yet another tunnel, he could see at the far end, a part of the tunnel that was even more luminous.

It was the object he'd been looking for and it was directly ahead.

He stopped the jeep and continued on foot. There was something not quite right with this picture. Why would anyone want to illuminate a weapon of mass destruction? Surely they would want to keep it hidden. Store it somewhere in a very dark corner.

Then he saw it, off to the left. It was a camera that had been fixed to the wall. They were watching their grim installation, making sure no one was messing with it.

He took a number of photographs of the installation and headed back to the cage. He was excited, he now knew it was possible to save Earth. He'd formulated a rough plan in his mind that should work, so long as there was enough time left. He was in the mineshaft now, ascending to the surface. Time was suddenly very important.

– Chapter Twelve –

Battle Plans

Z-Day plus two days...

Alan had already turned back into his normal shape by the time he got back to the boat.

"Bill, get us out of here and fast – don't worry about noise. There's no Zinden around. Speed Bill, speed!"

As he turned the craft around and stepped on the gas, Alan turned to Razor and Richard.

"It's the Earth Killer! Lads, we shouldn't have rested yesterday. We were fools to let that time pass by."

"We all needed a rest, Alan," said Richard.

"I hope that rest doesn't kill us all. We won't have many days before they'll depart. We have to get that device off this planet without them knowing."

"How the hell can we do that?" asked Razor.

"I don't know, I'm not sure—Razor, leave me alone, I need to think!"

Razor and Richard joined Bill at the helm.

"What's he discovered?"

"It *is* the WMD and he doesn't think we have much time to dispose of it. He says he needs time to think. I'm glad he's on our side, Bill?"

"We struck lucky there, Razor."

The journey back to the lakes was uneventful. They

used the same grouping as they did when they came down, only this time, Bill and Razor took the lead. Alan was demoted to passenger on Richard's bike. They figured Alan could think better if he was just a passenger, rather than thinking of the journey home. They were back at the side of Wastwater by nine-thirty that same night.

As the bikes pulled up in front of the cottage, Alan turned to Razor and Richard.

"Four hours rest, that's all!"

"Agreed, we'll warn the men."

The girls were there to meet their menfolk.

"No time to talk, Mary, Judy. We've found the Earth Killer. Everyone needs to get some sleep. They'll be up again in four hours. I don't need any sleep but I do need quiet and I mustn't be disturbed."

Everyone retired to bed, except Alan. No one slept well that night.

It was two o'clock in the morning when all the men assembled in the dining room. Alan was sat at the head of the dining table, maps and notes spread before him.

"You should all know that if this plan fails, all of mankind will be dead within the week. The reason for this early start is because we don't know when the Zinden will depart. It could be before we even get near them, although I'm sure that they'll want to stay a little while to see if their ruse has worked. The moment they are convinced that their plans have succeeded, they will move out. There won't be any warning. We need to execute our plan before that happens. Are we clear?"

Heads nodded around the room.

"OK! The basic plan is as follows: first, we retrieve the holographic cameras, the transmitter, receiver and the projectors from Razor's number one container truck, where he left it, down at the service station.

"Then, we steal the Scorch device and place it in the container on the back of the truck. Then, we set the holographic cameras up to film it.

"We then place the holographic projectors inside the salt mine and project the image of Scorch, sent from the container. We drive the container to the Zinden ship and persuade them to load it on board. It's as simple as that!

"If the plan works they'll think that Scorch is still in the mine, when it's really inside a container on board their ship. When they press the button to destroy Earth, BANG!"

"Wait a minute, Alan. That all sounds plausible when you say it quickly like that, but is it really do-able? How do we ensure they don't see us move Scorch?"

"Smoke and mirrors, Razor. Smoke and mirrors," Alan smiled. "OK. We go into the mineshaft, take a picture from their camera's viewpoint and place that picture in front of their camera. All they see, whilst we're moving Scorch and setting up the holographic projectors, is the picture we have taken. Once we're projecting Scorch we remove the still photograph."

"Why don't we just leave the photograph in place and forget the projectors?" asked Richard.

"Because while we're putting the photograph in front of their camera, and when we're removing it, their image will have to be cut temporarily. I think they'll send someone to check it out. If they find the photograph and no Scorch the game is lost. If they see Scorch there's a chance that they won't come near enough to notice it's a holographic image. That's the chance we have to take."

"OK. How do we transport it on the road? It'll jostle and joggle around!" asked Razor.

"It will but I have enough anti-grav buffers to smooth the ride out. It'll be fine."

"OK. So, how do we persuade them to take the container on board?"

"Well, I must admit that's the biggie that's kept me awake. We've heard, have we not, that they're taking souvenirs and artefacts."

"Yes, basically bits and pieces of Manchester," said Terry.

"Well, I'll persuade them that the contents of the container are the personal possessions of their leader. Well—something like that."

While listening to the replies to his questions, Razor had come to the conclusion that Alan had thought the whole thing through. There wasn't any more time for chitchat.

"OK, Alan, let's get to it!"

Alan retrieved a road map of southwest Manchester and shouted Lenny and Dave over to the table.

"Lenny, Dave – you two need to go and retrieve the truck. Lenny, use your bike to get down there. You'll have to approach from the south. When you get there, throw everything out of the truck other than the holographic gear and power supplies." He pointed to the map. "Then bring the truck south on the M6 to J18 and turn right onto the A54 towards Middlewich – stay on the A54 through Middlewich and into Winsford. Don't worry about the aliens – they won't be anywhere near there by now."

"What makes you so sure about that, Alan?" asked Lenny.

"They weren't there when I went down the mineshaft. I think they're drawing attention away from that area and thus they don't want to be seen in that place."

Alan went back to the map. "Keep on the A54 till you get to the River Weaver. There's a pub called the Red Lion. I looked it up on Orange Earth. You'll have to go all the way around the roundabout to park there – we'll meet you outside that pub."

"Who's we?" asked Lenny.

"Bill, Razor, Richard, Terry, Simon and me. We take the boat, as before, down the Weaver, past the mine and down to the pub. We'll load the holographic equipment onto the boat there."

"Why are we bothering with a boat? Why don't we just take the truck straight to the mine?" asked Razor.

"For a number of reasons: one, they seem to ignore anything we do if it's on the water, so let's keep to the water. Two, we can't be sure they're not watching the mine surrounds, from afar. The truck will eventually take the container to the main ship. If they spot that it's been near the mine, they might put two and two together."

"The boat may not take the weight of the Scorch device. We'll need to pick up a barge on the way down," said Bill.

"You say that like there'll be a load of barges just lying around waiting to be picked up, Bill," said Razor.

"We'll have no problem there," Bill smiled.

"When we've lifted Scorch, someone will have to stay behind in the tunnel. I need a volunteer for this."

"Stay behind? To do what?" asked Simon.

"Once we've removed Scorch, someone will have to go back in and take the truck we used to carry it back to where it was found. Everything must be in the same position as it was when the aliens left Scorch in there. This person will then wait where the holographic cameras and transmitters are, until I communicate with them.

"Once we are communicating, this person will get in a position so they can see the holographic image as it will be seen by the aliens' camera. He will then compare the still image with this view of the holographic image – they'll need to match.

"He will then advise us as to whether we need to change any angles to suit the image that is already in front of their camera. Once the images match, he will unplug the power to the Zinden camera, remove the photograph, then switch their camera back on.

"The moment he switches the camera off, it will trigger a response from the Zinden, such that they will have to come and check their device is still OK.

"When the Zinden come down the mine, if the deception worked, our spy will just remain quiet and do nothing. He will wait for around 20 minutes before coming out from the mine. If they are not fooled, then this person will attempt to get in touch with us as quickly as possible.

"It's a crucial job, you up for it?" Alan looked at Simon.

"Yes. I'm up for it."

"OK, let's get to it."

Lenny and Dave headed for the truck. They knew full well from what Alan had said that there would be no aliens south of the Thelwall Viaduct, or west of the M6. So they didn't need to be cautious until they were near the burnt-out services.

The truck lay undisturbed exactly where they had parked a couple of days before. Lenny opened the rear doors and started throwing equipment out of the back of the truck. Dave helped.

"I'll just do a final check of what's left inside, Dave. Then we'll get out of here."

Neither of them felt comfortable with being so close to the alien ships. Most of the fires were out but smoke was still drifting over the scene as they started the engine. The engine noise was so loud; they felt sure the aliens must have heard it.

"I'm going to miss that bike," said Lenny as he pulled truck one away from its parked position.

As he drove down the same ramp that the tour bus had driven down, he couldn't help but recall those terrible scenes that night. When it dawned on him that the remains of the bus were still there, he instinctively looked in his rear view mirrors to check there was no spaceship following. He hoped to God that Alan was right and that for whatever reason, attacking anything further south than the viaduct, was no longer on the aliens' agenda.

If it hadn't have been for seeing the carnage that the aliens had reaped in the two days prior, the drive to the Red Lion would have been quite pleasant.

They arrived at the pub some two hours before Alan, Richard, Razor, Terry, Bill and Simon arrived in the museum's boat. They were sat on the grass bank leading to the canal as the boat pulled alongside.

"Did you manage to get a barge?" asked Lenny.

"Yep! It's parked up near the mine entrance," replied Simon.

"OK. Once the holographic receivers and projectors are on the boat, everyone climb aboard. We're going to need all the manpower we have to load Scorch onto the underground truck and eventually the barge."

It didn't take long to load the boat and sail it up to the barge.

As they approached the mineshaft, Lenny and Dave saw the carnage for the first time.

"How could anyone do such a thing?" said Lenny.

"And the smell. It's making me feel sick," said Dave.

"I'm sorry lads, you'll have to get used to it. They murdered everyone within a few miles of the mine, including all the miners in the tunnels below," said Alan.

They reached their destination.

Once in the mineshaft a number of trips had to be made in order to get all the holographic projectors, receivers and power units down to where Scorch was.

"The truck the aliens used to take Scorch deep into the mine, is still parked near Scorch. So we'll take the holographic gear down to Scorch on a couple of those jeeps over there."

They drove down to Scorch. As the journey ended, Bill remarked, "Hell! That's quite a distance."

They climbed out of the jeeps, and Alan walked briskly over to the Zinden camera position and de-coupled the power cable. He immediately took a shot of Scorch from the camera's position and placed the photograph in front of the camera lens. He then switched the Zinden camera back on and hoped like hell that the lack of an image, for such a short period of time, wouldn't bring the Zinden down to investigate.

He was confident they would stay away this time since sending one of their ships to check on Scorch would risk their plan being uncovered. He didn't think the same logic would apply when he did the same action again in a few hours' time.

"We have very little time to get Scorch aboard the barge and over to the truck."

Lifting Scorch was easier than everyone anticipated. Yes, it was very heavy, but there were good grip points, just up from the base. They placed Scorch on the flatbed and took it to the mineshaft. As they pushed the device towards the lift entrance it became all too obvious that no one would be able to travel up with it.

"Do you think you and I can manoeuvre this thing into the lift by ourselves, Simon," said Razor.

"I would think so. It's only a bit of a shuffle."

"Then the rest of you will need to go up in the lift first. Once you're up there, send the lift down and we'll send Scorch up to you."

The others went up to the mine entrance and sent the lift back down.

Simon and Razor pushed Scorch into the lift, closed the safety gates and pressed the ascent button.

There was a loud buzzing sound, flashing red lights and a monotonous voice emanating from somewhere in the lift:

"Lift overload – reduce passenger numbers and try again."

"Shit! You've got to be joking!" exclaimed Simon.

They tried again but with the same result.

"Those floor boards look heavy, let's see if we can remove them," said Razor.

They wrestled getting Scorch out of the lift once more and started to remove most of the boards from the lift floor.

"Take care, Simon. We'll have to replace them once we have Scorch out of here. Remember, at least one Zinden is going to return for a last look."

Once most of the timbers had been removed, they returned Scorch to the lift. Now Scorch just rested on the metal skeleton of the base of the lift. Razor again pressed the button. This time the lift ascended, and Razor and Simon breathed a sigh of relief.

They replaced the timbers before they themselves ascended the shaft. By the time they had reached the surface, Scorch was on board the barge, covered in tarpaulin, and everyone was ready to go back south to the pub.

It was time for Simon to return to the mine. Alan came off the barge and moved Simon to one side to talk to him.

"Are you clear about what you have to do next, Simon?"

"Yes."

"Then tell me, nice and slow – no mistakes."

"I go back in and take the flatbed back to where we found it – near Scorch's original position. I then wait until you contact me.

"Once we can talk to each other, I get behind the aliens' camera and look at the holographic image you are sending me from the container on the truck.

"The holographic image you send needs to match the photographic image I already have in front of the aliens' camera. If it doesn't, I get you to adjust the angles in the container until it does.

"Once the images match, I unplug the power to the Zinden camera and remove the photograph. Then finally, I switch their camera back on?"

"Perfect, well done, Simon! But remember, the moment you switch that camera off, the Zinden will be on their way to check what's just happened. So what will you do when the Zinden come down the mine?"

"Hide and make sure I'm not seen. If I'm sure the deception has worked, I just sit tight for 30 minutes and then get out of that mine."

"You're the man, Simon. Good luck."

"You too, Alan."

Simon returned, via the flatbed, to where Scorch was, and awaited communications.

The others shipped Scorch down the canal to the Red Lion pub, where they placed it in the container, on the back of number one truck.

Lenny busied himself with getting the holographic transmitters set correctly. Alan and Razor worked on fitting the anti-grav corner units on the truck plinth. Fitting them was relatively easy – getting the settings just right, a damn site trickier.

He'd bounced the truck on rough ground several times and had Simon watch the live feed from the holographic transmitters. It took several attempts before the bounce was completely under control, but now it was and no matter how rough the road, the image remained rock steady.

Obviously Alan would be much more careful during the transportation phase but he knew it was imperative to make sure, no matter what the road surface, Scorch would look like it was on solid ground.

"OK, Simon if you're happy with the image match, then go ahead with the switch over."

Simon checked the images one last time. He was happy with it. He unplugged the Zinden camera, removed the photograph and holder, and plugged the aliens' camera back in again, leaving it a little slack so that it would look like it may have broken loose for a short time. He retreated behind the salt truck and waited.

* * *

"There! It's happened again, Zorn. I think someone should go in and check everything's OK."

"We've had strict instructions not to go in there again. I'll check with the commander."

Ribrek left the observation deck to check how they should respond. When he returned there was more than a little glint in his eye.

"Yes, we can go in. You watch the monitors and I'll go and check the camera. I'll signal you if everything is OK."

Ribrek took a ship and flew over to the mine. There was certainly nothing suspicious at the mine entrance. There was no sign of human activity at the bottom of the shaft either. He took a jeep down to investigate the camera.

When Simon heard the jeep coming, he was as scared as hell! He'd never been in this sort of situation before, where even just a little mistake, an accidental noise; a sneeze for example, would result in his death.

Again Ribrek found nothing untoward in the tunnel leading to Scorch. He moved over to the camera and looked at the power cable. "Ha!" he muttered to himself. "A loose cable."

He reconnected the power cable properly and waved at the camera, indicating that everything was fine.

Simon heard the alien muttering to himself and took a peep. He'd found the loose power cable, fixed it and turned around. Simon ducked back down quickly, as he was sure he'd been seen.

Ribrek heard a small rustle somewhere near the truck they had used to bring Scorch into the mine. He turned his light onto the truck.

He saw nothing, shrugged his shoulders, climbed into the jeep and headed back to his spacecraft.

Simon's relief was palpable. That was really intense, he thought.

He waited 30 minutes then sent the 'all clear' signal to Alan.

He drove back to the lift-shaft and took the lift back to the surface. As he walked quickly to his pick-up point, he prayed that the rest of the plan would be as successful.

– Chapter Thirteen –

Deception

Z-Day plus three days...

One deceit—

Baltire Adren's face was stern and menacing.

"To whom am I speaking?"

The Prime Minister was equally stern in response.

"I am Alexander Walken. Leader of the lands you are attempting to invade."

"The Zinden do not *attempt!* If we wished to invade your lands we would do so and we would be successful. Your puny attempts to stop us would not be sufficient."

"We have not attempted to stop you, as yet. Why would you commit this act of aggression, if not to invade?"

"We are a Zindorian expeditionary force. We look at the relative strengths and weaknesses of the worlds we encounter. Yours is particularly weak."

"You have no idea what our strength is."

"Strength is not just weaponry. Its reaction time, preparedness and much more. No, you are weak indeed."

"Enough of this posturing. What are your intentions?"

"To test your abilities."

"And if we do not wish to be tested."

"Then we will destroy this city!"

Suddenly the communications link went silent.

"I've lost the link, Sir."

The communications officer was frantically trying to regain the link.

"Did *they* cut the link?"

"I can't be sure, Sir. My guess is, they did."

"Put me in touch with Major General, Sir John Dowding."

"Yes, Sir!"

The Major General was in a helicopter passing over Birmingham. He was going north over the M6, on his way to join his forces, when the call came through.

"If you haven't already guessed it, John. The aliens aren't talking."

"Yes, I'd already assumed that would happen. Which option do you want me to pursue?"

"I think we need to exhaust our attempts to reason with them, before we go on the offensive. Just contain them for now. Cordon the area off and make sure they don't expand outwards from where they are already. If they attempt to break out then meet them with deadly force. Where's your front line, currently?"

"If you were to draw a circle around Manchester, you'd find our forces just north of Crewe. We haven't had any resistance, so far. We'll push on as far as Wilmslow and see if we can secure Manchester Airport. We'll not dig in until we meet sufficient resistance. At that point we'll look at the overall diameter of the cordon. That'll give us an idea of what we are up against."

"OK, all the best, John – keep in touch!"

Deserves another—

Alan had earlier sent everyone, except Razor back to base via the canal. Because Simon had turned off the Zinden camera for the second time, it made sense to Alan and Razor that they should keep a low profile until the Zinden had investigated the mine. He was sure they would investigate and until they did, they were going nowhere. Whilst they where waiting for Simon's 'all clear' signal, Razor turned on the radio in the cab.

"—An army spokesman has confirmed that ground forces were slowly making their way towards the outskirts of Manchester. Our sources say that the southern defence line is now north of Crewe and is steadily moving towards Manchester as we speak. The army insists that the slow progress north is part of the gradual tightening of the defence circle around Manchester and that going slow is part of the plan. They say it enables the aliens to pull back if they wish, thus preventing conflict and further loss of life. It also allows us to check for possible hidden pockets of resistance.

"Reports that the aliens are looting the city cannot be confirmed or denied by the military. Although they have said that strangely-marked container trucks have been spotted taking materials to a large spaceship on the outskirts of Trafford Park. The markings are the same design as those on the sides of their spaceship—"

"We could do with knowing what those markings are like, Alan."

"I've seen them. Photographic memory. I'll reproduce them on the sides and the top of the container before I get underway. You need to go and get some paint and some brushes. I'll need about ten litres of white, red and blue paint – quick drying if possible. Oh! And at least eight paint brushes."

Within 20 minutes, Razor was back carrying paint and brushes.

"Simon's sent the 'all clear', Razor."

"Great."

As he was opening the tins, he queried the eight brushes.

"They tell me this stuff needs an hour to be touch dry. Why eight brushes, Alan?"

"No choice. I'm the only one who knows what to paint."

Alan's shape was changing as he spoke. He suddenly had eight arms and the speed at which he was applying the paint was phenomenal. Within 15 minutes the painting was complete.

"I think with an act like that we could earn money."

Alan laughed. "We'll give it an hour to dry, then I'll be on my way. Fancy a pint?"

The two went into the Red Lion.

They settled down with their beers, in front of the clock.

"If I don't get back by around four o'clock then you should hurry back to the lakes and enjoy your last few days with Mary. Do me a favour, will you?"

"What's that, Alan?"

"Tell Judith we'd have made a formidable team."

"Now don't you go all weepy on me, Alan. You're going to make it and I'll be waiting here for you when you return."

As the hour mark came up, they finished their pints and went outside.

Alan had begun the day as an Earthling, now he needed to end the day as a Zinden soldier. Having marked the top and sides of the truck with the Zinden transport sign, he shape shifted into a Zinden soldier, choosing the rank of sergeant and pulled himself up into the cab.

"I've heard on the radio that the army are getting very close to this position, Alan. You'll need to get a move on if you're going to avoid them," called Razor.

"Get in that pub and pull yourself another pint. I'll see you back here in a few hours."

"I'll be waiting. Good luck."

Alan pulled away and onto the A54 towards the M6. As he took the slip road into Trafford Park, a spacecraft flew overhead but didn't fire – the paint job had worked. Alan could see the huge supply ship up ahead, and a queue of trucks dropping off cargo, ahead of him. He placed his truck at the back of the queue and waited in line. Further trucks lined up behind him. Slowly but surely he came to the front of the line and to the gatekeeper.

"You're not on my list, sergeant. What are you carrying?"

"Special delivery for Baltire Adren."

"Open the back, let's have a look."

"I have strict instructions not to let anyone near these objects. They are personal to Baltire Adren. You don't think a sergeant would be driving a truck like this if it wasn't for Commander Adren?"

"Open the back!"

"Do you want me to ask Baltire himself to intervene? I will say this only one more time; NO ONE must see the inside of this container! If you can't cope with that I'll personally phone Baltire myself."

Alan reached for the glove compartment. There was nothing in there; it was a gamble that thankfully paid off.

"No! There is no reason to do that."

The gatekeeper knew full well that if he made any kind of mistake as regards Baltire Adren, he would be executed. In these situations he'd always found it best to keep a low profile.

"OK, go ahead."

Alan drove the truck into the loading bay and waited for the container to be removed. He was sweating profusely. He'd never been so nervous in all his life. It wasn't for his own safety he was bothered, it was the fact that a whole planet's worth of life forms, depended on him getting this right.

The cab swayed from side to side as the container was removed and placed deep in the cargo bay. He moved his truck out, following the other trucks that had their cargo removed just prior to him.

Some of the trucks went to park on the roads leading to the ship. Others carried on, obviously going for more goods somewhere in Manchester. That's good, he thought, if they're still loading, that means departure time is not imminent.

As he rejoined the M6 on the southbound carriageway, his confidence was high enough to shape shift. Not back to Alan Smith the civilian but to Alan Smith the SAS soldier.

It wasn't long before he reached the front line of the troops coming north. He slowed down so that he would not be shot at. As he came alongside the troops he stopped the truck and leant out the cab.

"Hello there! Alan Smith – Special Projects Team SAS – I was on a reconnaissance mission with the rest of my troop when I got separated from them. Can you point me towards Middlewich?"

He knew full well where Middlewich was; it was just a way of deflecting the soldier's thoughts away from asking any awkward questions.

"Yes, go south and take the A54 turn-off, it'll be signposted. Have you drawn any fire from the aliens."

"No. But there's a lot of activity near the M6, M62 interchange."

"Thanks!"

"No problem mate!" and he drove off south, passing an enormous convoy of troop trucks, tank carriers and other armoured vehicles. He eventually turned onto the A54 and headed for the Red Lion pub, shape shifting back to Alan Smith the civilian as he drove.

When he reached the pub, Razor was outside, leaning on a wall with a pint of beer in one hand. There was another pint of beer next to him, with a beer mat on top of it.

"You're late. This beer will be getting warm if you don't drink it soon."

"No time for drinking, Razor. Take me to your leader!"

"Ugh?"

"Everyone on Earth knows who you are. You're my passport to the top. We need to tell your Prime Minister and his Generals not to attack that spaceship or the device stays on this planet – and if that happens—"

Razor jumped in the cab. "Head back to the M6."

As they reached the M6 they came across an army roadblock. Razor jumped out of the cab to talk to the sergeant in charge. Alan remained in the cab. It was obvious that Razor had been recognised. He jumped back in the cab.

"A Near Zero fan. He's taking us to General Sir John Dowding's field headquarters. Let's hope we can get to talk to him."

The sergeant climbed into a jeep and waved at the truck to follow him. The little convoy kept on the A54 past the

M6 turnoff and veered to the left onto country roads that were unfamiliar to both Razor and Alan.

"Damn, Razor. I should have guessed."

Alan was looking over the trees as he said the words.

"What do you mean, Alan?"

"That's Jodrell Bank – look over the trees, Razor. He's placed his field headquarters at Jodrell Bank."

As they turned left into the lanes that led to the radio telescope, Razor saw it in its entirety for the first time.

"Wow, that's quite a structure."

"I can't believe you humans are still using such primitive technology."

Razor let the little dig at the human race, pass. The convoy pulled up in the visitor's car park next to the arboretum. The sergeant led them into the facility and asked them to wait in the entrance.

Razor wasn't good at waiting, especially when the possible extinction of the human race was involved. He paced up and down in front of Alan, who was as calm as a millpond. This was worse than waiting for teeth to be pulled, thought Razor. After what seemed like forever, the sergeant reappeared, accompanied by a lieutenant. The lieutenant spoke.

"Sir John will see you now."

They were escorted into Sir John Dowding's office.

"Sergeant Wrigley tells us you've been into Manchester and have some important information for us that might help us get rid of these aliens."

Alan Smith spoke. "I'm afraid the information is so sensitive that I would request we be alone, when we speak."

Sir John looked across the room, "Sergeant!"

"Yes, Sir, on my way." The sergeant left the room.

"Now anything you tell me, can be said in front of the lieutenant, carry on!"

"I'm sorry to shock you but you need to know I too am an alien." Alan shape shifted into a copy of Razor. The lieutenant immediately took out his pistol and aimed it at Alan.

"I'm very different from the aliens that are attacking your city. I come in peace and with a view to getting rid of the aliens you are preparing to attack."

"Put the gun down, lieutenant. Why are you here?"

"To prevent you from shooting their cargo ship down."

"You're too late. An SAS team have eyes on the target. It's lying near the Old Trafford football ground."

He looked at his watch.

"It should be in pieces, any minute now."

"Call the attack off or we all die – the whole human race."

There was something about the gravity in his voice. Sir John believed him straight away. He looked at the lieutenant, "*Do it now*!"

The lieutenant dashed out the room, leaving Sir John, Razor and Alan Smith to stare at each other and just wait. Razor wasn't for standing still in these situations and was slowly pacing up and down. Alan counted at least 89 paces before the lieutenant rushed back in.

"The planes have been recalled, Sir. No missiles launched."

The relief on Razor and Alan Smith's face was obvious.

"OK, gentlemen, explain yourselves."

"The attack on Manchester is just a ruse, a diversion, so that you won't see what they're really up to."

"And what are they really up to?"

"They've planted a bomb that will kill all life forms, in what you call the solar system. They have made a mess of Manchester so that you would be distracted from them planting this bomb. Now the bomb is planted, they will leave in a hurry so that you would think that you had either defeated them or that it was just a raiding party. Once out of range from the deadly radiation that will ensue, they would trigger the bomb."

"So, why not shoot down the aliens?"

"We have smuggled the bomb back aboard that ship and they do not know this. When they activate the bomb, *they* will be destroyed, not us—so long as we don't down that ship."

Alan continued.

"There is an additional problem though."

"Yes?"

"I am aware that JISA (Joint International Space Administration) has a base on Phobos."

"Yes, they do."

"They will all die, unless you can get them back here before the bomb explodes. The worst of it is, if you communicate with them and the aliens find out, we're all doomed. So in the end you may have to choose between saving them or saving the whole planet."

"I suggest we get you two down to the PM. You can bring up the Phobos issue with him. Meanwhile, I think I'd better concentrate on attacking everything else they've got."

Now Sir John knew the objective of the alien force, he did not hesitate to attack. The sooner they were off the planet the better and a full-scale attack would help in driving them off.

Whilst Alan and Razor where airlifted to London to meet with the PM, Dowding's forces began their bombardment of the alien ships.

"Now Scorch is on board their vessel, we could do with them leaving ASAP," remarked Razor.

"I think they've been waiting for this attack on their forces. Without it I don't think they'd leave. I'm guessing that part of their plan is to be seen being driven away from Earth. The idea, a false sense of security to their opposing forces," said Alan.

"I suppose if we were to discover Scorch before they took off there's always a chance we could do something about it. With it being left on Earth after they take off we'd be well and truly screwed."

"That's exactly it, Razor. Now they're being attacked they'll be eager to get away."

Just as Alan predicted, by the time they both met the PM, the aliens had left Earth.

"We have already sent a code-red message to the team on Phobos," said the PM.

“Do you think they stand a chance, Sir?”

“There is a void at the centre of Phobos, it is just possible that they may be able to use that fact to protect themselves.”

“As soon as the aliens have detonated Scorch, I’ll take my ship up to Phobos. If there are any survivors I’ll bring them back.”

“Will we see the detonation from here?”

“I don’t know, Sir. I would think so. Even now the Galactic Enforcement Brigade is not sure how this device works. We are sure it must be pulsed in some way. We are sure it will be visible and will probably be a series of flashes,” said Alan.

“Now everything is done, Sir. Would it be possible to return to our loved ones in the Lakes?” said Razor.

“Of course, of course. We can talk more fully later. I’ll get a helicopter assigned to take you back.”

“Thank you.”

During the helicopter ride back to the Lakes, Razor noticed Alan looking wistfully at the scenery they were passing over.

“Worth saving, Alan?”

“Absolutely, Razor. Earth is considered to be one of the jewels of the galaxy. We’ve been watching you for a long time. We have shared in your growing pains and we’ve been hoping that you would survive. It is good that you have.”

“Are we to be members of the galactic empire?”

“I think so, but not yet. Maybe in 100 years or so, who knows? But yes, eventually you will be members. I’m sure of that.”

“And you, Alan. I got the impression that you and Judy were an item?”

“I hope she will join me on my travels, but that’s her decision, not mine.”

As the helicopter set down outside the cottage and Alan and Razor stepped down, everyone came out to greet them. Alan waved the pilot away and the ’copter disappeared into the distance.

Judy rushed over to Alan, and Mary and the children to Razor.

"When will we know?" asked Mary.

"I've estimated around eleven o'clock tonight," said Alan.

Razor turned to the children.

"We're having a star party tonight kids. We'll all assemble on the grass with a late night supper and watch the stars."

"Can I have jelly if it's a party?" asked Abigail.

Razor looked at Mary and mouthed, "Have we got some?" Mary nodded.

"Yes, Abigail. Lots of jelly."

– Chapter Fourteen –

Phobos

Z-Day plus three days...

To be honest, the base on Phobos was always considered a bit of a joy ride by most of the scientific community. That's basically because of Phobos's close orbit to Mars, which gives it a breathtaking view of the red planet, if ever the science team had enough time to relax and enjoy it.

Man has not yet set foot on Mars, even though most of mankind is itching to do so. The Joint International Space Administration: America, Russia, China, India and the EU, under the JISA banner, are still talking about another five months before the flight down to Mars will take place.

In the early days, Mars's moon, Phobos, was considered a better target than Earth's moon. It was certainly far less expensive to land on Phobos than it was to land on the moon, and thus it became one of JISA's main targets.

There were other reasons to choose Phobos as the precursor to any Mars mission. The fact that it was considered to be an organics-rich asteroid with frozen water ice was one. Large amounts of water will be critical in order to establish a base on Mars. Further, it may hold historic clues as to how water was delivered to both Mars and Earth.

Secondly, Phobos has collected ejected material from Mars, for billions of years. The stripes on Phobos are thought to be as a result of such ejected material from many impacts on Mars. Studying these stripes may prove to be useful.

The third reason was the fact that the current crop of Mars rovers would be better controlled with man on Phobos since there would be near zero latency between issuing commands to the rovers and the rovers responding to those commands, and the rovers were still sending JISA some valuable information.

Phobos is a good choice of name for this moon. In Greek mythology, Phobos was the son of Mars and in book 15 of the Iliad, Mars would summon Deimos (Dread) and Phobos (Fear). Now with Phobos there is something to be fearful about. The orbit of Phobos is decaying, and in the distant future, the 11-kilometre- (nearly seven miles) wide asteroid, will impact the surface of Mars.

Mathematicians have calculated that it is likely that around 7.5 million years from now, Phobos will break up and form a planetary ring around Mars but this will not prevent the continued decent of the matter into Mars. This would be a really bad time to be living on the surface.

The science base on Phobos is on the southern rim of Stickney Crater. The base consists of the lab itself and the Phobos return module that will be used to return to the mother ship for the journey back to Earth. The mother ship is not orbiting Phobos; it is orbiting in a high Mars orbit.

To date, the most interesting discoveries have nothing to do with Mars itself. As the science team predicted, they have found large quantities of water ice but in an unusual place; in a large void in the centre of Phobos.

The entrance to the void looks like a sinkhole, off to the northeast side of Stickney Crater, not far from the science base. There is a plan, already drawn up, to investigate the void in the near future, once the landings on Mars have begun.

"The message is coded, Levka?"

"More than that, Erika. It's coded red."

This was the first code-red message the team had ever received. Levka knew the drill, however, and pressed the emergency call button, as prescribed in the space station protocols.

"What's going on?" asked Enrico, bumping into Laurent, as they made their way to the central meeting room.

"Absolutely no idea. It's Levka that's called the meeting but he wouldn't tell me what it was about. Something about following protocol."

"It must be serious. Everyone's been called in."

As the two pushed the doors open to the emergency meeting room, they saw that the rest of the crew had got there before them. There were only ten individuals on the space station, currently two from each investing nation.

Enrico sat down next to Scott Parker and repeated his question, hoping for a better answer this time.

"So what's going on, Scott?"

"Levka has a code-red message from Earth."

"I thought they were only to be issued in life or death situations?"

"You thought right, Enrico. The code-red protocols also say that the message must be read out in front of the whole crew, and space station communications and communications with Earth, MUST NOT mention the subject matter in the message."

Enrico was just about to carry on his conversation with Scott when Levka stood up and addressed the gathering.

"Well done, everyone, for getting here so quickly. We'll get straight to business and look at the message now."

He punched in the decrypt code and went to sit in the audience with the rest of the crew. The 3D viewer glowed and the message began—

PRE-AMBLE: "This is a code-red message. It is likely that communications between Phobos and Earth are being monitored by an alien intelligence. It is imperative that they do not find the contents of this message. It would have grave consequences for life on Earth."

BODY OF MESSAGE FOLLOWS: "We believe that within the next 24 hours there will be the equivalent of a gamma ray burst that will deliver lethal quantities of radiation to Phobos. We have studied your predicament and have come to the conclusion that your only chance of survival – I repeat, your only *chance of survival – is to enter the void in the centre of Phobos and move as deep into the asteroid as you possibly can.*

"Do not expect the radiation shielding of the science lab to help you – it will not be sufficient. You will need to be underground to survive.

It is not possible to answer all the questions you will now have, and further communication may well be prejudicial to the survival of our species. So do not try to contact Earth until this is all over. If you survive we will be in touch. Good luck and God Speed—I repeat for your own safety, GET DEEP UNDERGROUND!!!"

MESSAGE ENDS

The whole room was shocked into silence. Rob Haddon was the first to speak.

"I've seen a plan somewhere on how to tackle the void. Which of you wrote it?"

"It was I," Aadesh Mehta stood up. "You must understand that the plan assumed ideal conditions and low numbers of participants. I don't see how all ten of us can do the trip."

"Having studied the problem, what do you see as the major obstacle?"

"Oxygen. Gravity is sufficiently low to ensure that the descent is not a problem, even if we all were really poor climbers, which we aren't. Obviously, I would still recommend the first two people to descend would need to be the best two climbers in our party. They could set up guide ropes as they descended into the void to help the others.

"Pressure suits are not the problem – in fact we have an extra two suits. *But*, we simply don't have enough portable oxygen for ten people. As you all know, each primary life-support sub-system only provides seven hours of oxygen and carbon dioxide removal. The secondary oxygen pack provides another half hour. So I would say we have six hours underground, absolute max."

"Is there no way of knowing when the radiation hazard is expected to occur?"

"None at all!"

"How wide is the opening to the void?" asked Levka.

Levka Asimov wasn't in charge of the mission by accident, he was not only the smartest man on Phobos but he could think quickly in response to changing situations. In just the short time they'd been talking, he'd formulated a plan, although there would be no guarantee of success.

"It's very much like a sink hole. Nearly circular and about 15 feet in diameter," said Aadesh.

"Have you been in it?"

"Only in the first two chambers. The first is quite small, the second quite large but our instrumentation suggests much bigger caverns further in."

"How do you get from cavern one to cavern two?"

"It's a small opening, but you can fit through wearing a pressure suit."

"And from cavern two to the next one?"

"Ha! That's different. The opening is quite small. There's no way through – unless we blast our way through."

"Perfect!" said Levka Asimov. He continued, "OK. This is what we do. First we prepare the return module for flight."

"Where the *hell* are we going to fly to, Levka?"

"After the rest of us have climbed down with the batteries and the extra life-support suits, you and Robert are going to plug the hole with it. You're flying it a few hundred yards that way," Levka pointed towards the sinkhole. "And you're going to make sure it's as good a fit as possible in that hole."

"We're going to use the escape module as a plug for that hole, why?"

"Because we're going to generate a lot of oxygen, using the space station batteries plugged into the ice within those caves and we don't want any of that precious oxygen to vent into space.

"Once that's done, *we* will start dismantling the engines from inside the cave and you will do the same from inside the module. In order to do this quickly enough, we will have to cut through vital systems."

"Then there'll be no way home, Levka," said Tsai Huang.

"Without surviving the lethal radiation, there *is* no way home, Tsai. I'm sure if we can survive the blast, someone will come for us. Our priority is to survive the blast.

"Once the hole is created in the escape module, Scott and Robert will join the rest of us and we will descend into the second cavern, to plug the hole that leads to the third cavern"

"We will freeze to death."

"We won't freeze whilst our suits are on and later we will have fuel from the escape module, to burn if necessary – Enrico and Laurent, that's your job."

They nodded.

"We keep our suits on at all times. We use the oxygen in our suits only if there is not enough oxygen being generated. Remember you will need to keep at least 45 minutes of oxygen left to return to the science station – assuming the station is still there after the blast. Is all that clear?"

"You know, we've no idea about the salt content in that ice, we may end up generating chlorine instead of oxygen," whispered Lin Lee.

"If that happens, Lin, then it truly is the end. At least it's a chance. If the green stuff *is* generated, it may be a better way to go, than frying in radiation."

"OK, let's get to it everyone, we don't have much time."

* * *

"Thank God for low gravity," said Aadesh. "There's no way I could have carried this battery otherwise."

"Levka is planning to use the station batteries as well," said Elise.

As the batteries were installed and the anodes and cathodes placed in the ice, large amounts of gases began to boil off. They paid particular attention to the hydrogen pipes to ensure that the hydrogen gas was pumped out into space.

Cutting the engines off had to be done in a particular order. First the propellant had to be separated.

Enrico and Laurent had come up with an ingenious idea for slowing down the rate of burn-off of the fuel. With hydrogen being deliberately created at one end of the void and later, rocket propellant being burned off for heat at the other end, although at a much slower rate than normal, the potential for a rather large explosion was ever present.

Separating the fuel tanks and engines from the escape module was proving to be a much more difficult task. At one point it was thought that Scott and Robert may be stranded but eventually they overcame the difficulties.

Slowly but surely the oxygen level rose, as did the air pressure, within the two caves.

There came a point when there was nothing left to do but wait, and hope that the systems they had put in place would, before the six hours were up, give them a chance of survival.

Everyone sat, relaxed their muscles and breathed as shallow as possible, so as to conserve oxygen, and as the hours went by the pressure in the cave system kept on rising.

Laurent Bonnet was the first to signal he had only 45 minutes of oxygen left. Elise looked at the pressure readings and signalled to him that he must keep his pressure suit on and use its oxygen supply until it ran out.

It was obvious to everyone that maintaining any oxygen within the suits was not going to be possible and slowly but surely they all used up their supply and reserves.

It was again Laurent who completely ran out of oxygen and had no choice but to remove his helmet.

"You're at the equivalent height of Mount Everest, with no ability to come down if you feel ill. You may not like this, Laurent, but I'm going to have to give you a mild sedative to put you to sleep," said Elise.

Elise repeated this with each member of the team. When Levka's time came, she plugged in the oxygen supply from one of the spare suits. When her time came, she did the same.

They were the only two awake when Phobos was illuminated several times, signalling the detonation of the Scorch device.

"It's like being in a large light bulb," said Elise.

A sudden rush of oxygen was generated.

"I think we'll be alright in here for several days, Elise. Let's hope they can get a rescue ship up here fast."

"My second supply is running out."

"So is mine."

They both removed their helmets.

– Chapter Fifteen –

Resolutions

Z-Day plus three days...

It wasn't possible to get a clearer view of the night sky, than the one that presented itself to Razor and his motley crew, on the night of the day that the aliens left Earth.

Alan had raised his spaceship and plotted the course that the aliens had taken, in order to make sure that everyone would be looking in the right direction at around eleven o'clock, the time he expected them to detonate Scorch.

The whole team had made a party of the event and the children were dancing with everyone and were running wild, until around ten o'clock. As usual, Abigail conked out first. She sat on Mum's knee and within a minute was fast asleep. Wendy brought a blanket and pillow and, of course, Emily out for her, and they settled her down between Mum and Dad.

Daniel was still wide awake.

"So, you've been to London, Dad?"

"Yes, to meet the Prime Minister."

"Did you see the fire?"

"What fire?"

"The Great Fire of London."

Mary just smiled.

"He's been learning about how dangerous fire is, and the Great Fire of London was part of the lesson at school, Michael."

"Ha! That explains it. I think they've put the fire out by now, Daniel."

"Oh? That's interesting. Do *you* have a fire plan?"

Razor thought for a moment.

"A fire plan, eh?"

"You have to have a fire plan, no matter where you are. If there's a fire you need to escape from it," said Daniel, earnestly.

"Well, yes, Daniel, I'm sure your right. We've been so busy with other things lately. What are you studying at school this year, Daniel?"

"Egypt," came Daniel's reply, at exactly the same time as Wendy's.

Daniel was obviously bored with the way the conversation was heading and immediately jumped up and went chatting to everyone else.

"Terry?"

"Yes, Daniel."

"Have they really put the fire out in London?"

Alan and Judy were stood, leaning on the wing of the spacecraft, talking to each other.

"So what are your feelings towards the only alien you know personally?"

"I don't think a lady should divulge her feelings just like that. Maybe a gentleman would divulge his first."

Uban became more serious.

"I would like you to join me on my travels."

"Is this a marriage proposal or do you just need another member of your team?"

Uban smiled.

"It is a marriage proposal. Although we would have to have two weddings; one on Earth and one on Calron."

The two moved closer.

"Then my feelings are very, very strong."

"But you would lose everything you have here on Earth; your friends, your belongings, everything."

"If I go with you I will have everything."

They kissed.

Simon and Dave were sat on a grass bank talking to Lenny.

"So what's it like being a roadie, Lenny?" asked Simon.

"If you don't mind late nights, hard work and lots and lots of girls, then it's not too bad."

"What's the pay like?" asked Dave.

"With a top band, and there's no band higher than Near Zero, you get top money. Not only that, you get all expenses paid, so when you're touring you can bank lots of cash for a rainy day."

"Are there any vacancies?"

"For you two – absolutely!"

"Can we say we've joined then, Lenny?" asked Dave.

"Consider yourselves to be on the payroll as from Z-Day."

"What the hell's Z-Day?"

"Zinden Invasion Day!"

Razor was sat with Mary and Wendy, everyone keeping a watchful eye on Daniel.

"So, Wendy? Are you still with us as a family, or has the experience frightened you off?"

"I'll be staying, if you want me, Razor."

"We want you," said Mary. "You can stay as long as you wish!"

"And I'll second that, said Razor."

Razor looked at the time.

"It's coming up to eleven o'clock everyone."

They all looked up at the sky.

"Now you're going to be embarrassed if those aliens don't press their button on time, Alan," said Richard.

Nearly on cue, several extremely bright flashes could be seen in the sky.

"A toast, ladies, gentlemen and aliens. May all aggressors light up the sky in that illuminating fashion!" said Bill.

"I think you've had too much to drink, Bill. Another toast, good riddance!" said Razor.

"Good riddance!" shouted everyone.

Alan and Judy came over to where Razor was.

"I need to go, Razor. If the science team on Phobos have survived they are probably in a bad way, I need to get there as quickly as I can."

"Do I get a ride?"

"Not this time, Razor – I'll need to concentrate on the rescue. I don't want any distractions. See you soon."

Alan returned to his ship, took it to the centre of the Lake and from there he launched himself into space.

* * *

Phobos...

"It's a shame we have to just sit here, Levka. We could have been exploring the large cave system beyond this chamber, if we could have kept the oxygen in the spare suits intact."

"Elise, have you gone crazy? We're lucky to be alive. We have carbon monoxide building up, nowhere to go and your still thinking of the next science project."

Elise shrugged her shoulders.

"How's Laurent?"

"Still the same, I'm not hopeful for his survival."

"I'm not hopeful of any of our survival, if we have to stay in this cave system much longer," said Enrico.

"I agree. We should attempt to get back into the Science Lab," said Erika.

"There's no way of getting to it. All the oxygen in the suits is gone. The lab is too far away," said Scott.

"I think it would be more comfortable in the ship than sitting in this cavern. It may also make rescuing us easier. There was mention of aliens in the communiqué – maybe there are good ones as well as bad ones out there."

"That's a little hopeful, Aadesh."

Suddenly there was a huge inrush of air into the cave system.

"Hello! Anyone home?"

Alan Smith's face appeared around what used to be the rocket bulkhead.

"Yes, down here!" shouted Levka. "How the hell did you get here so quickly?"

"Never mind that, we need to concentrate on getting you out of here. Are you all well?"

"Everyone's fine, except Laurent."

"What's wrong with him?"

"He was the first one out of his spacesuit and at that time the oxygen level and atmospheric pressure was quite poor. His life signs are not good, even now."

'Then we need to deal with him first. Can you haul him up here? We need get him into my stasis chamber."

"Into your what?"

"I'll explain everything later, once we are on our way back to Earth. Can you pull him up to me?"

"Yes, coming," said Levka. "Scott, I'll need your help."

The two scientists hauled Laurent through the science lab and into the alien spacecraft.

"Place him on that recliner, the one with the see-through canopy above."

As Laurent was placed into the stasis chamber, Alan set the controls for 'trauma regeneration' and closed the canopy over him.

"I've checked his life signs. He'll be fine in a few hours but it's good that we got to him when we did.

"You need to get the others to climb aboard, Levka. Make sure they leave their spacesuits in the science lab. It'll be crowded enough without everyone wearing those outfits."

On the way back, Alan explained what had been happening on Earth whilst they were on Phobos.

* * *

Z-Day plus four days...

The following day, Wendy woke early. It was probably around six in the morning. She peeped in at the children who were fast asleep. Creeping downstairs and tip-toeing through the forest of bodies, all of which were sound asleep, and most of which were snoring, she ambled into the kitchen and poured a glass of cold milk. As she ventured outside she felt the morning chill in the air. The sun hadn't quite broken through the mist as yet and as she walked further onto the dew-wet grass, it felt good to be alive.

On occasion, getting up early was magic. It felt good not to have the responsibility for the children, for a short time. It was great to think only of the beautiful countryside that surrounded the cottage, without having to constantly watch for dangers that might present themselves to the children.

She looked over at Wastwater and wandered to the place where she'd sat the previous evening. The sun was making progress now, the mist was clearing and she was beginning to feel the warmth of the sun on her face. The lake glistened in the sunlight, as did the dew on the grass. The silver grey mist was beginning to rise and dissipate. She sat watching a spider spin its web between the stem and leaf of a thistle. A blackbird alighted on the grass in front of her, tipping its head, listening for the slightest noise from under the grassy carpet.

If there was a heaven, then this was very much like it, she thought.

There was stirring in the cottage, she heard the kettle starting to boil and the low hum of a conversation. She thought it best to get back and get the children ready for the day ahead.

As she rose she could hear helicopter rotor blades getting louder and louder. She looked over the lake to see three helicopters approaching from the eastern head of the lake.

The only flat landing spot was in front of the cottage and by the time Wendy had reached the cottage, the helicopters had landed. On the side of one of the 'copters was the Sky News logo. The other two 'copters were plainly military. All three were disgorging their occupants at the same time and at the same rate—quickly.

Initially, the cameraman and the soundman were focussed on the news presenter, and Wendy was completely ignored, much to her relief. She instinctively avoided the press. It was just part of her job to keep a low profile. Whilst the news team were 'doing their thing', Wendy rushed past Razor, who was emerging from the cottage, and went inside to be with the children.

Razor immediately recognised Major General Sir John Dowding and was more than a little uncomfortable to be caught with a bacon sandwich in one hand and a cup of tea in the other. He managed to move his bacon sandwich to the hand that was holding the cup and after wiping his free hand on his pants, held it out to shake Sir John's hand.

"Sir John, What brings you here so early this morning – especially with a news crew?"

"Sky News has been told the whole story. We thought it would be good for posterity to film you lot 'in situ' so to speak, before telling the whole world what only a very few currently know."

He reached into his inside jacket pocket.

"I have a letter here that may explain a little more why we're all here."

He handed the letter over.

"It's from the Queen. I wanted to deliver it myself and thank your team, personally, for saving the planet."

Razor took the envelope, but didn't open it.

"OK, I'll promise 'access to all areas' so long as we suspend filming till we've all had breakfast."

"Yes, no problem."

"Then get the crews around the garden tables and we'll rustle up some food."

Sir John nodded at one of his lieutenants who immediately went off to inform the press.

Like the night before, everyone gathered outside the cottage for breakfast, rustled up by Mary and Judy.

Wendy and the children were sat next to Sir John.

"That was a good job, putting the fire out in London," said Daniel to Sir John.

"You mean Manchester?"

"Oh! Was there a fire there too?"

As everyone finished their breakfast, Razor stood up to address them.

"I have in my hand a letter from the Queen, no less. I would like to read it to you all."

He opened the letter and let the envelope fall to the table.

"It says, and I quote:

'Never has there been a more appropriate time to re-use the famous words of Sir Winston Churchill, never have so many, owed so much, to so few.

"'It is with enormous pride that the Queen and the Prime Minister invite you all to Buckingham Palace for a special awards ceremony and a celebration dinner.'"

They all cheered.

"There's no date. Sir John?"

Sir John Dowding stood and spoke.

"The whole world is waking up to the truth of what really happened yesterday. Within hours the enormity of what you did will sink in and thus the sooner you come down to London the better, tomorrow would be a good day. The Queen and the PM will drop their current itinerary to suit whatever suits you. You should know this is very unusual, I've never seen the likes of this before."

"Tomorrow it is then," said Razor

They all cheered, "Tomorrow!"

As the hubbub calmed down, the Sky reporter, Thomas Quick, stood to speak.

"Could we all assemble, over near the lake, for a group shot?"

The photograph was quickly taken, after which the news team started broadcasting.

"This is Thomas Quick reporting from Near Zero's hideout in the Lake District. We have an exclusive interview with the group that 'saved the planet' – and that's no exaggeration folks. Razor, tell me what happened?"

Razor carefully went through the story of what happened over the last four days. When he got to the part that included yet another alien from a different world, Thomas Quick was incredulous.

"We have yet *another* alien life-form on Earth?'

"Yes, but this one is much more friendly than the ones you are used to seeing."

"So can we speak with him, Razor?"

"I'm afraid he had to leave. You see, the intense radiation generated by the explosions that you saw in the sky last night, compromised the safety of the science team on Phobos. He's got the only craft that can get to them quickly. So, at the moment, he's attempting to rescue the science team on Phobos – assuming they're still alive."

Razor looked at his watch.

"He's probably just leaving the vicinity of Mars right now."

As the day progressed, more and more of the story of what actually happened came out on air. The whole world gasped collectively at how close Earth's population came to being annihilated. By late afternoon the world had new heroes and one of them was an alien.

As evening started to fall, Alan Smith's ship appeared in the darkening sky. It hovered for a short time over the lake and set down once more in front of the cottage.

In front of the whole world, the Phobos science team disembarked from this alien ship and welcoming them home was Sir John Dowding and the Near Zero team.

Alan was the last person to disembark. Judy rushed up to him and they embraced.

Thomas Quick went up to the pair.

"I hear that we have you to thank for rescuing our planet?"

"Not at all, it would not have been possible without Razor's team and Bill. Bill's local knowledge, especially where the ship canal was concerned, was absolutely invaluable."

"The whole world is curious to know more about the alien that saved the planet. Could you tell us more?"

"I don't think this is the time to be discussing me. It's a time for celebration of life."

"Have you heard that the whole group is to have tea with the Queen and Prime Minister tomorrow?"

"No, I hadn't, but I am pleased to see you are thanking the people who deserve your thanks. Now I must go."

Thomas was taken aback by the reluctance of the alien to talk to him.

Regardless, interviews with the other team members continued until around midnight.

"Well, it's been an amazing day up here in the Lakes. All is now quiet and the Near Zero team are having a well-deserved rest. We'll sign off now and be in touch early tomorrow morning."

It was six in the morning when the news crew began to wake. The news team and the army had brought their own tents and both were a hive of activity. At ten to seven, two of the helicopters struck up their rotors and left the cottage grounds, waking everyone as they departed.

Just as they were disappearing over the eastern shore of Wastwater, a Chinook appeared and carefully landed in the space the other two had vacated.

"It looks like our transport has arrived," said Wendy, bobbing her head into the room where Mary and Judy were still half asleep.

"Are the children up yet?" asked Mary.

"They've been up for ages, watching all the activity at the front of the cottage. I'm taking them down for breakfast."

With that, Judy and Mary reluctantly raised themselves and dressed for the day ahead.

"I suppose we should be dressing so that we're fit to see the Queen," Mary said as she slipped on her jeans.

"Not much chance of that," Judy replied as she slipped on her least dirty trouser suit.

Nearly everyone was eating outside the cottage again.

Judy found Alan away from the others, sat on the grass bank looking out across Wastwater.

"You, OK?"

"Yes, fine, Judy. I've decided not to come down to the Palace with the rest of you."

"The reason being?"

"There'll be too many questions that I can't answer. If it hadn't been for the Zinden invasion no one would know I was here. I realise I've blown my cover but to the peoples of Earth I need to remain an enigma. I don't wish to put meat on the bone. It's best to leave as soon as possible."

"Not without me, you don't!"

"Do you really still want to come with me?"

"Yes, oh yes!" she held him close.

"Then I have a suggestion—"

* * *

"Where's Alan?" asked Mary.

"He can't come with us," said Judy, almost tearfully.

"Why?" asked Razor.

"It's a long story. I don't want to talk about it now," said Judy.

As the Chinook took to the sky, with everyone aboard except Alan, a lonely figure watched the departure from the kitchen window.

Shortly after, the spacecraft took off, leaving the cottage completely deserted. There was very little sign of what had gone before.

The reception the group got in London was absolutely incredible. From the moment they arrived they were treated like royalty. The streets were lined with people all the way from the airport to the Palace.

Private rooms were booked at the Savoy so everyone could prepare for the night's presentation and the celebration dinner.

"Ma'am? We have the finest couturiers waiting to ensure you are dressed appropriately for tonight's occasion."

"Thank you! Someone must have realised that all we had to put on were jeans," said Mary.

As they were led to their rooms, Bill was heard to say, "Nay, lad, I can't afford to stay here!"

"It's all paid for, Sir. This includes your attire for tonight's dinner and anything you would like from room service."

"A cup o' tea, lad. That'd be nice!"
"I'll see to it straight away, Sir."

If it was at all possible, the crowds seemed even larger as the group were escorted to the Palace.

Everyone in the group received a bravery award, even Alan and the children.

At the dinner it was announced that the United Nations wished for them to attend a special meeting the following day – all agreed.

A specialist team from the foreign office was put in charge of their itinerary for the next few days, ensuring, as Razor insisted, that they be deposited back to the cottage in the Lakes, once 'the show was over'.

When the group flew into New York it was a full ticker-tape procession to the United Nations building.

After which they were given the freedom of New York.

Even though everyone in the group enjoyed the celebrity occasions, equally they were all elated once the little tour was over. Adulation is all very well in small doses, but as Razor put it, "You can't live off it."

So as the few days of hero-worship came to an end, everyone in the group was pleased to be deposited back to the cottage in the Lakes, all in their finery, and itching to get back to their normal lives.

As the Chinook took off, leaving the group back at the cottage, Mary said, "Did *anybody* think to pack our jeans?"

There was no answer, obviously no one did.

"I can't convince myself that this dress will look right on the back of a motorbike."

"Nor even in the Mini," said Wendy.

Before they had time to enter the cottage, the noise and smell of an old motorbike came wafting down the road, backfiring on occasion before it stopped in front of the well-dressed party.

The driver lifted the front of his goggles away from his eyes and stretched the elastic so that the lenses of the goggles rested over his crash helmet.

"I see I've just got here in time," he said. "I'm sorry I'm late."

"Late for what?"

"The marriage ceremony."

"What marriage ceremony?"

"I think you have the wrong address old chap," said Razor.

"No, this is the right address; I double checked it before I left."

"But if anyone here was getting married I would almost certainly know the guests and I don't recognise you, my man," said Mary.

"That's because I'm not a guest. I'm the preacher," and he removed his scarf to reveal his dog collar.

At precisely that moment, Alan walked out of the cottage and over to Judy.

"Will you marry me?" he said, looking lovingly into Judy's eyes.

"Yes, gladly," said Judy.

Everyone cheered!

– Chapter Sixteen –

Time Passages

Z-Day plus ten days...

As marriages go, this had to be one of the most unusual that Father O'Malley had attended. Everyone dressed up to the nines, with some of the richest people on Earth in attendance, yet no lavish banquet – in fact, hardly any food at all – and not a trace of alcohol anywhere to be found.

"Now that's what I call a real marriage ceremony," he remarked.

No one explained to him that he was marrying a human and an alien – maybe if they had he would have had reservations, but no one in the group thought anything about it. That's how integrated Uban Drix had become with his human friends.

Wendy and Mary were co-opted into being bridesmaids, and after a search by some of the menfolk in the party, a bunch of wild flowers was hastily put together for a very special flower girl – Abigail.

And would you believe there was suddenly a need for a pageboy, so Daniel wouldn't feel left out.

When it came to the ring, Alan had found a platinum, ring washer, which was probably worth a fortune here on Earth, but was a throw away item on Calron. It was noticeably too big for Judy's finger.

"We'll replace it with a better one before we leave Earth," said Alan, quietly to Judy.

"No you won't, we'll just get it fitted properly when we have time,"

Uban smiled. "Now I *know* I've chosen the right girl."

When it came to the vows, Judy insisted on Alan using his 'proper' name, Uban. She also requested, from that moment on, everyone in their group use it.

The toast was orange juice – on the rocks mind.

The best man, Razor.

The music was provided by the band, singing *Here Comes the Bride* – a cappella style.

After the ceremony, everyone crowded around the two to congratulate them and wish them well.

It was nearly sunset when the priest fired up his motorbike to leave the party, and it was nearly midnight when everyone retired to their beds.

Wendy and Mary slept in the same room as the children, leaving what was their bedroom for the married couple. Mary mused that she'd just been at the wedding of the century and no press were involved nor invited. That felt good.

The next day was the 'back to reality' day, when everyone started to plan his or her next move in life.

Judy had, what she considered to be, some good news for Cheryl. She told her she planned on being away for a *long* time and that she was the only person that could be trusted to run her business. She offered her 49% of the shares she owned and double her current salary, if she'd be in charge whilst she was gone.

Who could refuse such an offer? The deal was done.

Her first task was to organise transport for the group away from the cottage – that day if possible. Razor wanted to get back to 'normal' as soon as he could, which meant organising rehearsals and new tour dates.

Her second task was to ensure that no one lost out because of the cancellation of Near Zero's current tour.

Razor and Richard had grabbed one of Alan's downstairs rooms and were using it as an office. Richard was on the phone to Bill Evans of ElectricAudio.

"Bill, we need to audition some lead guitarists. Can you get the word out?"

"I know a couple of excellent players. One of them may want to join. I'll get in touch with them."

"OK. If anyone is interested give them a complete copy of our material. Then book him or her on a flight to the island. We're going to rehearse there before starting up the tour again."

There was a knock on the office door and Lenny walked in.

"You want to see me, Razor?"

"Yes, Lenny. First I want you to get as much detail off Judy, before she flies off with Alan, about the agreements we have with Bell Labs. Second, order up another complete set of holographic equipment from them and get it shipped to the island. Get Dave, Simon and Gary and take them to the island for some R & R and teach them as much as you can about the gear. If they have girlfriends or family, let them come also – just for two weeks mind, then it's back down to business. From now on, every gig we do, they get four free tickets each, for family and friends. That obviously includes you, Lenny. Oh, and by the way, tell them thanks for all they've done for the children."

"Thanks, boss"

"The thanks are all mine, Lenny. Well done."

"You wanted to see me, Uban?" said Bill.

Uban was down at his spaceship just checking in with Galactic Brigade HQ.

"Bill, Judy and I were thinking you helped so much in what we did that we'd like to give you something in return."

"I don't need anything, lad, I'm fine."

"I know you don't *need* anything, Bill, but you're getting our present anyway.

"Now this cottage here is sort of redundant now. We're going to stay here for around six months but after that we won't be back for maybe 50 years. I think that may cover the years you may have a use for it. So, we have a penny a year lease on the property for you and your family, starting when we leave. Use it how you will, for friends if you wish, that's entirely up to you.

"You must pay the penny each year to our solicitors though. The year you do not pay the penny, in person, we will know that you no longer require it."

Bill choked up.

"That's a wonderful gift, Alan."

"I'm afraid there's more, Bill. Razor tells me he is buying you a brand new car and a brand new canal boat with the moorings paid every year, for the next 50 years. You can't refuse them, Bill, because he's already placed the orders."

Bill burst into tears. "That's wonderful, Alan. How can I ever repay you both?"

"You already have, Bill!"

It was the following afternoon, just after lunch, when the fleet of helicopters arrived at the cottage.

Bill had left in his Mini the day before.

For all the difficulties they faced during the Zinden invasion, Uban and Judy had enjoyed the company of all their friends at the cottage.

It was a sad day indeed as they all gathered their belongings and climbed aboard their transports.

Razor, Mary, Wendy and the children were the last to depart.

Uban and Judy knew full well that they would miss the family the most.

Judy had asked Uban whether it would be possible to give Michael and Mary one of the wormhole communicators so that they could keep in touch now and again. His answer was an emphatic, no. The technology couldn't be passed on to Earth until it had become a full member of the Galactic Council.

There was some good news, however. Judy could keep in touch with Mary in a similar fashion to how he kept in touch with his solicitor and letting agent. Although that particular communications route could only ever be one-way.

The restriction wasn't technological. It was a restriction imposed by the Galactic Council, and it was protocol that could not be circumvented.

As the helicopters took off, Judy wept.

* * *

Z-Day plus 18 years...

"It's a good place to have a wedding," said Mary.

"Why's that?" asked Razor.

"Well, look, there's no press intrusion, there's only people here we want to have here."

"I'm not so sure about his cousin, Sam."

"You know what I mean.

Do you know, Michael, this reminds me of Uban and Judy's wedding."

"Well, I must admit, just like on their day, the preacher arrived slightly late for the ceremony."

"No, it isn't just that. I don't know. I think it's the atmosphere. It's so calm, just like the day they got married."

"Maybe that's actually because we've stopped the press from attending?"

Mary changed the subject.

"Doesn't Abigail look lovely in her white wedding dress?"

"Yes, maybe that's it. The wedding dresses are very similar."

"No, they're not, Michael," and she dug her elbow in his ribs.

"I never thought our little girl would grow up so fast."

"I never thought that we'd get so old, so fast."

"You're not old, you're just senile," Michael said in jest.

Mary laughed.

"You do realise, we're not only gaining a son-in-law but we are losing our baby?"

"Yes, I know, over time we seem to have lost an awful lot of people," and tears welled up in Mary's eyes.

* * *

Z-Day plus 20 years…

Abigail and Alex's baby girl, Brianna, was being bottle-fed by Nana. This was not unusual. Ever since the baby was born, Mary, when she had the chance, would take over feeding the baby.

Abigail put this down to the fact that, when *she* was the baby, her mother was so busy with the group that, most of the time, it was Wendy who held *her* bottle.

For Brianna's christening, Abigail was insistent that she did it all. Everything from preparing the food, to sprucing the house up, to organising the guest lists.

She was proud of the fact that it was all her, but it made her much more nervous about the outcome.

The result was that she was constantly asking for reassurance from her mum.

"Are the flowers OK, Mum?"

"Fine, stop worrying!"

"I've got us walking to the church. Do you think we should have hired cars?"

"What, for that small distance? No, I don't."

Abigail noticed the tablecloth was a little skewed to the table.

"Mother, put the baby down and come and give me a hand with this tablecloth."

"Stop fussing, the tablecloth is just fine."

The doorbell rang.

"Do you want me to answer that, dear?" said Mary.

"No, I'll get it."

She opened the door.

"Wendy, James, come in. It's lovely to see you – you're the first to arrive."

"I wanted to be the first to hold the baby!" said Wendy.

"Too late!" came the voice from the other room.

Mary came waltzing in with baby in her arms and gave Wendy a peck on the cheek.

"Are we fighting, or are you surrendering that baby to me?"

Mary handed the baby over.

"Hello, James," she gave James a peck on the cheek also.

The doorbell rang again.

The guests assembled in Abigail and Alex's entrance hall. The church was only a five-minute walk down the road, so 15 minutes before the service, they processed to the church.

Brianna had two godmothers, Alex's sister, Sarah and one of Abigail's close friends. Daniel was her godfather.

After the service, the guests walked back to the house for the feast Abigail had prepared.

"I thought Lenny was coming to the christening, Ab?" asked Dad.

"He's not well. *He* tells me he's suffering from taking too many drugs when he was young, but maybe it's just old age, eh, Dad!"

"Well, besides the drugs, he has done a lot of hard work during his time!"

Razor looked over at Mary and raised his glass.

"To absent friends, Mary."

"To absent friends, Michael."

* * *

Z-Day plus 53 years...

There is something about black that shows off the beauty in a woman. Certainly Abigail was a very beautiful woman and wearing black definitely suited her.

She was really hurting now. Her parents had been so good to her and she missed them like hell.

On one arm was her brother, Daniel; on her other arm was her daughter, Brianna. Both were holding her tight and keeping her upright.

It was only a few weeks ago that she was talking to them, about how 70-year-olds are the new 40-year-olds. They were both laughing at Abigail telling them how young they acted and how young they looked. In fact, she'd laughed at the fact they still liked going out on the motorbike.

She wasn't laughing now. The police said that they would have been fine if the same crash had happened whilst they were driving a car, but they had no chance on a bike.

The officer said they died instantly; there would have been no pain.

There was pain for her, however, and it was hurting deep inside.

Sky News was covering the funeral.

The event was being broadcast simultaneously, on all channels all over the world and on every Earth colony in existence. Earth's Council had declared a world day of mourning and there were very few who were not watching.

It was Alistair McBride with his low-key, calm voice that was speaking. The pictures were coming from a helicopter flying over the procession:

"Today the whole world is in mourning for two of its most loved citizens. It should have been impossible for one man to fit all that Razor did, into one lifetime, but somehow he did it.

"As the cortège passes through the centre of London, let us reflect on his life.

"The son of one of the wealthiest landowners in Wales, he grew up in idyllic surroundings in, what can only be called, a privileged household. He could easily have sat back and enjoyed the role of gentleman farmer and led the good life. But no, that wasn't for Michael Jones.

"A fierce competitor at school and later, an Oxford Blue, he had always been an active child.

"His degree was in Sports Science. He was fluent in several languages, including German, French, Spanish, Italian and Russian.

"Like so many young men, when the terror campaigns of the 21st century turned into all-out war, he joined up. Because of his language skills he was recruited by Special Forces and ended up working with the Russians.

"He was awarded the military cross together with his lifetime friend and soulmate Richard O'Shea, both of them

showed extreme bravery under fire. Russia bestowed the Order of St George (1st Class) on the two.

"After the terror wars and like thousands of other soldiers, they were both demobbed at the same time. For some reason, even they couldn't explain why, they stayed together. Razor had always played the piano but with Richard's help he started playing the guitar in his post-war years. He always said that he didn't start writing 'proper' music until Richard O'Shea (FourLeaf) started writing with him.

"He met Mary when his group, Near Zero, was auditioning for a keyboard player.

"Whilst gigging in Manchester, he was caught up in the Zinden Day Massacre. He managed to escape, with Mary and the children, and was the leader of the group that literally saved the human race from extinction.

"For a long time after Z-Day he continued to write songs and further his music career, but a few years ago he decided to pack it all in.

Since that day little has been heard of him or Mary. We were informed that they were enjoying their retirement somewhere in Brazil.

When word of their fatal accident came through, we all found out that, unbeknown to us, they had been staying in a castle in the Scottish Highlands for the last eight months."

By now the pictures from the news helicopter were showing that the cortège was closing in on the airport.

"The cortège is now arriving at Heathrow where, as you see, a private plane is waiting for them. The pipes of the Queen's Own Highlanders, who make up the guard of honour, can be heard as the cars approach the plane.

"Don't they look resplendent in their kilts?

"We're told that both Michael and Mary made it clear that they wished to be buried on their tropical island paradise where they spent so much time when their children were growing up.

"The family have indicated that the burial itself should be a private matter and so once the aeroplane is in the sky we will be respecting their wish."

Both coffins were drawn from the car by pallbearers and lifted aloft. Slowly they were carried to the aeroplane.

"The Queen and the Prime Minister offered the use of a Hercules to transport the coffins but it was refused by the family, simply because the runway on the island was too short to take that size of plane.

"The mourners are now boarding the plane. One can see their daughter Abigail and her husband Alex. Behind her are their son Daniel and his wife.

"You may know Daniel as the Chief Executive of Zero Industries. He took over the family business when Razor retired a few years ago and he's really taken the business to new heights.

"Behind them is a who's who of their rock star and film star friends."

Once all the mourners had boarded the aeroplane, Alistair McBride on the Sky News helicopter just watched in silence, as the aircraft took off and disappeared into the blue.

Later that day on a remote island in the South Pacific, an aeroplane touched down with two coffins. Returning, probably two of the most famous people in the Sol system, home to rest.

"They've left a parcel, you know," said Abigail.

"Yes, I know, Abigail. Do you think Uban and Judy will ever return to open it?"

"*They* thought so and that's all that matters."

Abigail broke down again as the coffins were lowered into the island soil.

"I loved them *so much.*"

"I think the whole world did!" said Daniel.

– Chapter Seventeen –

The First Ark

Z-Day plus 15 years...

The experiments on Gorizon Prime had brought on a new impetus to the Zinden 'Sol Project'. Even though his ancestors were well aware of the difficulties, it had only just become apparent to Sagar (Pasreen the sixth) how difficult an undertaking it was to ship 40 million-plus inhabitants from Zindor to Earth.

The first ark, which was still just a shell with propulsion units attached, had not yet been spun up so there was no artificial gravity on board as yet.

The ark is basically a four-mile diameter toroid attached to a central hub by eight spokes. The central hub houses the nuclear power unit and the main propulsion units. The spokes that attach the central hub to the toroid, hold the docking stations and the embarkation ships, of which there were very few at present.

On each quadrant of the toroid lay a set of spin-up jets. These could be rotated both to aid propulsion and improve the manoeuvrability of the ship. When used in conjunction with the main propulsion units, they helped to relieve stress on the spokes, during periods of maximum thrust. Their natural alignment was, however, tangential to the toroid.

With such a large structure it isn't just that the quantities of materials are huge, it's also the fact that the time to build each one is significant. Being that this is the first one, even the Zinden don't really know how long it may take. The lowest estimate is 350 years but their worst-case scenario is a staggering 570 years.

It doesn't take a genius to realise that the 9,000-year Sol Project timeframe, will only allow for a finite number of ships.

"Are you suggesting that we leave some of the population behind, Ediene?"

"Of course not, but we can't possibly go with Cazein's suggestion, that we should build 80 arks. That's just plain ridiculous. For the love of Nigor, the planet hardly has the resources to build ten ships, never mind 80."

"So, what are you suggesting?"

"It's obvious. If we can't build a fleet of ships for a single trip, we will just have to make many trips. I estimate that each ark will have to do at least eight trips, possibly nine."

"Is that feasible?"

"In theory, yes, but we don't actually know. The sheer size of the structures may present us with a problem or two and it may be that some hidden design flaw, some unexpected stress, will lead to a catastrophe. It's a risk everyone is going to have to sign up to."

"You understand that the loss of just one ship would mean the loss of half a million Zinden? That's an awful lot of the populous. Is there nothing that could be done if an emergency of that magnitude arose?"

"It's the sheer scale of the problem, Sire!" Ediene's tone darkened. "There are too many bodies, Your Highness. Even if we could rescue them, there's nowhere out there to put them."

"OK, back to the issue here. Let's take the worst case scenario; so we're talking about a ship that can travel around 35% the speed of light, having to traverse over a distance of three point eight light years. So each trip will take 11 years?"

"Yes, then there's the journey back with the empty ship, giving a round trip of 22 years. In all, eight journeys will take 176 years. Let's say we err on the cautious side and make that 200 years."

They both looked at each other, pondering whether the total transfer time was reasonable or not.

"It doesn't sound unreasonable," said Sagar.

"No, I agree," added Ediene. "But it may be that building ten ships is still too high a target number. It may mean that there has to be ten trips for some of the arks."

"I think we can live with that, but no more!"

"Well, I must admit I think eight arks, maybe as many as is achievable."

"Then that's what we will settle on, Ediene."

"OK!"

"I do have one worry, Ediene. How will you ensure that the last to arrive do not get the worst deal, as regards land, etc?"

"Yes, we've given it some thought, Your Highness. There are two points to remember here. First, there is plenty of land – we have a population measured in millions. Earth's indigenous species is numbered in the billions. Secondly, we will form a land registry so that we can ensure that the land is split up in a fair manner."

"By fair, you mean that it will be split in favour of the ruling elite, Ediene?"

"Of course, Your Highness."

The King smiled.

"Good. So how's the work on the first ark coming?"

"Well, that's why I'm here. I estimate we will fix the last base plate in place within the next few weeks. Once the structure has been pressure checked and then spun up, we will need to have the handing over ceremony."

"Handing over?"

"Yes, Your Highness. The hull construction director will officially hand over the ark to the internal construction director and the hull construction team will leave to start the second ark. We are hoping that you will attend the ceremony."

"My calendar's full this month, Ediene. I won't be available until the 14th of next month."

"That sounds about right, then let's make that a date. An extra few weeks on top of 278 years is hardly worth worrying about, is it!"

"For the love of Nigor! Has it been that long?"

"Yes! The first rail structure was shipped aloft in the time of Aldeen the Second. He knew when the project started that even his grandchildren's children, would never see the day the structure was finished."

"So what's the next step?"

"Sandor's battle ship is towing the first captured comet fragment, into synchronous orbit with the ark, as we speak. The number two nuclear plant was switched on last month, to heat the central water basin. It's just a matter of getting the water in there now."

"I heard a rumour that the water ice was quite dirty."

"It is, but it's nothing the filters can't handle and the dirt will help bulk up the soil required for the agricultural bays."

"OK, Ediene! I will have Anheime arrange my visit for the 14th of next month. You may leave."

"Your Highness."

Ediene bowed and left the room, relieved and eager to get back to work. He didn't much like having to report to the King every month. He felt it was far too big a project, to have to report so regularly. Once a year would have been much more sensible in his eyes, or maybe even less. Simply as problems arose, would be a much better option.

After the meeting with the King, it was customary to follow up with a general meeting with the project management team involved with the Sol Project. The meeting was at the Core of Engineers Building. Ediene thought that this stemmed from the time of Margnon the Third, who reputedly beheaded a number of engineers because of their slow progress during his reign. He imagined, in those days, there was a high degree of interest following any meeting between the chief engineer and the King.

The core building wasn't far from the Palace. Ediene was looking forward to seeing his 126-strong management team again. He'd only just come back from a short holiday and even though he knew, within a very short space of time, that he would be snowed under with work-related matters, he was still looking forward to getting back on the job.

A round of applause greeted him as he walked through the door and stood in front of his team.

"Well, comrades, as you are all aware, the sealing of the ark will occur in two weeks' time. We will then spin the ship up and initiate oxygen enrichment. By the 14th of next month I will be standing beside you all, in the belly of that ark, without the need for a spacesuit or magnetic boots and standing with all of us will be the King of Zindor."

A large cheer rang out from the gathered team.

"As for today, unless there are outstanding emergency issues, I only wish to see the teams involved in final closure, spin-up, oxygen enrichment—Oh, and water management. I'll see the other teams after the 14th. Well done, everyone. You may now go."

Most of the management team rose and filed out of the room. Ediene recognised at least one team member that should not have remained seated.

"Is there a problem, Sorel?"

"Yes, but I need to speak with you privately!"

"OK! The rest of you chat amongst yourselves for a few minutes – see if you can prioritise the session for me."

Ediene could tell from Sorel's demeanour that there could be a significant problem. Sorel was head of security for the team and not prone to chasing ghosts.

"What's the problem, Sorel?"

"A few years ago, not many years after the events on Gorizon Prime, our chief of security, a man called Slevin Binx, found an alien intruder on the hot side of the Deepfall."

"Yes, I've heard of the incident, Sorel. Why do you bring it up now?"

"Well, to cut a long story short, when he retired he asked that the hot side of the Deepfall should be scanned on a regular basis. He thought that just once a month would do the trick, just in case the aliens returned. So we agreed to do that.

"He also said that if we register a contact, that we mustn't try to contact them in any way. This was because the last attempt to do so ended up with them committing suicide. Slevin Binx thought that it was because they didn't want their technology ending up in our hands."

"That is a reasonable assumption, but you haven't, have you?" Ediene said with some glee.

"Yes. There is a contact currently there. We discovered it yesterday. We have done nothing to raise their suspicions. So far, there has been no attempt to leave or enter their ship. Have you any suggestions or thoughts as to what we should do next? Should we have acted differently?"

"No! I guess they're already out of the ship. You're doing exactly what you should be doing, waiting for them to return."

Ediene paced up and down and muttered to himself.

"Of course!" he exclaimed. "Do you know what disguise the aliens assumed, last time they were here?"

"They pretended to be archivists."

"Then check whether we have any new archivists at the central museum. If so, find out their names and where they live. Then get back to me as quickly as you can."

Ediene returned to his meeting, ignoring completely the list that the assembled project teams had drawn up.

"Answer me a number of questions. Is closure and pressurisation running to schedule?"

"Yes, everything is going to plan, Ediene."

"Will the comet fragment arrive before the 14th, Eraxen?"

"No, it will be clearly visible by the naked eye but it won't be here. It's still moving far too fast for docking. The actual estimated time of arrival is around three months."

"Are the nuclear plants fully operational, Cantor? And if so, will the place be sufficiently oxygenated and warm, on the King's arrival?"

"Yes. It'll be like being close to the Deepfall, Ediene."

"OK, comrades – I'm sorry I can't spend more time with you today but I have other meetings to attend. You know how to get in touch with me, if there is a problem. Thank you for your time. You may leave."

As the project management group filed out of the room, Sorel came in, pushing past the stragglers.

"There's two of them, husband and wife."

"How predictable is that? Where do they say they live?"

"In an apartment close to this building, near the Deepfall. They *do* live there, we've checked."

"It's too obvious. It *has* to be them. Arrange for them to be followed when they leave the museum. So long as they're heading home, then we leave them alone. If they start to head for their ship, we arrest them. You and I, Sorel, will be sat outside their house when they arrive home tonight. I want to look at these intruders."

* * *

"There has to be evidence here somewhere, of what they plan to do next. That enormous spaceship up there isn't being built for fun. The Zinden are planning something big, very big."

"We've been searching for nearly four days now, Mistree. There's no obvious evidence in here and we know for sure that they've not attempted to use Scorch again."

"Yes, but we *have* found that there is still one device missing. They built another two devices after the genocide event on Gorizon Prime. As we know, even though they don't as yet, one exploded near Earth, Paakel. That's no coincidence. They're going to use the other. I can feel it in my bones."

"Maybe the details of the event they're planning aren't contained within the central archives."

"That's not their way, Mistree."

"That *wasn't* their way prior to Shezar and Rial's visit. But maybe they learnt from that and decided to keep their most sensitive secrets top secret and away from the archive."

"So, are we wasting our time here?"

"I think we are," said Mistree.

They both looked at each other and at that moment the decision to get away from the planet, and rethink their strategy, was made. It was still important that they kept up their disguise – so leaving early was not on the cards. Archivists have far too much work to do, to leave early in the day, so any attempt to do so would generate suspicion.

It was suppertime before Mistree called on Paakel to leave the museum. As they walked the short distance to their apartment, their senses were tingling.

"Something doesn't feel right, Paakel."

"I agree, Mistree."

"Can you see anyone watching us?"

"There's a man across the road near the street lamp and someone in the car we've just passed."

"When we turn the corner, change."

As they moved out of sight of the stranger in the car and the man across the street, they shape shifted.

As the two detectives turned around the corner they were shocked to find their subjects had disappeared. After much searching in doorways and alleyways the man in the car radioed in to HQ. He didn't notice the two small, dog-like creatures, which crossed the road only a few yards behind him.

"We've lost them, Sorel!"

"How?"

"They were heading towards their apartment; they turned the corner and just disappeared."

"That may mean they're heading for their ship. Meet us near the ship's co-ordinates, close to the Deepfall."

Sorel immediately contacted Zinden Air Command.

"We need the Deepfall extractor at these co-ordinates."

Sorel sent the precise co-ordinates of the alien craft. Ediene was well aware of what Sorel was doing and was already driving like hell, to the alien ship. Sorel and Ediene arrived just in time to see the huge Deepfall extractor bring the alien craft out from behind the Deepfall. As the extractor came nearer, with the alien craft in its jaws, Mistree and Paakel appeared, walking in the middle of the road, straight towards where Sorel and Ediene stood. All of the firearms held by the assembled security personnel, turned and aimed at the two aliens.

"If you attempt to enter that craft, it will self-destruct," Mistree said calmly.

"What is you purpose here?" asked Ediene.

"To find out what you are about to do with the two remaining Scorch weapons you possess."

Ediene wasn't surprised that they knew about Scorch, but he was surprised that they knew how many were remaining. He was delighted that they had not uncovered the invasion plans.

"Of what concern is it of yours?"

"It is of concern, to all free worlds."

"We intend to destroy the devices."

Mistree and Paakel knew this was not the case.

"Do you mind if we witness their destruction?" said Paakel.

Paakel knew that at this stage, the Zinden did not yet know what had happened to their first invasion force. They'd been sent out on a 30-year mission and had simply vanished.

One day the Zinden would discover what happened and then, everyone was sure, they would send their remaining device to Earth.

"Not at all. It's just that you may not be around to see the event."

"You must understand that our survival is totally irrelevant. You have produced a weapon of mass destruction that endangers all the worlds about you. Surely even creatures as arrogant as you, can understand that this cannot be tolerated. If you continue on your path, then worlds more powerful than yours will eventually have to stop you."

Ediene ignored the implied threat. Paakel continued.

"I have a simple question for you, Sir. Why did you destroy, rather than settle on Gorizon Prime?"

"There was nothing useful on the planet and to be frank it was a perfect test site."

"It is estimated that there were over three trillion individual life forms on the worlds you destroyed."

"There was no dominant, intelligent species."

"A lack of intelligence in a species does not mean it forfeits the right to live."

Ediene shrugged the reply off with a hand gesture.

"It was a perfect test sight!"

He started to walk away and added, "Arrest these aliens," to the assembled security forces.

Mistree and Paakel had agreed, long ago, the signal they would give each other if the time came to self-destruct. The mechanism was easy but both had to do the gesture simultaneously. Paakel was holding his belt buckle. Mistree touched hers.

The explosion killed everyone in their vicinity. Simultaneous explosions occurred on the shuttle and the main spaceship. If Ediene hadn't been walking away, he too would have died. As it was he just had a feeling he was dead.

When Ediene eventually opened his eyes he was being rushed to the central medical facility.

"What happened?" he gasped.

"You were too close to the suicide bombers when the explosion happened. You are not seriously injured, just concussed."

"Where are you taking me?"

"The central medical facility."

"No, I'm fine. Take me to the Palace. I need to speak to Sorel. Where is he?"

The medics looked at each other.

"He's dead, Sir. He did not survive the blast."

Ediene sat bolt upright, he remembered now, "Damn!"

"Pasreen the sixth is asleep, Sir. Waking him may give *you* cause for concern."

"You mean he may have my head chopped off?"

"It has been known."

"I'm sure it has. Wake him, I insist!"

Very well, Sir." Anheime led Ediene to the library.

"Please wait in here, Sir. Make yourself comfortable."

Ediene wasn't at all sure he was doing the right thing, and without doubt it was still possible to lose one's head by royal decree, even in these modern times. He waited nervously for what seemed like hours.

The King came in, in his dressing gown, with Anheime following.

“This had better be worth it, Ediene.”

“Sire, I have just encountered two alien beings. They have just killed a large number of our security personnel and the head of security for the Sol Project.”

The King noticed the shakiness in his voice and the weakness in his legs.

“By Hal, Ediene. Sit down. I’ll have Anheime get you a drink – he nodded towards Anheime. Tell me what happened.”

“You know we’ve had visitors like this before?”

“Yes, before Baltire’s force left for Sol Three.”

“These behaved identically with the previous pair. They must have been from the same alien race.”

“What did they want?”

“They were trying to discover where the two remaining Scorch devices where.”

“We only have one, Baltire’s group took the other!”

“They obviously knew nothing about Baltire. They thought there were two remaining. They said they would not stand idly by and watch us use them. There was an implied threat. That’s why I came here. Should we abandon the Sol Project?”

“How can we do that?”

The King paced the room – he threw his arms in the air.

“Look at the effort the population has put into the scheme. There would be riots in the streets if we abandoned the invasion. Not to mention the military. They’d be up in arms also – literally.”

“But what if these aliens have the power to destroy us, before we can invade?”

“You’ve seen our military might, Ediene. It would take something to overcome us. No, we carry on. It’s too late to reverse that particular decision.”

“I’m happy that you woke me, Ediene. I will think further on the matter. You may go.”

The King left the room.

* * *

This was only the second time that the King had been up to Ark One. The first time, he hadn't even stepped out of the shuttle, he'd just flown around the outside of the enormous structure. This time would be different; he was going to stand inside the torus without the aid of a spacesuit or weighted boots. Quite an occasion.

As his ship flew into Spoke Seven's docking bay, the bay nearest the torus, he couldn't help but marvel at his people's endeavour and ingenuity. The fact that you could actually see the rotation of the ark before the ship roto-synched, made the scene even more impressive. By the Sons of Hal this was an enormous and magnificent structure.

As the auto-lift system deposited the King and his entourage onto the floor of the torus, the assembled crowd chanted and cheered.

The King addressed the assembly.

"Well, I wasn't sure you would reach this milestone whilst I was alive, but you have and you have done it in style. So I congratulate you, the astroworkers of Zinden, and I name this ship the 'Ixes Pen' and hope that the fitting out of the vessel will be as quick as the hull construction."

He raised his glass, "To the Ixes Pen and all who dwell in her."

"To the Ixes Pen," came the reply from the assembled workers.

The cylindrical diameter of the torus was approximately four miles. I say approximately, because the shape wasn't a precise circle. The outer hull (the floor, when the ship was in spin) was much flatter than the rest of the structure. This was to ensure that there would be more space for the building structures to come.

In the centre of what was now known as the floor, was a 30-foot deep basin that ran all the way around the outer skin of the ship. Known as the central canal, this would hold the majority of the water supply for the trip. It was estimated that the water in the comet fragment was more than enough to fill the basin.

A number of water-based ships would be used to move goods and people around the ark once the journey to Sol Three had begun – none had yet been flown aboard.

Once the ark is on its way to Sol Three then, except for the barges, only pedal power and leg power will be allowed on the ark.

For Ark One, the trick now was to get the water from the comet fragment into the basin. Once that was complete, the hydroponics systems could be installed and then the replenishment of oxygen around the torus could be stabilised. Whilst they were this close to the planet, growing the food and planting the trees was much more about generating a stable atmosphere, than it was about generating food to be consumed.

Once the above was concluded and the farms were built, they could start building the cities.

Ediene's current estimate for completion of the internal structure of the ark, was around 110 years.

After the ceremony, the King took Ediene to one side.

"I have some grave news, Ediene. Baltire's mission must have failed."

"Why do you say this?"

"He was due to send us a coded message. It has not arrived?"

"Could there be other explanations?"

"No! The message was to be sent no matter what his circumstance and whether he succeeded in his mission or not. No message has arrived. He and his mission must have been destroyed."

The two walked together for a moment.

"Just look at this magnificent structure, Ediene. The people won't be stopped now. It's too big. Instead of you and I turning our thoughts to stopping this project, we should be using our talents to prepare for the second mission to Earth. We have one remaining Scorch device, let's use it!"

* * *

"A hundred and thirty four deaths in one day. By the mists of the Deepfall, Hzax, what is it?" said Shrayth.

"I don't know. It's very flu-like. They seem to come down with what appears to be a cold. Within the hour they can hardly breathe and within 12 hours they're dead."

"What's the death rate, can I see a survivor?"

"No."

"I'll wear a mask."

"No, you don't understand. I mean there *are* no survivors. It's 100% lethal."

Shrayth's nose started itching.

– Chapter Eighteen –

Galactic Enforcement

Z-Day plus four months...

Considered by many as one of the great strengths of the current Galactic Empire, was the fact that it was not centralised. The inability to travel at greater than light speed meant centralisation was next to impossible. So from the beginning, the empire founded itself on autonomy.

This resulted in a constitution that was designed around non-interference of one race upon another, around non-aggression, and common values.

The ability to communicate via wormhole technology – so that simply talking and seeing each other was instantaneous, no matter where in the galaxy you were, helped to police those values.

De-centralisation meant that the Galactic Council was truly representative of the people it spoke for.

The council was literally spread throughout the galaxy. The council chamber was effectively a virtual space. Each council member having an avatar, controlled from whichever planet the member was on.

The council sat in a vast spherical-shaped room. Each local group had a member present in the chamber. A local group could easily encompass thousands of stars and thus membership of the council was a great honour.

The leader of the council, Lorana Syne, was overseeing the current debate.

The floor of the debating chamber itself was just a plain circle. The number of virtual podiums on the floor depended on how many speakers were involved in the debate.

Currently there were only two podiums present. On the first was Trelain Ronke, residing on Seran Four in the local group, Ramos. On the second was Plotely Rahn, residing on the moon of Trual, in the local group, Rintac. The two advocates were nearly 100,000 light years apart, yet immersed in real-time verbal combat, that in the end, would decide the fate of the Zinden race.

Rahn's voice was piercing under normal circumstances but this was far from normal and his voice was getting louder and louder—

"How many more lives are we to lose to these barbarians?" Rahn shouted at the top of his voice. He continued, "The genocide event on Gorizon Prime resulted in the biosphere of every planet and moon, I repeat, *every planet and moon in that star system*, being sterilised!

"At the other end of the scale, 4,228 humans died on Sol Three in the attack on the city of Manchester, and four of our own Galactic Enforcement Officers have been killed on Zindor itself.

"Not to mention the fact that Zindor actually planned, and still is planning, to destroy every living thing in the Sol system anyway! There can be no further evidence required – the population of Zindor should be terminated immediately.

"I rest my case."

Rahn had been chosen to represent the life forms of the Gorizon Prime system and the murdered citizens of Manchester, all of which had been killed by the Zinden. He was well known for his passionate presentations.

Trelain Ronke, however, was the calm and quiet defender who would have no truck with any argument that could result in a complete race being summarily executed.

"Council members, I implore you, give the peoples of Zindor a chance. You have to understand the hardship that they have suffered, living on such an inhospitable planet such as Zindor.

"It is my conjecture that a large proportion of the peoples of Zindor didn't even know the plans to de-populate Sol Three. In fact, I put it to you that they still do not know what their leaders are planning. How can you condemn the innocent women and children of the Zinden race, when it was just the ruling elite that plotted the deaths on Gorizon Prime and Sol Three?"

"Balderdash!" shouted Rahn. "It is not possible that the general population did not know what was being planned. At the time they were, and still are, building an enormous structure called an ark, in the space above their planet. It is so big that it can clearly be seen from their planet's surface. Nearly a quarter of the population on Zindor is working, either directly or indirectly, on this project. Everyone on Zindor knows that the ark is intended to carry half a million Zindor inhabitants from their world to Sol Three. *They know this!*"

Rahn's voice took on a darker tone.

"What do the citizens of Zindor think will happen when that ship reaches Sol Three? Where do the citizens of Zindor expect the citizens of Sol Three to move to?"

"This is sheer conjecture. Yes, the general population know of the ark project, but the leaders haven't told them where they are going or what is needed to be done to establish their planet on another world."

"NO! It is not possible to start such vast projects unless the population has a clear view of what they are for. Projects like these use enormous resources and consume vast amounts of wealth. So much so that the rest of the economy, and therefore the people, suffer. The population has to believe in the purpose of such a project or there would be riots on the streets. They know! They know!"

Rahn knew this particular argument would be the main one used by Ronke and had prepared for this eventuality.

"Would the council allow me to bring a witness forward?"

"Of what relevance would this be?" said Lorana Syne.

"The witness is a native of Zindor. He does not know that the council is watching him. He thinks he is simply having a conversation with another Zindorian."

"How do we know all this is correct?"

"We have a lie detector attached to the chair the witness is sitting on and a stress analyser focused on him, so that you can be sure that he is not being coerced or put under duress during the interview."

"Then we will accept his testimony, carry on."

"Council members, I must object—"

"Sit down, Ronke," said Lorana Syne.

A holographic scene appeared on the debating floor. It was some sort of drinking house. The two appeared across a table, a pint of liquid in each of their hands.

"So what do you make of the invasion of Sol Three, Alreda?"

"Absolutely necessary – we need somewhere better than this dump to live on, do you not agree?"

"It's just that we're talking about exterminating more than eight billion people."

"It's them or us. We can't be soft if we're going to become the dominant species in the galaxy."

A gasp of shock filled the room.

"Is taxi driving your only job, Alreda?"

"Haven't got time for anything else."

"So do most of your customers feel like you do?"

"All of them! Well—I've had a couple, like you, who'd prefer not to sterilise Sol Three. Most have no problem with the idea though."

Whilst the conversation continued in the ale house, Rahn left the picture running but turned the volume down.

"So much for the populous not knowing, Ronke. On worlds I've frequented, if a taxi driver knew what was going on, the whole world knew. And councillors, I point to the fact that the taxi driver showed a complete lack of concern, when it was mentioned that eight billion humans would have to perish—need I say more?"

The last few words were uttered with a degree of exasperation in his voice.

As Trelain Ronke rose again to speak, Lorana Syne shouted him down.

"Enough! I have no doubt that there are innocent people amongst the Zinden but this does not mean that they do not pose a threat to the rest of the galaxy.

"We will have the vote. Cleric, Ezat read out the charge."

Ezat stood. "The Zinden race is charged as follows:

1. *That it carried out an act of genocide on all of the life forms indigenous to the system known as Gorizon.*
2. *That it attempted to carry out the same on the system known as Sol.*
3. *That during its attempt to carry out genocide on the Sol system – 4,228 humans were murdered on Sol Three.*
4. *There is still a plan in motion to terminate all the life forms in the Sol system.*

According to the laws of the First Galactic Empire, the above charges call for the annihilation of those responsible.

If you vote yes, you are voting for the implementation of this sentence. You will now cast your vote!"

As in all votes of the Galactic Council, there are only three possible choices laid out in front of each council member: Yes, No or Abstain. Within a few minutes the result was in.

Ezat stood again. "All have voted. The result of the ballot is as follows:

"*The Zinden race is to be terminated!*"

There were mutterings and signs of approval from most of the council members. Lorana Syne stood up and spoke.

"The sentence will be carried out by the use of lethal virus. Authorisation for its development is now officially given. The chief scientific officer in charge of the virus project must seek further approval before deployment."

"May I speak to the council, Councillor Syne?"

Lorana Syne looked up from the paper she was reading, to see one of the most respected council elders, standing to address the chamber.

"I give way to Councillor Ramadis."

The old man bowed his head towards Lorana.

"This is only the second time since the council was formed, that such action has had to be contemplated. I have read the historic documentation and I have seen the visual archives and believe me, they do not make for comfortable viewing."

"What's your point?" asked Lorana Syne, fearing that this may just turn out to be the reminiscence of an old man.

"There was a great deal of soul searching and regret, after the first time we committed our *own* act of genocide. Although entirely legal, there were suicides and sections of the Galactic Empire that revolted in disgust. I would like to propose a minor change to what has been voted upon."

"You have our attention, Ramadis," shouted another, even older-looking councillor, off to the right.

"We feel no comfort in this verdict, Ramadis. Anything you may suggest, that may make the verdict easier to live with, would be most useful."

"Then I respectfully suggest that in the years needed to develop the lethal virus strain and of course its antidote, we attempt to find the innocents amongst the population."

"How are you suggesting we do this and what would we do with the rescued population? Their planet would be in no fit state for them to remain."

"I have given this some thought. First, we would need a shape shifter from Calron to work with the anti-war, anti-genocide, protest groups. The obvious choice is Uban Drix. He did a remarkable job on Sol Three and anyway he's the most experienced officer we have, close to Zindor.

"Second, we isolate one of their small colonies that has potential for growth. We organise the dissidents to move there. We encourage them to remain distant from the rest of the populous and surreptitiously place the antidote into their food chain. We then introduce the lethal virus strain onto Zindor and its colonies.

"I would suggest that this is the only additional action we take, the rest is up to the Zinden population itself."

Ramadis sat down.

At first the rest of the council remained silent but it was as if Ramadis had uncorked the bottle. Slowly but surely the council members started to stand up and applaud him.

Lorana Syne was smiling – she stood.

"This is a worthy suggestion, indeed. We will take an immediate vote. Those who are in agreement with this proposed change to the plan, raise your hands."

Nearly everyone on the council raised his or her hand.

"Those against?"

There were only three dissenters.

"The alternative plan carries the day. Well done, Ramadis. Let us hope that there is someone down there that is worthy of redemption."

* * *

For the last four months Uban had been awaiting instructions as to his next posting. He had informed central command that he now had a permanent partner and two months ago she had been sworn in, over the wormhole link, as a recruit to the post of Galactic Enforcement Officer.

Judy's following two months were busy with learning the ways and principles of an officer in the Galactic Enforcement Brigade, and taking exams to that effect. She was hoping by the time the next posting came through, she would be ready for her final exams.

"Well, here's our next posting, Judy. We have instructions to fly to Zindor. Are you really up for this?"

"I can't think of a better way of learning how to fly that machine of yours. You have to promise that I can take my exams before we go into stasis though, *and* promise to come out of stasis a few weeks early to check the results, before we start our mission."

Uban smiled, "Of course my love!" They embraced.

"Why Zindor, Uban?" she said quietly.

"We are to see if we can start a counter movement against the genocide. The ones who join us are to be saved from their extinction event."

"How long before the extinction event?"

"Approximately two years to develop the virus and antidote. I would guess around eight years testing and then around four years, maybe a little more, to deliver it to Zindor and the colonies."

"How long will it take for us to get there?"

"Well, it's six light years away and we can attain a speed nearly 65% light speed, so we should be there in around nine and a half years. With stasis you'll be around nine hours older but I'm afraid all your friends will be nine and a half years older."

Judy wasn't thinking about the age of her friends at that moment.

"So we'll have about five years to start the movement."

"That should be long enough to drag in the decent people of Zindor, don't you think?"

"I would have thought so. Do you think there are any?"

"I'm sure there must be."

* * *

"Please unfasten your safety harness and do your reanimation exercises. You have been in STASIS for nine years, five months seven days, five hours and three minutes. It is possible that you will suffer from nausea and dizziness for the first hour. Your first meal should be small and you should take your time eating it. Tomorrow you may eat as normal. Do not have a large meal for at least five days.

"The ship is now in the Zinden system and we are currently on time for orbiting over the main population centre, in the next two weeks. The ship is in stealth mode. It will not be detected."

Judith felt quite sick. In the first few minutes of her awakening she wasn't quite sure if the invasion of Earth had ever taken place. Where exactly—

Then it all came flooding back. Her mind was racing. Alan—Uban, where is he? As she started to sit upright, Uban dashed over.

"How are you feeling?"

"I need something to be sick in."

"It always feels bad the first time you face it. You need to get up and exercise, as quickly as you can. Then we have to eat a small meal. Once you've had your first meal you'll start feeling normal again."

"Then can I have a love off my husband?" she said.

He smiled and gave her a hug and a kiss. Then she remembered.

"Did I pass my exams, Uban?"

"Yes, I checked earlier."

"Hooray! Ugh—I feel horrible!"

– Chapter Nineteen –

Zinden Resistance

Z-Day plus ten years...

It had been a long time since Uban and Judith had landed on a planet. If there was one thing they'd learnt about Zindor from the earlier failed missions, it was to avoid the Deepfall. Thus, this time the ship came in vertical, but fully cloaked, directly to a large cave system in the southern highlands.

Most of the time Judith had to remain within the ship. There were two facts that were ingrained on both their minds. One was the fact that no Zinden must see an Earthling on their planet and two, none of them must know that Bahra Torane, Urban Drix's name whilst on Zindor, was not from their planet. Judith had it in her mind that this was going to be a lonely and claustrophobic few years, but it had to be done. Earth and a whole lot of good Zinden lives, were at stake here.

In the first month, Bahra Torane had moved into Hisce, the largest township on the southern continent, lying in the foothills of the southern highlands. He'd arrived looking for work as a forester, saying his speciality was tree logging. He hadn't found much work but a reasonable number of the locals needed a handyman. So that's how everyone saw him making ends meet.

Right from the start, he had made it plain that he did not believe in what the government was doing.

"Don't get me wrong," he would say. "I would like a better planet than Zindor, but killing other intelligent species was not the right way of doing things."

It was a line he was to repeat time and time again. He was so well known for his anti-government views, that at one time he was targeted by a bunch of roughnecks who collared him outside a bar he was drinking in and called him an "Earthling lover" and "a traitor to the Zinden race".

A heavy brawl resulted and to his surprise, a mountain of a man came to his aid, and the roughnecks disappeared just as quickly as they'd appeared.

"Thanks, fella!"

"No problem, my man, I don't believe we should be killing these Earthlings either. The way I see it, if they haven't done any harm to us, why should we harm them?"

"A noble sentiment my friend. Let me buy you a drink. What's your poison? In fact, more to the point, what's your name?"

"Laron-Tero. Yours?"

"Bahra Torane."

Over the course of the next few evenings the drinks flowed freely, and slowly the two became close friends.

The rhetoric between the two became more and more anti-government and they were beginning to gather a small following. Someone had filmed their anti-genocide arguments and had posted the film on Zindernet. Their following was small and hardly growing, but it was a following. Mainly consisting of young teenage Zinden. At one time the government was sufficiently rattled to arrest Bahra, for incitement to plot against the government.

The judge laughed the charge out of court. Suggesting that there were not enough followers to start even a small riot, never mind an actual plot against the government.

On that day, as Bahra left court, two very surly Zinden males accosted him.

"Mr Yoleta wants to talk with you."

He had no idea who Mr Yoleta was, but regardless,

there was no arguing with these two. He was bundled into the luxury transport, a 'heavy' on either side of him.

Eventually the vehicle turned down a long driveway and into what could only be described as a palace courtyard. The 'heavies' got out and escorted Bahra to a sumptuous hallway where a man was standing waiting for them. He bowed.

"Would Sir kindly follow me?"

He led Bahra down a long, carpeted corridor and into a large library room.

"Mr Bahra Torane, Sir."

"Thank you, Alsed. Welcome, Mr Torane. Would you like a little refreshment?"

"No, thank you, I'm fine. To whom am I speaking?"

"My name is Corante Yoleta, I own the estate you are on, most of the southern highlands and a large number of the outer colonies."

"I can see you are rich, Sir. But what do you want with me, a mere forester and a pain in the government's side?"

"I would like to offer you a small, off-world estate where you and your followers can flourish."

Bahra thought that the offer would have been absolutely wonderful, had it been made in a few years time; it was far too early in the project to accept at the moment. There was no way he was going to directly pass up such an offer. Could it be delayed, he thought?

"Why am I so suspicious of such a generous offer? How could a rich man like Corante Yoleta gain from such an arrangement?"

"It's quite simple. I am a businessman. I grow richer when situations are stable. I grow dramatically poorer if activists stir up movements that bring chaos or violence."

"Mine is a peace movement, there will be no violence."

Corante Yoleta lost a little of his cool demeanour.

"*You are naive indeed* if you think your stance against the genocide will not result in violence."

Perfect! Bahra thought, absolutely perfect. Of course, in all forms of protests one gets the violent types. Sooner or later it will happen. Once it does, the movement will become newsworthy, really newsworthy, if his plan was successful. He now knew how to react.

"If violence occurs I will consider your offer, but not until. Tell me, Mr Yoleta, do *you* believe in the genocide plan?"

"My belief is irrelevant, I just believe in stability. I make no moral judgements."

"In not making a moral judgement, Sir, you are making a moral judgement."

"Enough. I will hold you to that promise, Mr Torane. Alsed!" he shouted.

Alsed duly arrived.

"Escort Mr Torane from the building."

"This way, Sir," said Alsed.

He was escorted back to the transport and duly dropped back on the outskirts of the Hisce forest. He made his way back to the little shack he called home. Laron-Tero, was awaiting his return.

"What did they want, Bahra?"

"They want to buy our silence because they think we will turn violent."

"We've no intention of turning violent."

"On that, you and I agree, but maybe there are others who prefer violence. I think we need a rally. Let's get some press attention!"

The message went out on the Zindernet that there would be a rally in four weeks' time. The message gave the exact date, time and place. The message stated categorically that the protest march was to be peaceful, and activists who wanted violence, should stay away.

The protest day started well. Nearly 100 Zinden had turned up. They were to march on the Redus Tower. Bahra was sure that the protest march would be completely ignored. In fact he thought it was much worse than that. He was sure that, unless there was some sort of violent event, they wouldn't even make the news at all. He was desperately hoping for a violent event. World news was the only way he could get the message out to the whole of the Zinden race, that there was an alternative to the planned genocide.

Violence wasn't a thing he could organise himself. It was too dangerous to his cause. If they were all seen to be violent, they'd end up in jail rather than moving off planet.

Just before the start of the march, Bahra lifted himself onto the top of a particularly high goods transporter and addressed the crowd.

"Do we believe in exporting death to other worlds?"

"No!" shouted the crowd.

"Do we want the people of Sol Three to die?"

"No!" shouted the crowd.

One of the crowd shouted, "Down with the Government!"

As the rest of the crowd was starting to respond, Bahra stepped in, "No! We don't want to change our government. We just want to change their policy. NO TO GENOCIDE!"

The crowd cheered, "No to genocide!"

"Let's get this march underway and let's keep it peaceful!" shouted Bahra, and he repeated, "No to genocide! No to genocide!"

Again the crowd joined in the chant, and the march began. "No to Genocide!"

The distance from City Park to the Redus Tower wasn't great, but the walk around the base of the tower would take most of the morning.

As he walked past the green mass-transporter, he thought it unusual to see it above ground. They tended to be used on service roads, deep under the city.

He was probably only a block away when the explosion occurred. The green pieces of metal from the transporter flew towards him, scything through bodies as they went. A head off one, an arm off another, the fragments weren't for slowing down. Luckily, the blast had knocked him to the ground, so he received only a quarter of the fragments he would have done, had he remained upright.

The pain in his back, neck and head was excruciating, but as he lost consciousness he knew his plans were beginning to work.

He awoke, face down, in what looked like a sterile room.

The medic, who was removing the shrapnel from his back, noticed his eyes move.

"Ha! Glad you could join us, young man. The police say you're an important witness and that we should take care of you, so we're doing just that."

Bahra tried to move, but the pain from his neck as he tried to turn, was too severe.

"What happened?"

"You don't know? You're not going to be that good of a witness then, are you?"

As the larger piece of shrapnel was pulled from his right shoulder, he again felt the dizziness that was to lead to the loss of consciousness. His body had had enough pain for the moment. It had decided to shut down again.

When he awoke the second time he was lying face up in a small one-bed room. He noticed a policeman standing guard outside his door and a very familiar face staring at him, from a comfortable chair in the corner of the room. The familiar face noticed he had awoken.

"Should I be saying, I told you so, Bahra?" said Corante Yoleta.

"It would appear that way, Corante. Did you put someone up to this?"

"No, that's not my style. And your promise?"

"Will be kept. In fact, now is a perfect time for me to speak to my people. Will you allow this?"

"Who am I to stand in your way? Are you strong enough to face the press?"

"I think so. I think the image of me hurt in a hospital bed, whilst renouncing violence, will get through to the dissidents that matter."

Corante Yoleta went to get a selected number of the press corps – the ones that would gain Bahra the most publicity.

The press corps filed in quietly and stood at the end of his bed, cameras rolling.

"As you can see, gentlemen, my cause promotes extreme emotion in the general population and I would like to state categorically that I deplore this violent action.

The dissidents who did this are no followers of mine and should be hunted down and thrown in jail.

"This incident has changed everything and today I announce that my followers and I will no longer remain on Zindor. Corante Yoleta has most generously allowed us to use one of his estates on Shelta-Shon, where we can study and preach our non-violent philosophy. I urge anyone and everyone, who believes in our non-genocide policy, to come and join our community as a protest against the desecration of Earth that is to come."

The first question from the press was addressed at Corante Yoleta.

"You believe in this movement, Mr Yoleta?"

"No, I do not."

"You're a hard-headed business man, Mr Yoleta. What could you possibly gain from helping this movement, if you don't even believe in their cause?"

"Stability. I know these citizens to be peaceful, yet because of their protests, we have bombs going off in the streets. Bahra and I agree this is no way to proceed. By isolating them, we will isolate the extreme elements.

"Bahra and his followers will still have access to the Zinden Free Press, but they will not be blamed for the activities of their more aggressive followers."

"Are you and your followers not just being sidelined, Bahra?"

"In a way, yes, but we don't mind that. At the moment the movement has less than a few hundred followers. If we grow in number, we will be listened to. If we do not, we will be ignored – sidelined as you put it. Let history decide our fate. How many good Zinden are out there?"

The next morning the news coverage was phenomenal. Every TV station and newspaper, on Zindor, was covering the event.

In homes all over Zindor, there were people packing their belongings and heading for the spaceports, to embark on the journey to Shelta-Shon.

It was obvious that the Great Division, as it would be known in the distant future, of the followers of Bahra

Torane, had also hit a raw nerve with the more aggressive side of their movement. One of the ships, full of 'the good of Zindor' and destined for Shelta-Shon was blown up as it left the spaceport.

Eventually as Bahra Torane and his followers assembled on Shelta-Shon it became clear that a total of some 6,500 followers had arrived.

The estate they were given was vast and green. There would be no problems farming the land. In the centre of the estate was Lake Eiron, some 20 kilometres in length and 15 kilometres at its widest point. The lake was filled with melt water from the glacier on the Pinnacle mountain range. The water supply for the community housing was taken directly from the lake.

The whole transfer from Zindor to Shelta-Shon happened much more quickly than Uban Drix had anticipated. Much to Judith Wells's delight, they were probably a good two years ahead of schedule, which meant her isolation would be coming to an end soon.

The killer virus and its antidote had been ready for some years now and were in the midst of being transported to Zindor right now. The delivery vessel was due to off-load the anti-viral drug, when it rendezvoused with Judith, sometime in the next 24 hours. The rendezvous point was just off-world, around 150,000 kilometres from Shelta-Shon.

"I'm just standing off the co-ordinates, Uban. I don't want to be hit by the incoming ship."

Uban was talking to Judy via his wristband. The other colonists were quite a distance away and couldn't hear him.

"When are you expecting them?"

"Any time now. If they are on schedule, I would expect them here in around 40 minutes, but you know yourself if the ship sees gravitational anomalies in flight, it could be any time between yesterday and three or four days' time."

"OK! Send me three pulses when the flight arrives."

If Judy needed to talk to Uban, she would send pulses that made the wristband tighten. It was a way of communicating, even when he was in the midst of the Zinden.

"Will do, take care."

"You too."

Even Uban was feeling Judy's loneliness by now, but there was nothing they could do. It wouldn't be long now before they would be together again.

It was around three hours later that Uban felt the tightening on his wrist. Everyone had retired for the night, so rather than take the call in bed – he quietly slipped out into the fields and walked over to sit on the edge of the lake.

He raised the wristband to his ear, as if he was just cradling his head in his arm, and said quietly, "Go ahead Judy, I'm receiving you."

"The shipment's here, Uban. It's in three very large containers. I won't need your help to move them. They have their own anti-grav packs. I have to put them in the lake tonight and they will seed the lake, over the next few months, with the anti-viral agent. The medics have said that there may be a few in the population that will become slightly ill, and just one or two that may have a bad reaction to the drug. There should be no fatalities, except yours."

Uban was not sure he heard correctly.

"Come again, Judy."

"There'll only be one fatality. You!"

"Explain!"

"Well, we need to extricate you somehow, from your exalted position. The powers that be, seem to think dying would be good. The scientists have included a toxin, which once absorbed by any 'being' from Calron, that's you, by the way, Uban, will make it appear that you have suddenly died. Your body will shut down. To you, it will feel like you are simply in stasis.

"You will be pleased to know that the Zinden do not cremate or embalm their dead. They don't even bury them. Your body will be placed in a tomb. Even if you're sealed in a tight space, you will be using so little oxygen, unless you wake up, that you will not suffocate."

"What do you mean, unless I wake up?"

"Well, if you wake up you'll use more oxygen, so you may suffocate. So don't wake up!"

"I have a feeling I won't be in control at that moment."

"No, you won't be. Stop worrying, I won't let you suffocate."

"Someone's coming, speak with you later—"

"Can't sleep, Bahra?" said Laron-Tero.

"Too many things going round in my mind, Laron. What's woken you – old friend?"

"I keep wondering whether we're doing the right thing, not fighting against the government on the genocide issue."

"You have to trust me, Laron. We'll win in the end. They'll not carry out that threat."

"You seem so sure of that, Bahra. I wish I could be that sure."

"I'll tell you what, Laron. If I'm not proved right before the year-end, then we'll all join the activists. Agreed?"

Laron-Tero suddenly became more cheerful.

"You have to promise me – no action before year's-end."

"Promise."

Laron and Bahra shook hands and walked back to their rooms.

It was a few days later that Laron noticed the increase in admissions to the little clinic they'd set up, only a few months before. There were lots of people with flu-like symptoms, the symptoms disappearing within 24 hours. Two of the followers had to be admitted. They seemed much more serious at the time, but even they were now recovering.

"Laron, quickly, quickly! Bahra is dying."

Laron rushed to his friend's side, not believing for one minute he could possibly be dying. As soon as he saw his face, he knew it was true. From being normally orange in colour, his face was almost blue. His eyes were grey and he was sweating profusely. When he spoke it was with a much-weakened voice.

"Laron, I'm not going to be around for much longer."

Laron-Tero was filling up with emotion.

"What's wrong, Bahra?"

"It's just my time, Laron. You mustn't worry about me. This was foretold to me a long time ago. I have some instructions for you."

"Tell me."

"First it is you who must now lead our followers. But you must remember your promise. You must maintain the peace. It is very important. Do not side with the extremists until after year-end."

"We've talked of this before, Bahra. I will not side with the extremists."

"I have a request, for me personally, Laron."

"Anything."

"When you place me to rest, leave my wristband on my wrist. It will guide me through the afterlife."

Ever since Laron had known Bahra he had never seen him without his wristband. It was an easy promise to make.

"I will do this, Bahra. I will miss you, old friend."

"I will miss you, Laron."

Bahra closed his eyes and was gone.

The next day the whole of the community gathered to pay homage to the great Bahra Torane. A silent procession made its way from the village around Lake Eiron to the caves on the lower slopes of the Pinnacle Mountains.

As the body was laid down, one of the followers removed his wristband.

As the body lay in state, Laron-Tero came to pray over him. He glanced down and noticed that the wristband was gone.

"No!" he bellowed, as if in pain, "who has removed the wristband?"

"I have, Laron. I didn't know it was important."

"Where is it, my child?"

She reached in her pocket and gave it to Laron who immediately place it back on Bahra Torane's wrist.

"No harm has been done, my child."

Bahra Torane's body lay in state overnight, so that his followers could see him. There were many tears.

The next day Laron laid the first rock and then each member of the sect filed past, to place their rock in front of the cave entrance. By the time the last of the now nearly 7,000-strong, anti-genocide sect had filed past, the cave was sealed.

Uban was due to awake late in the day, the day after the funeral, or early the next day, depending on the amount of toxin he had ingested.

Judy had pulsed Uban's wristband many times without a response. As yet she wasn't worried, but as night fell she knew she had to open the tomb to set him free.

She landed their spaceship a few hundred yards away on the other side of the hill and walked over to the tomb. There was no one about so she climbed to the top of the stone pile that sealed the tomb and began to scrape an opening in the very top of the rubble pile. It took nearly an hour to create an opening large enough to squeeze inside the tomb. Uban was still lying there inert as she clambered, torch in hand, down the other side of the stone pile.

She shook him.

"Uban, wake up!"

Uban could hear her and he was trying to stir, but he couldn't quite come out of his stupor.

"Uban!"

He managed to move slightly. He could feel the grip of the toxin lessening.

"Uban, wake up!"

"Wow! That's powerful stuff, Judy. Sit me up."

As Judy sat him up he realised how much his body was aching. It felt like he'd been jumped on all night, and he had a headache like he'd consumed two bottles of Ashalte rum the night before.

"Your colour's returning."

"Don't talk so loud, Judy."

"I'm whispering."

"It doesn't feel like that."

"C'mon, Uban, we need to get out of here!"

"Yes, OK."

The two of them slowly climbed the rubble pile and after covering the opening with the discarded stones, quietly made it back to their spaceship.

"It's damn good to get back here, Judy. Any news of the viral delivery?"

"It's on target to arrive in about three months. Should we stay around to see how the colony reacts?"

"I don't think we've any choice."

"Does that mean I have your full attention for the next three months?"

"Well, we could park the ship near the Celestine Nebulae and unwind for a few months. A sort of second honeymoon?"

"I think we deserve it."

"So do I."

* * *

"This is Xia Nam calling Galactic C3012. Uban, Judy, where are you?"

"You're early, Xia. We weren't expecting you for another nine hours. We're on our way – we estimate we'll be with you in a couple of hours. Judy's just told me to say hello!"

"We're looking forward to meeting the first Earthling Enforcer."

"How is Yin Shu?"

"I'm fine, Uban. It's good to know you've settled down at last. See you in a couple of hours."

When the two ships docked, the two crews embraced like long lost relatives.

"It's good to see you again, Uban. How the heck did you pull that off?"

"Pull what off?"

"Saving Earth from the Zinden Scorch weapon?"

Uban explained what happened and the importance of Judy's technological breakthrough in the scheme.

"Now that was a good plan."

The four discussed their journeys over the last 40 years. To Judy, she was like a child learning a new language. She had no idea, until now, how many civilisations existed out there. As the tales of 'daring-do' ground to a halt, Uban indicated it was time to resume his mission.

"You know you're about to kill over 40 million Zinden, Uban?"

"Xia, I saw what they did on Earth. I know what they intended to do. I know what they did on Gorizon Prime. I've read the transcript of the Galactic Council debate and seen that they have no intention of stopping their murderous ways. The good of Zindor are safe on Shelta-Shon.

"I'm not killing 40 million Zinden; I'm saving billions of lives that they will claim, if they are not stopped now.

"Where is the virus and how is it to be administered?"

Yin opened a small silver case and lifted a green-coloured phial from inside it.

"This is it. You simply land and break the phial in the atmosphere. It will have no effect on any other species. Any Zinden that has received the antidote will not be harmed."

"OK! Yin, Xia. It's time we left and did the deed. Hope to see you again, under better circumstances."

"Bye, Uban, Judy. Stay young and healthy."

The two ships separated and C3012 headed to the northern highlands of Zindor. On landing, Uban Drix came down from his ship and removed the green phial from its protective case.

"For all the harm you've done and all the harm you intend to do, I break this phial."

The green liquid spilled out and instantly evaporated into the atmosphere of Zindor.

Uban and Judy were nearly back on Shelta-Shon when they started picking up telemetry between Zindor and her colonies:

"This is an emergency broadcast from the planet Zindor. Do not attempt to land. We have a flu virus that is 100%

lethal. No one who has had the disease has survived. It has not yet reached the colonies. If you are inbound, try for one of the colonies. Do not land here – I repeat, do not land here."

As Uban and Judy's cloaked ship, circled Shelta-Shon, the disease had reached the inner colonies and as expected, remained 100% lethal.

"Judy, take the ship down to an unpopulated area. I'll change into a Zinden again. One of those I met on Earth. I'll pretend I'm from the other side of Shelta-Shon."

Uban casually walked into the anti-genocide colony, along the banks of Lake Eiron.

"Hello there, stranger. Have you come from Zindor?"

"No, I've been on a camping trip on the eastern flank of the river. I've heard there's a problem on Zindor."

"How long have you been out there? Everyone on Zindor is presumed dead."

"Did no one get away?"

"Not one, the colonies are dying the same way. We've had several people from Zindor come here, but they all died. Only the colonists that have been here for a long time have survived."

"Who came from Zindor?"

"Corante Yoleta, his family and their entourage. But all of them perished. It is a great shame. He was a good man. He gave us the lands on which we developed this colony."

"He was a good man. This news fills me with great sadness. I must return to the hills."

"May, Bahra be with you, my friend."

"And with you."

* * *

The intergalactic database entry for Zindor now reads:

Zindor

The nearest planet to the star Ustulo, a red dwarf. The planet is tidally locked to the star and now contains only primitive life forms, on the dark side of the planet. There was once an advanced civilisation but the species died out some time ago, from a particularly virulent strain of Zinden flu. Survivors of this apocalypse are thought to have migrated to Shelta-Shon, a small M-Class planet in the Nixor System.

– Chapter Twenty –

Inclusion

Z-Day plus 283 years...

Andrea was completely out of breath as she dashed into the house. So much so that the shout she intended, so as to gain everyone's immediate attention, was only just audible to those sitting in the living room.

"Mum, switch the holo-array on, quickly!"

Mum was in no mood to be rushed, and in no mood to let Andrea waste her time in front of more holo-games or movies.

"You've seen enough rubbish today, Andrea. You have work to do for college, you haven't yet finished."

"Mum, it's the news. A delegation from the Galactic Council, whatever that is, has just landed on Earth and guess what. Someone called Uban Drix is in the delegation."

Andrea knew there was something significant going on. It's impossible for a young Earthling of the Jones clan to forget a name like Uban Drix.

Mum was galvanised into action. The array burst into life. Mum was pacing around the holographic image, studying the delegation. She grabbed the holo-array's remote and pressed alternative camera angles. She selected the preferred angle and focussed in on the two delegates in the centre of the party.

"It's them alright. They're a little bit older, but it's definitely them. Grab your coat and contact your dad. Tell him we'll pick him up, on the way down to the spaceport."

Andrea's mother, Mary went to the safe and removed a small package. By the time she reached the car, Andrea was already sat in one of the other passenger seats.

"Find Andrea's father, Charles."

The auto-drive kicked in, and after a short journey, the car parked outside the penthouse office suit of Zero Industries. Andrea's father climbed aboard and sat back in the last unoccupied passenger seat.

"The spaceport, Charles," he said.

"Can you believe it's happened on our watch, Mary?" he said.

"Will we even be able to get close to them, that's the big question, Michael? Zero Industries may have some clout on Earth and the colonies, but the Galactic Council is a completely different proposition."

"I think just the mention of Razor's children, will hit a nerve. They'll see us."

The spaceport was completely over-run with newsmen and paparazzi. Michael had never seen so many pressmen being held back by so many security guards. There was absolutely no way he would get to see the delegation, if he approached them in the normal way.

"What are we going to do, Dad? We'll never get to them, through that lot."

"I have an idea, Andrea. Mary, wait here!"

Michael went over to the arrivals desk and was quite animated as he spoke to the girls behind the desk. One of them was writing down what looked like instructions. Michael came back.

"What was all that about?" asked Mary.

"Listen to the announcement!"

The PA came to life:

"Would, Uban Drix and Judith Wells please report to the arrivals desk. Razor's children would like to speak with you."

The message cut straight through everything – red tape, security and the press corps. They were all suddenly irrelevant to Uban and Judy.

As the two groups came face to face they looked at each other.

"You have to be Razor's descendant. You look just like him," said Judy.

"Thank you!" said Michael.

"We have a 280-year-old photograph and holographic image of you two, and you've hardly aged at all."

"Well, I can see that it may take a little bit of explaining, this lack of aging," said Uban.

"This is my daughter, Andrea. She has something for you," said Michael.

Andrea stepped forward, holding a package in the palm of her hand. She offered it up to Judy. "This is a present for you, from Mary and Razor. It's been a family heirloom for quite some time, but every generation has taken care of it, so that you would receive it in pristine condition, when you arrived back here on Earth."

Uban and Judy looked at each other and smiled.

As Judy took the present, she said, "I think we owe you a great deal of gratitude, for keeping this safe for us for such a long time, Andrea."

The President of the World Council had been with Uban and Judy as they met the Jones clan. Uban took the President to one side. "Is there a private room we could use, whilst we opened this artefact, Mr President?"

"I'm sure we can find one." The President nodded to one of his aids who quickly ascertained where a suitable room would be and led the President, Uban, Judy and the Jones family there.

"Would you like me to stay outside?" said the President.

"Not at all, Mr President. You're most welcome."

There was a table, at the centre of what looked like a small conference room. Everyone sat around it, as Judy opened the package.

"What is it, Andrea?"

Andrea couldn't answer the question. She did not know what it was, either. "All I know is that the instruction handed down with the artefact, was to simply press the top."

As she was speaking, Andrea demonstrated the action and pressed the top.

Some sort of dynamo or motor, spun up in the base of the unit. The power surge switched on the holographic projector and there, sat before everyone's eyes, were the 3D images of Razor and Mary.

Razor spoke first.

"Hello, everyone. We're hoping that within the group of people that are seeing this image, there are two very close friends of ours. Two people who helped to save the planet from the evil that was the Zinden.

"As you can see, we're a little older than when we last met, Uban, but we'd like you to know that we had a full and a happy life. Abigail became a doctor and Daniel started a company called Zero Industries, which we're told is doing rather nicely, thank you. This device you're viewing us on, is one of their products. It's called the Holotub.

"We just wanted to say hello for one last time, old friend. Tell Judy not to underestimate her contribution to defeating the Zinden. If it hadn't been for the early development of the holographic projectors, we would have lost the fight and she's the one that had the foresight to see the potential of those devices—Mary?"

"Hi, you two! We send you all our love. Take care of the people that brought you this Holotub. They are family. As a well-known science officer once said – live long and prosper—Razor?"

They both waved goodbye and blew kisses to the viewers.

Uban turned to see Judy tearful, and moved to hold her hand.

"Would it be OK if the Jones family tagged along, during our visit to Earth, Mr President?" asked Uban.

"It would be our pleasure, Councillor. Should we address the members of the press now?"

"Yes of course, Mr President."

The two leaders, Judith Wells for the Galactic Council and the President of Earth's Council, walked to their respective podiums, in the VIP lounge of the spaceport. Surrounded by the world's press, the President was the first to speak.

"It is with great honour, that we welcome the representatives from the Galactic Council, to Earth.

"Earth applied to join the Galactic Federation of Planets, some 50 years ago and even though this visit concerns other matters, I'm sure that having the delegation here, will allow us to further press our case for inclusion.

"It is a sobering thought that Earth nearly succumbed to the Zinden genocide plan, and we are all pleased to see that the council wishes to place a memorial here on Earth to honour the fallen."

The President looked towards Judith Wells and waited for her to speak.

"Thank you, Mr President. The Galactic Council has, for a long time, wished to commemorate the events that led up to the defeat of the Zinden, but circumstances beyond our control prevented us from doing so, until now.

"Two hundred and eighty three years ago, an aggressive race called the Zinden, attempted to wipe out all life on Earth. They did not succeed because of the courage and bravery of a handful of men, and a single member of the Galactic Enforcement Brigade. We gather here today, to uncover this monument in honour of the courage of those few, and the sacrifices made by the people of Manchester."

As she pulled the chord that uncovered the monument, the assembled crowd cheered and clapped. Uban Drix stepped forward to address the crowd.

"People of Earth, over the last 300 years, your world has become a very different place than it was when we were last here, and Near Zero were at the top of the hit parade.

"Global temperatures are under control, the great stockpiles of nuclear weapons have been destroyed, there is a world council ensuring peaceful solutions to problems between nations and acts of barbarism and terrorism have all but disappeared.

"Lately you have gone much further by starting the difficult and long-awaited terra-forming of Mars. A truly selfless act, since no human currently alive, nor even their great, great grandchildren, will see the results in their lifetime.

"It is because of these changes that the Galactic Council has agreed that the Sol system is to become a full member of the Galactic Federation of Planets."

An enormous cheer erupted in all corners of the planet. The euphoria was tangible and Uban had to stop speaking for a good three minutes.

"This delegation has been given the authority to sign the treaty between Earth and the Galactic Council and we have come with knowledge and equipment that will allow Earth to communicate with all of the other planets in the Federation.

I am sure that this marriage between cultures will benefit all, and I am pleased that Earth's own council has chosen such a wise course of action over the last three millennia.

May all our Gods bless Earth, and all who sail on her."

* * *

Uban and Judith found it very difficult to find a working motorbike from the prime ministerial periods of Earth's history. The earliest bike they could get their hands on had been an Apple Turbo Thrust, built some 120 years after the Earth Council was born. It didn't even have wheels, as such; they were holographic renditions of what wheels used to be like.

As they powered along the old road system, towards the Lakes, they wondered how the old cottage had faired over the last 300 years. Yes, Uban had kept in touch with his solicitor, accountants and letting agent, and there was a huge stockpile of money that had accrued whilst he was away. But he hadn't seen the old place for nearly 300 years, so he was more than a little curious to know how the years had treated it.

It was great to see how Earth had protected its natural resources. How it had expanded its nature reserves. Uban found the Lake District, as beautiful as ever.

As they pulled in front of the cottage, both Uban and Judith felt the years between fade away. They were back at Z-Day and aching to see their long lost friends.

"It hasn't change a bit," said Judith, as she took her helmet off.

"The front door is bio-entry. I sent our bio-data over around three years ago, so we should be able to just walk in."

Uban was right, the door unlocked as Judy approached.

"Very 'today', Uban."

"Yeah, I thought so – a nice touch, eh?"

They both went through the lounge into the kitchen where so many of the really important decisions had been made. There was no kettle or oven. The kitchen was extremely modern.

"OK, I give up. How do I make a brew?"

"I just knew you were going to ask that, Judy."

"Well, answer me."

Uban smiled and grabbed her by the waist.

"You just ask," he whispered, and gave her a kiss.

She gave him a hug and said, "Two brews please!"

A voice from somewhere in the kitchen said, *"Imprecise data. Please state the type of liquid refreshment required."*

"Two coffees, please," said Uban.

"Would that be with milk or sugar?" asked the voice.

"Milk, no sugar, please," said Judy.

The two brews appeared on the kitchen work surface.

Uban and Judy grabbed their drinks and slowly toured the whole house, reminiscing as they went.

By mid-afternoon they were sat by the lakeside looking out over the exact same view they had looked at some 300 years before.

"It's nice to know that some things hardly change at all. No matter how much we rush around, no matter how far we travel, it's nice to have a place to come back to."

"I agree, Judy. You know, here is where the plaque should be. Not at the spaceport. Not even in Manchester. It should be here where the plan to save Earth was finalised."

“I think maybe the authorities have got it right, Uban. Why would a place so beautiful and so unchanging want to have imposed upon it the transient nature of intelligent life? We should always leave these places and spaces untouched.”

As the sun went down over the ridgeline, Uban and Judy just sat there in the cool evening breeze, surrounded by beautiful countryside, waiting for the stars to appear.

They just held hands, loving every minute of being back with a planet that was well worth saving.